I0675950

Forever Twilight

Jerry Lambert

Copyright © 2024 Jerry Lambert.

All rights reserved. No part of this book shall be reproduced, stored in a retrieval system, or transmitted by any means, electronic, mechanical, photocopying, recording, or otherwise, without written permission from the publisher.

This is a work of fiction. All incidents and dialogue, and all characters with the exception of some well-known historical and public figures, are products of the author's imagination and are not to be construed as real.

Library of Congress Cataloging-in-Publication Data is available upon request.

Trade Paperback ISBN: 978-1-7325378-7-3

V112524

Contents

Chapter 1
Les Revenants

Pointe Cèdre was a sleepy town on the edge of the bayous of Terrebonne Parish. It had existed in some form since the eighteenth century when French colonists had invaded. And then, when Jefferson paid the French handsomely for The Louisiana Purchase, it officially became part of America. The parish's prosperity had originally been built on fur trade, with an abundance of seafood and game. But time and population growth had not been kind to those trades and industry demanded more. Then rice and sugarcane became the most lucrative crops for the landowners.

One of the wealthiest of these had been George McCambridge. His rise to fortune had begun with his sugarcane plantations in the Caribbean and had moved to Terrebonne where he was able to raise a family. Before the Civil War and other tragedies had ruined him, he built a monument to his own wealth called Bridlewood House. So called after his mother's maiden name. And on that property, he had built a monument to his own death in the form of a capacious marble mausoleum.

Some things about Pointe Cèdre were timeless. The people

1

were largely poor and uneducated. The population had given over to a small ruling class that had inherited thriving farms and sawmills and plantations. They had given over to churches and preachers who told them that these heirs of prosperity had been chosen by God and that if they worked harder, he would bless them in the same way. The fact that this never seemed to come to pass did not alter their faith or allegiances, rather it was considered to be a test of those values.

There was a stunning natural beauty which was the domain of all who lived in Pointe Cèdre. Lakes and trees and endless green. Even the oceans of brackish swampland had its own haunting gothic allure. Where Cyprus trees were draped with Spanish moss and moonlight was often the only light at night.

Pointe Cèdre had its beauty, but it also had a pointless malevolence. It's natural beauty was endangered by those same miniature titans of local industry, the sawmill owners, and the pig farmers. The men who cared more for profit than the water their families drank.

Reported crime was low because crime was rarely reported. Criminals were cousins or cousins of friends, and it was dealt with, as with all things in Pointe Cèdre, privately. Closets in this small, idyllic town were known to overflow with bony truth and no one wanted outsiders to open them.

But there were some crimes so heinous that the very memory of them was an apparition. A ghost of a tale that everyone in town seemed to remember a piece of. Something dark and sinister and too deliciously timeless not to be retold by grandmothers on crisp fall evenings as the days shortened.

One thing that was not timeless was Bridlewood House itself. Time and lack of care had devastated the mansion and left it in a state of disrepair beyond any mere handyman. A confection of stone and plaster sat melted in the elements with the waters of the bayou lapping at its doorstep.

Early in the renovation it became clear to Craig Jones that things were different at Bridlewood House. The place had sat empty for a century, so things were already going to be dicey. He had been in the construction business for long enough to know what to expect with abandoned properties. If they had followed his advice, they would have demolished the house and just started fresh.

But the new owners would not hear of it. They insisted that they wanted to restore the old-world charm of the building. And he did see their point. The place was going to be stunning. But right now, it was a disaster. A mass of disintegrated plaster, warped woodwork, and no electrical wiring. The lack of electrical was almost a blessing. It would perhaps be easier to start from scratch anyway. Besides, who was he to argue with seemingly bottomless pockets?

As soon as he stepped into the cavernous house the echo of emptiness surrounded him and swallowed him whole. He had seen many an empty house in his time, but this was the grandest by far. The foyer was littered with the debris of an ancient broken marble urn. It had been a thing of great beauty at some point but was long past repair. It was shattered in parts into pieces no larger than dust, and the dust of it long since blown to the four winds. It looked as though it had been pushed over the balustrade upstairs. But that would have taken enormous strength to accomplish that feat. The house had long been empty and therefore the refuge of many a local kid. No window remained intact.

Craig looked down at his clipboard, then up at his assistant Jim.

"Get that out of here." He pointed to the remnants of a shattered marble urn.

"Sorry, chief," Jim said. "I wasn't sure if that was on our list of repair projects."

"No, I wish, but this one is well past what we can repair. The interior designer wants it sent to a restorer. I need to see what shape the floor is in underneath. Bound to be more shattered marble.

"Is it true what they say about this place?" Jim asked.

"What?"

"About the thing that supposedly happened here back in the day."

"Oh, that. Yeah, my grandma told me that story. George McCambridge built this house and apparently there was a murder suicide that took place here involving his daughter."

"Money ain't everything, I guess." Jim said.

"Nah, these people aren't any happier than you and me."

"Think its haunted?"

"Jim, you're a grown ass man." Craig scoffed.

Jim nodded and moved on to another room with his clipboard.

Craig was in awe of the stairs. They had been a masterpiece, that much he could tell. They curved up to the second floor in sweeping grandeur. The finest Carrara marble had been pieced together by masters of their craft. The stairway needed a bit of refurbishing but remained surprisingly intact. No noticeable destruction of treads or balustrade. It was filthy but had stood up well against the test of time.

Craig looked up and surveyed the upper stories of the foyer. Deteriorating plaster walls soared up thirty feet or so. Remnants of a chandelier dangled above the room. Ropes of crystal hung down like raindrops.

As he looked more closely, there appeared to be a basketball wedged in it. The ball was red, white, and blue, like the bicentennial balls from 1976. Then he realized it probably was one of the bicentennial balls and had been lodged in there for decades.

Craig moved on into the drawing room to the left of the foyer.

He examined the doorway. He tested the pocket doors and found one surprisingly functional and one off its tracks. It would all be rebuilt anyway. If the pocket doors were any good, he might just save them for a home project of his own. Or perhaps even his wife's architectural salvage business.

The entire project seemed to be the vanity project of some rich kid architect with more money than sense. Everyone knew the Huston name. Even out here in the sticks. They were a family of hoteliers from New Orleans. He had seen them in the papers many times. Craig had been surprised when he had gotten the call but found the guy easy to deal with. He needed a contractor who would not say *no*, and Craig had been a contractor long enough to know not to say no. Rather he would just find a way to make it work. He always did.

What he did not know, or really care, was why anyone would spend this kind of money on a house this far away from everything. They were hours away from New Orleans by car. They would have to helicopter in when they visited for a weekend. Though that seemed well within the abilities of the Huston family. Their wealth and influence were legendary. And like most people of legendary wealth, they were legendarily tight fisted. But on this project, he had been given free reign.

The drawing room was a large area with paneled walls. The plaster had been painted an eggshell white at some point. The old paint was lighter in rectangles and squares where paintings had probably once hung. The floor was marble, like the foyer, also in surprisingly good shape. There was furniture left behind, but the fabrics had mostly turned to dust as well. Nothing was to be saved, all of it would be hauled away.

One sofa looked salvageable, and Craig looked long and hard at it. He considered that it might be a worthwhile home project. He walked around it. It had once been a beautiful divan. He hoped that he would find the interior bones of the piece to be in good shape. He loved a home project. But if he brought home another worthless piece Terri would kill him. Still, it was too good a piece to throw away without trying, and the new owners did not care about saving any of the furniture. He took out his phone and snapped a photo to show Terri.

In the corner of the room stood two young people. One, a tall dark-haired man. He was quite handsome. Beautiful, one might think, and dressed in the livery of a footman with dark gray cutaway jacket, matching breeches, and burgundy waistcoat. The other, a stoutish creole woman with her hair piled wildly atop her head, wrapped in scarves. She wore an elegant dress of colorful silk. They regarded Craig, who could not see them, with concern and interest.

"What do you suppose he is planning to do here?" The dark-haired gentleman asked.

"They seem to be considering renovating this house."

"Why don't they just go away." He stated more than asked.

The woman shrugged.

"Don't you think it will be nice to have people in the house again?"

The handsome footman seemed to think a moment and appeared to decide that it would not.

"They bring trouble." He spoke. "They always seem to."

The creole woman nodded, as there was some truth to this.

Craig looked up from inspecting the sofa and began to cross the room toward them.

Each gentleman had a slightly alarmed look on their face. He was coming right at them and seemed to be looking right at them. Just as the footman was about to say something, the man walked right through them. The man shivered briefly then produced a tape measure from his pocket and got down on his knees. He had neither seen them nor sensed them. He was simply headed to the corner of the room for measurements.

"I hope they don't turn it into a whorehouse again." The footman said.

The creole woman laughed.

"I doubt that it will, but that was rather an interesting time."

"What a *strange* time that was."

"And what a strange time it seems to still be."

"True." The footman said. "The gentleman who comes here, he seems well bred but he could still be the sort to open a brothel."

"I suspect it will not be a whorehouse," the woman said, "at least not the traditional kind."

The two walked through the room and directly through the wall into the corridor.

"It is exciting to be around people again, though, is it not?"

"It is, I suppose." The footman replied, cautiously optimistic.

The creole woman closed her eyes and seemed to be anticipating a message.

"Can you feel it?" She asked.

"Feel what?" The footman replied.

"The energy is returning to the house. I have a feeling that the other residents will begin to stir."

"You're probably right." The footman replied.

Almost as if on cue the form of the original ghost of Bridlewood appeared on the stairs.

"Good day, sir." The footman said.

"What's goin' on here?" He asked.

"Hard to say, Mr. Spall."

"How did you know my name?" He asked.

"Abel Spall." The footman said. "You were the original ghost of Bridlewood. We've not forgotten you."

"Ah, yes." Abel said. "Seems like a lot goin' on around here."

"Whatever it is, she isn't going to like it."

"Who?" Abel Spall asked.

7

"Your memory is failing you."

"No, I've just been in a slumber for some time. It creates a fog that lifts after a bit."

The footman and the woman exchanged looks like longtime companions.

"She. The lady of the house."

"A lady?"

"Yes, they can own property now."

"My word, I have been asleep for a while."

Chapter 2
La Fête

The afternoon appeared calm and indolent, the late spring skies clear and blue. A temperate southern breeze blew in and the leaves of the willows rustled across the estate with a flourish. Brackish water rippled in bright diamond waves across the bayou of Lake Marchant as they caught the last of the afternoon sun. A normally quiet transformation into early evening was abuzz with activity. Tonight would be magical.

The grandeur of Bridlewood House was well known to all in the parish, though few had actually seen it themselves. Therefore, its mythology among the locals had grown over the years. Some believed that it had a ballroom the size of a cathedral. Or a private theater. The fact that it had its own chapel with its own minister was true, and an unimaginable luxury for most.

The mansion sat at the bottom of a hill. Anatole remembered the first time he came to Bridlewood House they came up over the hill and suddenly, as they crested, the house was visible. The estate, like the McCambridge fortune, was as new as it was legendary.

The lawn was vast and flat and was bordered by the bayous of Lake Marchant on one side and forest on the other. On clear days you could see out to Terrebonne Bay from the house. A folly had been built, just as they had seen in European estates, that accommodated groups for outdoor luncheons when the weather was amenable. There was the small chapel just for the family. Even the stables and outbuildings were remarkably beautiful. Designed by one of Europe's most sought-after architects.

Anatole Blanchet carefully tied the line of Chinese lanterns to the massive oak tree. Standing on the ladder, he turned awkwardly back to look upon his work. Tables with white linens flapped in the breeze under his crisscross of lanterns that would look enchanting against the twilight and dark southern night to come.

He could see his friend Emily Delphin approaching across the lawn. She was wearing her somber gray lady's maid attire. Her uniform ever at odds with her broad and sunny smile.

"It all looks so beautiful." Emily said as she approached.

"Thank you." Anatole replied.

"You know what Spring social means to Miss Charlotte."

"I do."

Spring social was a time for the McCambridge family to shine. George McCambridge was the sugar baron who had built the plantation, but his wife had always managed the social side of their lives, having come from a family of some note. But now that she was gone their daughter Charlotte had been left to replace her mother as the leader of Pointe Cèdre society. Spring social was for her girlfriends to appear in their finest gowns from Paris. For the men to look perfectly turned out by their valets.

The party was already legendary in Terrebonne parish. A collection of the local well to do. Young ladies who had already debuted into society and the young gentlemen who wished to woo them. Or at least dance with them. Charlotte had managed to create the event and then make it a social requisite within the last three years. Social connections were the domain of her mother's side of the family. Her father was rich, but he came from a poor family of no repute, so he did not know of such things. It seemed to be the way of society to raise children who intended entirely to build their futures on the familial wealth and, short of that, their connections.

"The lanterns look wonderful." Emily beamed.

"Thank you."

Anatole smiled with pride as he climbed down off the ladder and faced Emily.

He had worked hard since he became employed at Bridle-wood House. He had no choice, for he had gone into service after his own mother. She had been the head housemaid here for many years. And now she was the housekeeper. She knew everything about Bridlewood House. She had encouraged him to work there, but ultimately, he had been hired by the butler, Carstairs, as coal hallway boy then worked his way up to footman.

"What is Miss Charlotte wearing tonight?" Anatole asked.

If Emily thought it was an odd question from a young man, she did not show it. They had all grown up together and they were not *just* servants to Miss Charlotte.

"Oh, it's so beautiful." Emily said with great excitement. "It is a pink confection of silk organza. She will look like a princess."

Emily had a way of getting as excited for things that were happening to Charlotte as if they were happening to her. And Anatole realized that perhaps he did the same thing. His own mother had warned him against that as a pitfall of service.

Know your place, she would say.

"Will you be staying throughout the party?"

"Yes, I'll be here in case she has any hair or gown needs." Emily said. "She'll be changing gowns halfway through the party."

Anatole knew that she meant that Miss Charlotte might have to use the bathroom and no human alive could get in and out of a gown without assistance.

"Indeed." Anatole said.

"Of course, as a footman you'll be here all night."

"Oh yes I will," Anatole said. "And I cannot wait."

"Have you ever been to a party where you were a guest?" Emily asked.

It was a good question, as most servants had not.

"Charlotte's birthday parties when we were kids."

"That doesn't count."

"Oh." He said. "A wedding and a baptism...and a funeral if that counts. But not parties like this that are just for amusement."

"Not just for amusement." The voice startled them both. They turned to see Miss Charlotte McCambridge standing behind them.

"I beg your pardon, Miss Charlotte."

She laughed.

"As I was saying, not *just* for amusement" Charlotte continued, "also to help the girls of this parish meet men who have manners and can dance so that she may find a decent husband."

"Of course, Charlotte. Um, I mean, Miss Charlotte" He corrected himself.

"It's alright, no one else is around."

"Sorry. Charlotte."

"And stop apologizing."

He nodded. He would not tell her that his mother had repeatedly told him to ignore her and call her Miss Charlotte. Because his mother understood that if Mr. McCambridge heard them call her Charlotte they could well be sacked.

"Everything looks perfect." Charlotte said as she surveyed the lawn.

"Thank you, ma'am." Anatole said.

Charlotte smiled and turned to Emily.

"I just had my hair done by Miss Marie," Charlotte said, "when shall we get me into my dress?"

"The party starts in a couple of hours so well get dressed about that time. They need to wait."

"But I have always greeted people as they arrived."

Emily gave her a look with downcast eyes.

"That was when your momma was alive." Emily said. "Now you're the mistress of this house and you want to let Mr. McCambridge greet them. Or your cousin Bernadette or your cousin Beulah?"

"I wouldn't let Cousin Beulah greet the coal man."

"But you are now the head of society, and your entrance should be anticipated."

"I suppose you are right." Charlotte conceded.

She turned and headed back to the house.

"I guess I should get going." Emily said.

"Who is Cousin Bernadette?" Anatole asked.

"Yes, she and her twin brother Beau will be staying here at least through the month."

"Twins?"

"Yes. They're about our age. I haven't seen them in a few years."

"Nice folks?"

"Nice enough, I guess."

Anatole shrugged.

"Well, I have to get back up to the house before the wind disturbs my hair." Charlotte said.

Charlotte turned and made her way up the slight hill to the terrace and then inside the house.

"By the way," Anatole said, "her hairdresser Marie?"

"Yes?"

"Is she *that* Marie? The one they call Queen Marie?"

13

"Yes," Emily laughed, "just because we're creole doesn't mean we have to believe in all that voodoo business."

There was no one around them, but his voice lowered.

"They say she can see things. She *knows* things. She can make things happen."

"Oh nonsense." Emily laughed.

"Don't laugh," Anatole involuntarily smiled, "maybe she knows if you laugh at her."

"She sees things because she owns a brothel, and she knows things because she is the hairdresser for every rich old cow from here to New Orleans."

"I see what you mean."

"Sex lives and natural hair color are the only real secrets left and she knows them both."

"Well, I have to get back to the house." She said. "I still have to get a few things together."

Emily turned and headed back up to the house.

As she walked, he looked up ahead at the house itself ahead of her. He saw movement in the glass cupola at the top of the mansion. A round room on top of the mansion that was glass walled and looked out for miles around, he imagined, though he had never been in there. He saw a flicker of movement. Someone was up there, and then they were gone. Lightning fast. Probably just a play of light, but his mother had instilled a belief in a haunting at Bridlewood House. He took it seriously because his mother was not the kind to tell stories.

He had heard his mother speak of it in hushed tones with her friends, but nobody spoke of it anymore. There was an understanding that you may hear or see something unusual in the house and if you did you kept it to yourself. Except they never kept it to themselves. He could think of many nights when his mother and her friends would talk quietly about something they had experienced in the house while cleaning or cooking. He himself had seen nothing and wanted to keep it that way.

One night he hid around a corner as his mother told a tale. Quietly, so that he had to listen intently. A tale of how she had encountered a man in overalls. He was dressed as a worker, but he was in a place where no work was being done. She had been delivering linens to Mr. McCambridge's suite of rooms when she encountered him. She went to stop him and ask him what he was doing in the master suite. He turned to her and simply...evaporated before her eyes.

She said that a deathly silence had fallen all around her as the apparition dissipated. Felt the presence leave the room. It was as if a cold draft had surrounded her and passed through her. The air was electric and frosted. And in an instant, it was over.

He believed the story because his mother did not lie nor tell stories for entertainment. She was stern but loving. And while she enjoyed sharing a story or two with her friends, she did not retell the story for show at parties. She merely told the story to a friend over coffee while he listened in from around the corner. And she never spoke of it again.

"Stop daydreaming."

Anatole was startled out of his reverie by a male voice. The voice of the Charlie Mayes, the first footman.

"Carstairs wants to see you." He said bluntly, then walked away.

Mayes was an absolute jackass, but he was, at least for now, Anatole's superior. His mother was head of household, but Carstairs, the butler, was his and Mayes' boss.

"Thank you." He said to Mayes' disappearing countenance.

Anatole moved quickly because making Carstairs wait was never an option.

Chapter 3

The Footman

Anatole had often felt that he had been raised by a family other than his natural birth family. How could they be related when he seemed to have nothing in common? He often felt like a stranger in his own family. His mother was only interested in work and his father was a wastrel by anyone's definition. And yet the resemblance to his father was so strong as to be undeniable. His bastard fantasy was blown whenever he saw his father's eyes which were exactly like his own. Almond shaped and strikingly blue green. They were the honey trap that his mother had fallen into. They portended a depth and a mystery that she could not resist. She had often told the story. His eyes were an ocean and she had foundered on their shore like the story of the Sirens that she had read to him. Trapped by an intangible promise and an intractable curse.

"He was once as handsome as you are." His mother would say, and Anatole would blush.

Andre David Blanchet had been worthless most of his adult life, in Anatole's opinion. Anatole mostly remembered him as a drunk and an abuser. He claimed to lose memory of the attacks, yet somehow, he had enough control to hit Anatole's mother in places where it would not show when she was working. He had never had a work ethic and had leaned on his hard-working wife to provide for their family.

Anatole had only distant memories of a time when his father had not been a drunk and an abuser. Things had been different in the beginning. He had remembered when his father had worked and made a living. His father had worked as a carpenter in Pointe Cèdre. He had built more than a few of the houses there, and even done work on Bridlewood House itself. But then something had happened. He had turned dark, and Anatole never knew why. He had never asked his mother, and perhaps he did not want to know. He only knew that suddenly his father would stop coming home and he would be found in the houses of ill repute of the local wealthy who had convinced the poorer man that equality would be achieved by wasting his own meager earnings in their sporting houses. Though perhaps they did not need convincing. Perhaps the escape from their own dreary lives had been invitation enough.

His mother put up with it for reasons that no child could understand, though as Anatole matured it became clearer. Perhaps there was an expectation that a boy needed a father, even if the father was not an agreeable example. Though he did begin to realize that a woman had no real choices in society. At least not a woman of no means nor station who worked as a maid. A woman like that was almost property, and since his mother was creole, it was even worse for her in many ways. She had come from a family with some small means, but it was all lost. She had been given an education, and she passed that education down to Anatole. She taught him to read and write and she taught him manners. That education is how she rose to the station of housekeeper. While it may not sound like much to some, the position was well respected. She was head of a great household.

That education had made it possible for Anatole to mingle with his betters and for him to one day be able to be employed in a great house such as Bridlewood. This was the only gift she could give her son and it was a greater one that he could have realized. Had he had a better father perhaps he would have taught him a trade. Carpentry or hunting. But Anatole had a mother who was strong and had taught him a work ethic that his father never could have.

When he was a young man, his mother had walked in on him acting inappropriately with a playmate. She stopped them immediately and chastised them. Boys don't kiss boys; she had told them. Anatole had understood the message and it had never happened again. Sons learned from their mothers, and he had listened appropriately.

Anatole had learned that his feelings were not appropriate for his current life. His attractions were incorrect and were the pitfall of a life lived in non-Christian way. How could he ever live up to what God expected and also find happiness? Perhaps happiness was not important. Perhaps it was merely a construct, as his mother had often intimated, for the wealthy to achieve and the poor to strive for. Why should he bother?

As he aged, he found that many comely young women were interested in him as a husband. He was handsome, apparently, and had a good position in a fine house. He would be able to provide well for a family one day. But he was not yet certain that he wanted any of that yet.

The only thing that he knew he wanted was to work hard on his career and to become a valet and then butler someday. From where he sat the position of butler was so high up as to be unfathomable. And Charlie Mayes had his sights on that position before Anatole would be able to achieve that. And anyway, Carstairs was still alive and healthy and not going anywhere yet.

When Anatole was not studying or doing chores he was reading. Books of adventures in jungles he would probably never see in countries he could only hope to visit. Though he had often traipsed through the subtropical forests of southern Louisiana and imagined the stories of Melville, Thoreau, or Stephenson as he pushed past the palm fronds and banana trees. The bullrush and the duckweed. The areas around the bayou were rich with subtropical growth that echoed the books he had been reading.

He would sit for hours on a blanket that he had brought with him. Under a tree with his book and his sandwich and an eye that was ever aware of movement around him. He had alligators instead of tigers; they were slower, but they were persistent.

One day things changed. He was sitting in his room in their small house just off Beech Road when she came to him. He was reading one of his books and was immersed in an alternate world. A world where he had outgrown his mother and father and was independent. A world where he was master of his own destiny. Something he could not imagine happening in his current world.

"Hello, mon cher." His mother said quietly.

He had been so engrossed in his book that he jumped at the intrusion.

"Sorry." She laughed.

Anatole laughed and blushed.

"There has been an opening that has come available at Bridlewood House. For a job."

"Oh?" He barely looked up. "Are you going to offer it to Janelle?"

"No, this is not a job suitable for your cousin."

"What is the job?"

"Hall Boy."

"What is that?"

"A Hall Boy is the lowest rung on the servants' ladder, but it is a start. It's a position for a young man who may want to get into a life in service."

Anatole looked at her quizzically.

"What do you mean?"

"It means that if you are interested in a life of service in a great home that this would be your opportunity. I know there are a lot of adventures you wish to go on in life, but here is a real opportunity to become part of something bigger than you. Something with a future. Bridlewood House."

"What does the job entail?"

"It is fairly horrid." She smiled. "You will sleep in hallway at night and be prepared for if someone should knock in the middle of the night. Or if someone should want something and not be able to summon their servant. A hall boy also empties chamber pots and attends to every little terrible chore that no one else can or wants to do."

"It sounds awful."

"Oh, it is." His mother said, as she brushed his hair out of his face. "But Gerrard, the first footman, will be leaving in a year or two to join the seminary and I think you could become second footman. But you have to start somewhere."

Anatole had often considered what it would be like to be employed at Bridlewood House. To see his friends Charlotte and Emily each day and to be a part of the daily goings on of the great mansion. But what of his dreams of adventures abroad? They were nothing but dreams if he never worked to achieve them. And perhaps this would put him on the ladder toward that goal. Certainly nothing else that he was currently occupied by was furthering that goal.

"Alright." Anatole said. "If you think I can really do it."

"I know you can do it, Anatole. But I worry that you are too smart to endure the first year of this most menial work. But if you do I believe there will be great rewards for you."

"What do you mean?"

"I worry that you cannot put your pride aside and do a job

that is tough and inelegant. I worry that I have taught you too well and that you know too much about the world to be able to empty the chamber pots of other servants. I worry that the books I have taught you to read and the ideas that they have given you have ruined you for the world you were born into. I am your mother and first and foremost I want the best for you. So, I have tried to raise you to appreciate things above your station so that you may strive to achieve *more*. More than what your father and I could achieve. More than what your father could imagine. You are *my* hope for the future, and you always have been.

Anatole was stunned for a moment. He had never heard his mother speak this way. That she might depend upon him for anything was shocking. Unreal. But he allowed himself to imagine for a moment what it might be like to work in such a role in the great house. The house of Bridlewood. The house that was known near and far for its beauty and its grandeur. The house that he had practically grown up in because of his mother. And now he might also call it home. The thrill was almost too much.

"Mother," he said cautiously, "I think I would like to do this job."

"Alright, mon cher. But first you need to apply and show them that you can do what is needed. And you must follow all rules and never ever think that anything is beneath you...even when it is. That is a what makes a good servant."

Anatole looked at her and thought about this moment.

"Yes." He said. "Yes, I can do this."

She smiled. He could tell that it made her happy to know that he would have a career. People like them did not have a lot of options. She had made that clear to him without ever making him feel hopeless. He would work in this great home, and he would build a career and a life for himself where the work was the center of everything. Because anything else would be a slap in the face to his mother. And his father had delivered enough disgrace to the family that he was determined to be the end of that.

Andre Blanchet would be an unmemorable smudge on history. But Michael Anatole Blanchet would be welcome remembered as a dependable servant of the great house of Bridlewood. And then he would save his money and use it to fund passage to Europe, and then to Africa, or India. Somewhere far away where he could walk into the jungles and live amongst the locals and forget about Pointe Cèdre forever.

Chapter 4
The Lady's Maid

When Emily Delphin was ten years old she would run through the dense forest of the Bridlewood Estate with Charlotte McCambridge. They would jump and play and get muddy and dirty. Back then they were just Lottie and Em. Best friends. And Anatole would often join them. They did not have jobs or positions to worry about. Mrs. McCambridge encouraged their friendship, though Emily's parents did not. Her father had worked at the estate and worried that she and Charlotte would fall out and that he would be fired from his position at the estate. He was a creole, after all, and knew that men of color had little to no standing in the eyes of the law. A man of any color could be fired for any perceived offense. And Emily, as a young woman of color, was the most vulnerable of all.

Emily Delphin did not believe as her father did. She had not had the life experiences that he had. All she knew of social standing was that her friend was rich, and she was not, though she did not yet understand what that meant. They were merely words that she had heard her parents say. And it had not had an impact on their lives thus far. While she had been raised in the house as a child of a servant, she had never felt like one.

When her father left employment at Bridlewood House, she had stayed on working as Charlotte's companion and occasional scullery maid. When they both reached their teenaged years and it became clear that Charlotte would need a maid, they both begged for Emily to be allowed to do the job. It seemed a perfect arrangement for best friends.

Today the best friends prepared for a big party.

Emily pulled Charlotte's gown together and began buttoning the long row of buttons. She caught the button hook on one of the flowers and before she realized it, she had pulled it loose.

"Oh."

"What is it?" Charlotte asked.

"I'm so sorry, Miss Charlotte, I pulled this rose loose. Let me just grab a needle and fix it right up real quick."

"Please hurry."

Emily's heart began to beat faster as she frantically searched around the room for a spare needle. She'd just have to run down to Miss Blanchet's office to get another needle.

Emily Delphin rushed through the house avoiding the tremendous amount of activity in her path. The party would begin shortly and soon all the effort would be seen by all. And with any luck it would appear completely effortless. She had run downstairs to fetch a needle and thread.

Emily knocked on Fabienne Blanchet's office door. The housekeeper was at her desk signing receipts for things as they arrived from the vendors. She was a plump woman of fortyish. Smooth complexion, somewhat darker than her son Anatole. But with the same bright disposition. She had been the housekeeper at Bridlewood House for as long as Emily could remember.

"Child, you really have to learn to make a more graceful entrance."

"Sorry, I am in a hurry."

"Ladies are never in a hurry. Lady's maids may often be in a hurry, but they manage their time, and they hurry in a more graceful manner. Like an elegant swan who appears calm as it crosses the lake, but beneath the surface it is paddling its heart out. *You* are that swan."

Emily looked at her quizzically.

"Are you the swan?"

Fabienne asked, lowering her glasses.

"I'm sorry, I am having an emergency."

"Well, that's different, I guess. What's your emergency?"

"I broke my last needle, and I need to make a quick alteration to Miss Charlotte's gown. One of the flowers was a bit loose."

"Oh dear." She said, "Guests are already arriving. That Miss Bouchard is doing shoddy work if the dress is already falling apart."

Emily looked down.

"No, ma'am, it was my fault, I snagged the dress when I was fixing the buttons in place."

"Well, thank you for being honest. But you've got to be careful, child. You're very young for a lady's maid and you've got to be perfect. I know you and Miss Charlotte are friends, but she's still your mistress."

Emily nodded.

"Yes, ma'am."

Fabienne stood and retrieved a box of sewing needles from her desk.

"Take the box but see that you get it back to me."

She punctuated with a stern look to know that she meant business.

"Of course. Thank you, ma'am."

Emily smiled, her gratitude beaming as she rushed out of the office. She rushed down the corridor of the downstairs kitchens, dodging multiple scullery maids and cooks. Charlie Mayes was in the way chatting up one of the maids. He winked at her as she passed by. She ignored him, as she always did. He had some crush on her that would always remain unrequited. She knew what he got up to with every single available woman who crossed his path.

"Slow down, now." Charlie called to her. "You don't want to crash into someone."

She slowed herself and turned to nod at him. She could not afford to antagonize a superior. She could not decide if he was her superior or not, so decided to defer to the safe side.

"So sorry, I am in a rush to get something for Miss Charlotte."

"A lady is never in a rush." He parroted Fabienne's well known line, "Fortunately, you are not a lady."

He smiled and winked.

She found him to be quite disgusting but would not allow that opinion to color her manner. She had been taught to be polite to everyone in the household and she would maintain that stance even if they did not return the favor. Everyone here is working toward the same end of making Bridlewood House the shining example of this parish, and indeed this entire state of Louisiana. She repeated this mantra, taught to her by Miss Blanchet.

"Of course, I will be more careful in the future."

She nodded and went on her way up the stairs resurfacing back into the rarefied world of *Upstairs*. Where maids were quiet and composed. She was reminded of Miss Fabienne's words about the elegant swan. She glided across the floors and up the back stairs to the private rooms of the house, coming out into the main corridor.

Emily continued down the hallway to Miss Charlotte's rooms. She knocked once and entered. Miss Charlotte sat at the mirror admiring her jewelry.

"I have the pins; it will only take a moment."

"That's fine. But you really should be more careful."

"I am very sorry, Miss Charlotte."

"It's fine, just fix it." Charlotte was terse but tried to recover. "It's alright, just finish so I can get down there."

Emily quickly threaded the needle and tacked the flower perfectly back in place. Charlotte stepped into the gown and in minutes was secured into it and standing before the cheval mirror. Charlotte stood before her as a transformed beauty. Hair perfectly coiffed by Miss Queen Marie herself, and the gown and the jewelry. Everything was perfect.

Their childhoods had been side by side as best friends. Her mother had constantly warned her that she would have to defer to her friend as a "better" and that she could not be honest with her the way she was with her other friends. But Emily had never wanted to believe that. She refused to. The Charlotte she had always known was still there and she did not believe that anything would change her. The death of her mother had thrown her off. Had sent her spiraling down into dark places, but Emily had been by her side and tried to help with a pain that she could not comprehend. But nothing would change the real Charlotte McCambridge, that much she knew.

"Did you notice if people are arriving?"

"Oh, yes." Emily said. "They're just beginning to. I saw the first coach pull up as I was coming back up the stairs."

"Who was it?"

"I don't believe I recognized them."

"It may be my cousins Bernadette and Beau. They were arriving a bit early to freshen up just before the party."

"Yes, I imagine it was them. I'd recognize just about anyone else."

"You've met them before, Em."

"I have, but it has been a few years."

"Have you heard about what happened to Bernadette?" Charlotte said conspiratorially.

Emily smiled deviously, as she sat down to put the pin back in its box.

"No, I haven't."

Charlotte sat down next to Emily in their usual disposition for gossip.

"Father said her engagement was broken off."

"Oh, my!"

"Yes, and it apparently it wasn't by her!"

"Oh, dear! What happened?"

"Father wouldn't say." Charlotte whispered.

"Maybe he doesn't know?"

"If mother were here, she would know. She always knew what was going on."

"Yes, she did." Emily smiled. "So, what do you think it could have been?"

"I'm not sure, but it's a bit of a scandal. As you know it is very unusual for a man to break off an engagement. It can ruin a woman, which I certainly hope has not happened."

"Of course, that would be terrible."

"So, I have invited she and her brother Beau to stay here at Bridlewood for bit, in hopes that things might quiet down there among New Orleans society."

"Do you think it might blow over?"

"Not likely, I'm afraid. But it cannot hurt. And hopefully she'll tell me what happened."

"What about her brother?"

"He's a nice enough young man. He reads a lot."

"He's quite handsome, as I recall."

"He is, yes. And he has an engagement to a woman from a wealthy family from South Carolina."

"Anyone we know?"

"No, they are not a known family, but plenty of money, I hear. Hopefully whatever this scandal with Bernadette is does not interfere with his engagement."

"Could it?" Emily asked.

She was constantly surprised at the unforgiving nature of high society and supposed that she was quite glad not to have to worry about such things.

"It could indeed." Charlotte said. "Fortunately, the Chenevert name still carries enough import to save the engagement."

"It is kind of you to take them in for a while."

"They are good people, and more importantly they are family."

Emily nodded.

"I think it's time to go downstairs." Emily said.

"Oh, the jewelry first!" Charlotte remembered.

"Stay there, I'll get it."

Emily walked over to the side table and picked up the tooled leather box. It was hinged it on either side and opened from the middle. She carried it carefully over to the dressing table. She set it on the table and opened the box. The jewels inside sparked a blinding green.

She lifted the bracelet first. The heft of the bracelet was a sign of the quality, like nothing, she could ever dream of owning. She wrapped it around Charlotte's waiting wrist then locked the clasp. Next, she picked up the necklace and draped it over Charlotte. She locked its clasp as well. When she was finished, they both were quiet as they looked at Charlotte's reflection in the mirror.

The emeralds glimmered around her neck and wrist. Their

facets each refracting the lights of the candles and gas lamps. They both knew but could not say that the emeralds had transformed her from a mere girl into a woman. For the first time Charlotte began to reflect the confidence that she may indeed be able to fill her own mother's shoes in society. Emily could feel that tonight would be her night.

Chapter 5
An Evening to Remember

Charlie Mayes and Anatole Blanchet stood in their livery like a well-groomed pair of matched lions guarding the entry and greeting each guest and directing them to the champagne. They wore the livery that was reserved for special occasions, grey breeches, and burgundy coats. Each with his hair tied back in a burgundy ribbon. Charlie with his straight brown hair and Anatole with his creole waves controlled by pomade, as Carstairs had taught him.

Footmen were chosen for looks and height, they were symbols of their employer's power and prestige, so Charlie and Anatole had elicited their share of looks of appreciation over the evening. Charlie seemed to have *known* a number of the women. He often regaled Anatole with his tales of romps with the ladies who visited and left subtle hints that they would welcome a late-night visitor to their rooms. But now that he had seen the looks exchanged between, he and some of the ladies he began to realize that those stories were likely true.

Anatole, being only nineteen, had not experienced that yet, and was not sure what he would say if it happened. He had not physically lain with a woman, knowing that he had no opportunity to marry or support a wife and children yet. His mother had often warned him of the dangers of knowing a woman biblically and having to get married. However, these women were so far above him in station that he knew that would not be the consequence. The consequence of getting caught would be loss of job or death. Charlie Mayes clearly thought this was a small price to pay.

By the time Charlotte McCambridge came down the stairs the back lawn vibrated with an air of festivity and, the life's blood of a good party, anticipation. The *beau monde* of Louisiana society awaited her. No one would dare be late, even fashionably so, to a McCambridge party. The invitations too dear to appear even remotely blasé about the event. The tiny social register of Pointe Cèdre and Terrebonne Parish was represented in the assemblage as well.

Miss Charlotte looked magnificent in her pink gown that Hermione Bouchard had designed for her. Emily had done her best putting her together this evening. She was new at being a lady's maid and she was very critical of herself. But when she stood back and looked at Charlotte she was impressed with her own work and devotion to detail. She smiled demurely to herself.

Emily seemed to be the perfect companion for Miss Charlotte. They were close in age, though Emily seemed slightly more mature, and she was very good with Miss Charlotte's hair and clothing choices.

Outside, once the guests had all arrived Anatole and Charlie were done with the role of footmen. Now they joined the ranks of the wait staff passing drinks and canapes in the crowd. Anatole was the tallest servant there, so he stood out in the crowd.

He made his way through the crowd and found Miss Beulah Sugarbaker entertaining a group of young listeners who were able to at least appear enthralled with her story.

"And then I reminded him that I was a lady," she said.

Everyone laughed uproariously. He had missed the story but seemed to blush.

"Thank you, Anatole." Beulah said as she snatched another champagne from the tray.

Beulah Sugarbaker was full figured young woman whose unsuppressed appetites were not limited to the dining room. She had a large bosom and a large bottom and a personality that people of high society would call vivacious. Her appreciation of men was well noted, though she often found herself surrounded by the kind of men who did not appreciate women in that same way.

"Yes ma'am." Anatole replied, ignoring her wink.

Several of the other guest took a glass as well and returned empty glasses. He turned and headed back up to the house with the tray of empties. At nineteen he was still unaware that he cut such a dashing figure, or that there were people who admired it.

Anatole set down his tray at the makeshift station and picked up another that had been filled for him. He realized that he needed to relive himself after this tray. Heading across the lawn again he saw a beautiful couple chatting with Charlotte. He made his way to them to offer them a refill of their sparkling drinks.

"Miss Charlotte, I just picked up a tray of your favorite sparkling rosé just for you."

Charlotte's eyes lit up at the proffered champagne.

"Thank you, Anatole."

Charlotte took a flute of champagne. The other young woman followed, and then the young man.

"Anatole, I don't know if it has been mentioned yet, but these are my cousins Beau and Bernadette Chenevert."

Anatole nodded in their direction.

"They will be staying a while and Mr. Chenevert's valet has taken ill. I would like for you to act as his valet during his stay."

"Of course, ma'am."

"I hate to trouble you, cousin." The young man said. "I can manage without a valet."

"Don't be ridiculous, Beau!" His sister replied. "A man of your standing cannot be expected to wash out his own linens every night."

She laughed in a brittle manner that set Anatole's teeth on edge, yet he smiled the mirthless smile of a servant.

"It's no trouble at all!" Charlotte added.

And to Charlotte it was no trouble. But Anatole was already trying to imagine how he would juggle that duty with everything else he had to do. Helping the man dress was only the beginning. He would also have to clean up after him and launder his clothes for him if the staff was too busy. Some of the men he had valeted for couldn't be bothered to clean themselves properly and their clothes reeked. This gentleman certainly did not look like that sort, but still Anatole wondered why he had chosen this career.

Bernadette smiled awkwardly. He suspected that she was quite astonished to be having a conversation with the help.

Anatole nodded and stepped away and continued circulating around the lawn. The day was heading into night and the lanterns around the yard flickered magically in the darkening twilight. Guests all had just enough champagne to set them in the right mood for merriment. Some more than others.

By this point his tray of sparkling flutes was now full of dirty empties. He dropped tray off at the bar station and stepped into the woods to relieve himself, as the other facilities had been reserved for the guests and the ladies.

The woods were dark, though a few lanterns had been placed to make it easier for those who needed to be able to see. Branches cracked underneath his feet as he made his way just out of view into the darkness. He unbuttoned his breeches and pulled out his member to relieve himself.

"A beautiful evening, wouldn't you say?"

Anatole was startled by the voice, and he turned quickly, almost pissing on the gentleman's shoes.

"Beg your pardon, sir!"

"Quite alright." The man said.

Anatole did not know him but recognized him as a guest. Not a name that he was familiar with.

"My, but you are a tall gent, and I see that the equipment is commensurate with your height."

Anatole laughed nervously; he did not know what else to do.

"May I have a closer look at that?"

"Oh, I have to get back to the- "

But the man did not take no for an answer. And even if he would have Anatole had never been taught how to say no to his betters. Before he could do anything, the man had reached out and grabbed his manhood. His stream of urine, long since stopped.

"Sorry, did I interrupt something."

The voice startled Anatole and he jumped back. The man who held his penis turned around in shock.

"No, sir!" Anatole said.

He realized how it looked. Standing in the woods with his dick in a stranger's hand. It was dark, but there was enough light from the party lanterns and gaslights around the property for him to have a good idea what was going on. Anatole quickly put himself away and began buttoning his elaborate footman's breeches.

He then realized in horror that the man who had come upon them was none other than Miss Charlotte's cousin, Beau Chenevert. The man he was supposed to be acting as valet for during his stay. He would certainly never allow that now that he has every reason to believe that Anatole was some kind of catamite.

The green jacketed guest excused himself and left them there together.

"Sir, this was not what it looks like."

"It is none of my concern what you do. But I understand that people can get rather forward after too many drinks."

"It was as you say, he was emboldened by drink."

Anatole's face burned hot knowing that there was no way to explain what had happened. He was merely a servant and there could be only one conclusion. Anatole realized that he had been gone from the party for far too long. He excused himself and made his way back to the yard and to the bar station to pick up another tray of champagne before dinner was served.

As the guests began to make their way into the ballroom for dinner, Anatole and Charlie stood sentinel at the doors. Once again, a matched pair. They had each memorized the table number of each guest so that they could direct them as they passed through the doorway.

The ballroom was warm with the glow of hundreds of candles. The glittering crystal and gilt of the room

The man in the green jacket. The man from the woods who had taken him in hand stood before him. He was a rather handsome man of over forty. Anatole realized that he did not know his name and needed to tell him where he was seated.

"Dr. David Vandenberg and Miss Beulah Sugarbaker." The man said, his eyes lingering longer than they should in appreciation of Anatole, this stranger knowing things about Anatole that no person had ever known. He had touched him in a way that was wholly inappropriate, though it had not been unpleasant. Anatole shut the thought from his mind.

"Well, shall we stand here all night?" Beulah Sugarbaker chimed in.

"Pardon, ma'am," Anatole apologized, "you are at table thirteen with Miss Calais and Mr. Johnson."

"Thank you, Anatole, are you getting forgetful at such a young age?" Beulah chided. "At least you're pretty."

"Isn't he?" The doctor winked as he led Miss Sugarbaker into the ballroom to her seat.

"Try to keep up, you fool." Charlie Mayes, ever helpful.

"Sorry." Anatole said.

The guests were all safely inside the ballroom and Anatole finally had a moment to step outside for air. He went downstairs and stepped outside into the cooler evening air.

"Come in and eat."

He recognized his mother's voice immediately. He turned to see her standing there with a plate piled with food.

"I'm fine." He spoke. "It's nice just to be outside in the air."

"Then eat out there but eat. You're a growing boy and you need it. And eat fast, you'll be needed again soon."

He smiled and took the plate. It wasn't the same food as the guests were having inside. He smiled because it was better. His mother had somehow found a moment to fry him some chicken. The side dish was the fancy creamed spinach that he had first grown to love at Bridlewood House.

He had so many fond memories of this Bridlewood and yet he longed for more. Somewhere else. The man in the green jacket had somehow reminded him how much he wanted to escape to freedom. A place where he would not feel that he was a trophy on display to be touched or admired with no consideration for his own desires. The man in the green jacket had awakened something inside him. A realization that he did indeed have the capacity for carnal lust, but also a reminder of his need for independence. But how would he ever obtain it in this gilded cage?

Chapter 6
Dressing the Part

"Carstairs wants to see you."

Charlie Mayes said with no preamble, as usual. He had manners but he did not bother wasting them on Anatole.

Anatole would be lying if he said that he had not been expecting this, but his blood still ran cold. He immediately knew it would be about the incident in the woods at the party. He had done nothing wrong, and yet he was about to get fired and he would never work again because it would become gossip. And gossip was one thing he knew was inescapable. He would pay for someone else's actions for the rest of his life.

"If you value your job you'll get moving, foozler."

Charlie Mayes said with his usual delight at his own perceived wit. His insults were as nonsensical as they were poorly timed. Anatole had just finished helping the maids clean and put away all the crystal from the party and had not a single broken glass, nor had he ever in his tenure at Bridlewood House. So, a foozler, he was not. But his own opinion of Charlie Mayes was such that any insult that came from him was immaterial. Charlie Mayes enjoyed whatever slight advantage he had over him, but Anatole promised himself that he would never treat anyone else this way. The only person beneath him was Tilly the hall boy, and being mean to Tilly did not seem like much sport.

Anatole's role at Bridlewood House was something that seemed ever evolving. As second footman he was regularly called upon to do any manner of task. From opening doors, to going into town with Miss Charlotte to carry parcels, to laying the table for meals, to bringing in firewood. Generally anything that Charlie Mayes, the first footman, thought was beneath him. Decorating for a party was something that Miss Charlotte herself asked Anatole to do because he did a good job and because she knew that he enjoyed the task. And on some rare occasions he would be called upon to be a valet when guests were staying on for a longer period. That was beneath the dignity of a *first* footman.

So, it was not unusual when the butler, Mr. Carstairs, sent for him, but the circumstances were. After what had happened in the woods the night of Miss Charlotte's party. His office was located downstairs near the kitchens of Bridlewood House. His mother Fabienne was the housekeeper. She and Mr. Carstairs ran Bridlewood House like a well-oiled machine. Her office was next to his. From there she organized all manner of housekeeping duties and paid the bills.

As the tallest of the Bridlewood House staff, Anatole often felt like his head would hit the beams in the lower ceilinged areas below-stairs. Still, he made his way along the main passage of the kitchens. The cook's domain was on one side, with cooks and scullery maids hard at work. On the other side of the corridor was the housekeeping rooms with laundry and ironing seemingly constant. All cleaning supplies were kept there. Great airing cupboards were banked along the walls there and all the linens of the great house were kept there. Stored after laundering and ironing.

By the time he reached Mr. Carstairs' office his melancholia had blossomed into a full-blown attack of neurasthenia. He knocked lightly then opened the door. Mr. Carstairs was in the middle of a swig from a whisky bottle.

"Jesus Christ, knock and wait!" Mr. Carstairs bellowed. "Otherwise, what's the bloody point of knocking!"

Mr. Carstairs was not English, as far as Anatole knew, but as a butler he did fall back on what he had learned were English turns of phrase. And his accent was not Louisiana.

Carstairs then calmly replaced the lid on the bottle and slid it back into the drawer.

"Sorry sir," Anatole apologized, "Charlie said you asked for me?"

"Yes. Mr. and Miss Chenevert will be staying on for a few weeks here at Bridlewood House and Mr. Chenevert has not brought a valet."

"Sir, I- "

"Anatole. You have been given a golden opportunity here at Bridlewood House. One that exists entirely because of your mother. If you play your cards right, you will be first footman one day and then perhaps a valet or even butler. But you will never achieve these things if you whine."

Anatole froze again, but this time in astonishment.

"I'm sorry sir, I did not mean to appear to whine. It will be my honor to take care of Mr. Chenevert for the length of his stay."

"That's more like it."

"How..." He stammered.

"Spit it out."

"How is he?" I asked. "Is he decent to be around?"

"He seems pleasant, I think. I don't think he will be difficult.

43

He has not yet struck a servant in my presence if that's what you mean."

Anatole was not pleased that he was going to be taking care of Mr. Chenevert. He already had so much to do, and he had not done a lot of valeting in his time here. But he would brush up and make it work.

"That's good," he said, "I'm just surprised that a gentleman like that is traveling without a valet."

"The youth today," Carstairs bemoaned, "do not hold to the same standards, I fear. Also, the Chenevert family is related to Miss Charlotte on her mother's side." Mr. Carstairs shared. "I believe they have a prestige name but not a lot of money left to go with it."

"I see, sir."

"One dissuades gossip below stairs, but that is what Miss Bernadette's maid implied to Charlie."

No wonder Charlie didn't want to valet for him, Anatole thought to himself, he knew there would be no great gratuity at the end of their stay.

"Anyway, I'd like you to make your way to the velvet room now and see to him before the tea."

"Yes sir."

Anatole nodded and excused himself. Carstairs had given him his instructions and despite the added extra workload Anatole was elated to not have been fired yet.

His mother had recommended him, and she had put herself on the line with Mr. Carstairs and Anatole could not disappoint her or shame her in any way. Anatole was determined that he would take care of Mr. Chenevert with no complaints.

After running up the backstairs two flights and walking calmly down the wide marble corridors Anatole arrived at what they called the velvet room. So called because of the black and purple velvet flocked paper that seemed impossibly elegant to

Anatole. It was dark and mysterious and masculine and was his favorite room at Bridlewood House.

He knocked twice and waited a moment. After not hearing a response, he entered. He found it empty and proceeded to prepare the room. No fire had been laid, and the evening could turn cold. So, he laid the wood and prepared it for the moment Mr. Chenevert might request it be lit. He then took the gentleman's valise and began to lay out his clothes. He hung the jackets and shirts individually or folded the underthings and placed them all in the wardrobe.

He had seen a lot of fine clothing in his time at Bridlewood House. Mr. McCambridge wore fine clothes that were made for him in town. A tailor named Mr. Randy came out regularly and brought bolts of fabric with him. Mr. Randy always called him into service as his assistant during those times. He had even made the very footman's livery that he wore each day. But Mr. Beau's clothes were very fine and of styles he had not yet seen. He was admiring the stitching on one of the jackets when the door opened.

Anatole was startled, he started speaking before he even turned to greet him.

"Sorry sir, I was just putting your things away."

"Quite alright," he said.

Anatole hung the jacket and turned to greet him properly. In the morning light he was much younger than Anatole had thought before. Probably twenty or so years old. Perhaps younger. About Anatole's age. He was blond and quite handsome. His eyes were a cornflower blue that were not unlike his own blue/green eyes. But as a creole Anatole's skin was dusky tan. And Mister Beau's was light and smooth as marble, but tan from afternoons spent outdoors.

"Shall we get this thing going?" He asked.

"This thing?" Anatole asked.

He smiled.

"Shall we get me dressed for the tea?"

"Of course, sir." I replied as I blushed. "Would sir like a bath?"

"No, I just had one this morning."

"My apologies, sir. I was only just now made aware that you would require a valet."

"I normally dress myself, but my sister insists that I have a standard to maintain."

"Of course, you do, sir."

"You manage to dress yourself every day, I presume."

"I do, sir."

"I do not think I need assistance in that area, but I am occasionally inclined toward laziness, so I do appreciate you hanging my clothes for me."

He nodded and gestured toward the wardrobe.

"If I may, sir," Anatole said, "I hope you know that what you saw in the woods the other night was not what it looked like."

"And I believe I told you that what you do is your own business." He said. "Let us not mention it again."

Anatole was quiet for a moment.

"You have some very fine clothes, sir."

"I had these made for me on Savile Row."

He assumed Anatole would know what that meant, but he did not want to ask and appear ignorant. Anatole had heard Mr. Randy mention it as a place in London.

"Which suit would you like to wear for the tea?"

"You decide for me, I never know about these things."

Part of a valet's job was to know men's style. Anatole was merely a second footman acting as a valet. Everything he knew about style he had learned from Mr. Randy. He hoped that he had paid enough attention.

He returned to Mr. Beau's wardrobe to have another look at

what he had brought. The tea would be black tie, of course. He had brought a black suit and a dark navy suit and a gray suit with a cutaway jacket. The blue suit was perfect for blending in with the rest of the gentlemen, but the gray was dark enough to be correct but would let him stand out a bit.

"Sir, I think this gray blue suit and black tie and waistcoat would be ideal for your skin tone, eye, and hair coloring."

Beau laughed.

"I don't think I have ever put that much effort into it."

Anatole suddenly felt as though he had overthought the whole thing. Anatole was sure that he could sense that.

"No, no," he said, "that's perfect. I was just reminding you of my laziness again."

Anatole nodded in relief. He did not get his sense of humor, perhaps because he was in such a state to impress him and his employer and to make his mother proud.

He began to undress, and Anatole turned toward the wardrobe to offer him some privacy. When he was undressed down to his underwear Anatole brought his stockings to him first. He knelt to put them on him, but he dissuaded him with a hand.

"I'm not a complete invalid just yet."

He pulled on the hose and snapped them into place. He then pulled on the fresh undershirt Anatole had folded for him on the bed. While he did that Anatole prepared his dress shirt. He held it as he put one arm through each hole. He then turned to Anatole, and he secured the buttons.

Anatole held his trousers for him to step into. He pulled them up and for a moment he was at a loss as to whether he was meant to button them for him. He held them up and waited a moment to see what he would do. Mercifully, Mr. Beau buttoned himself and Anatole was relieved from wondering.

"Would you mind taking care of this?"

He was nearly as tall as Anatole was, so he stood in front of him and began to tie the tie for him. Anatole had never tied anyone else's tie for them, so it was very awkward for him. What resulted was like trying to tie a tie with two left hands. He had to immediately untie it.

"Sorry sir."

"I have found that many valets find it less awkward if they stand behind and tie it as though they were tying their own."

Anatole moved behind him and attempted it again. It was a bit awkward at first. Anatole was careful not to get too close to Mr. Beau. He did not want the misunderstanding of the other evening to resurface. With the new technique he found immediate success.

"If sir would sit for a moment." Anatole gestured toward the chair next to the mirror.

He sat and Anatole brushed his Brutus style haircut into place. His sideburns had already been impeccably trimmed.

With the addition of the jacket, he was then the picture of the perfect southern gentleman.

"If you have everything you need, sir, I will be required elsewhere but I will see you before dinner tonight to prepare you."

"Thank you, Anatole."

"It is my pleasure, sir."

This gave Anatole just enough time to run up to his rooms and get into his afternoon footman's attire. He made leave and walked calmly down the hall to the doorway that led to the servants' backstairs. He then ran up the stairs to his room to make the change as quickly as possible. Guests would arrive soon, and he needed to be there before any of them did.

Dressed, he ran back down the stairs and practically slid into place at the front door next to Charlie, the first footman mere moments before the first carriage arrived.

"You were nearly late, idiot."

"Sorry, Charlie, I had to dress Mr. Beau."

"I don't care."

And with that the first guest arrived at Bridlewood House. Charlie opened the carriage door for the well-heeled couple who emerged. Anatole opened the front door of the house and we both escorted them inside where Mr. Carstairs would properly greet them and direct them toward the Champagne.

Chapter 7
The Belle of Terrebonne Parish

The morning had started off with an overcast sky and Charlotte worried that her tea would be spoiled by a melancholy air. So much so that she eschewed the ornate gray gown she had intended to wear for a somewhat simpler, yet cheerier one in violet. The sun, however, seemed like it might cooperate after all.

Emily finished pinning up Charlotte's copper locks in a fashion she had seen in The Saturday Evening Post. The magazines were kept in the library as they were quite expensive, and no one was allowed to touch them until after Charlotte's father had read them. They occupied a table with the day's paper. Emily completed the look with a small, jeweled pin as she had seen in the illustration in the magazine. Emily had once explained to her that most people had never even seen a magazine but her position at Bridlewood House allowed her to casually peruse a copy. She knew that many people read a paper to know what was going on in the world but access to popular stories of culture and entertainment were rare for most. The fact that Emily and Anatole were allowed to learn to read was an exception from many great houses. One that her mother had insisted upon.

She finished her masterpiece just as there was a knock at the door.

Emily stepped away from Charlotte and opened the door to her bedchamber to find Charlotte's father standing there. Since Charlotte's mother's death his attention to his own grooming had declined. But today his valet had gotten him together well enough for the tea.

"Papa!" Charlotte called from her dressing table, standing to receive him. "Come in and make yourself comfortable."

Charlotte gestured toward the sitting room of her bedroom suite. She stood up and crossed the room to him and planted a kiss on his cheek.

"Good to see you looking so well for the tea today."

"Well, you know I will only make a brief appearance."

"People will be so glad to see you."

"No, my darling, they are coming to see you, not some old fossil. They want to see what the Belle of Terrebonne Parish is wearing and serving and thinking and saying."

"Just a simple dress."

"It isn't the dress," he said, "it's how you wear it."

Charlotte blushed.

"Oh my, your hair looks fine today."

It was Emily's turn to beam with pride.

"Emily always keeps up on the trends, papa."

Mr. McCambridge rarely came to her rooms without purpose, so the room was weighted with the portent of his visit.

"The Mayhew boy is coming today. He's growing up to be a fine gentleman, don't you think?"

"I suppose so, father."

Charlotte knew where the conversation was going, though

she did not especially wish to have it at this moment. She had guests to receive shortly.

"He seemed very much in control of himself at your party."

"Indeed, he did."

"He is exactly the sort of young man you should be marrying."

He was, in fact, exactly the kind of man she *should* marry. She had never heard a bad word about Robert Mayhew. But she had not heard much of anything about him. She had been raised around him, but they did not have a lot to do with each other. There was nothing particularly wrong with Robert Mayhew, but would it be so wrong to get to know him first? Not that she would ever disagree with her father's instructions. He had given her the life of a luxury where she had never wanted for anything. So, to disobey him now would be unimaginable.

"Father." Charlotte began, though she realized that she did not know how to continue.

"Yes, my dear?"

She struggled to find a way to say what she needed to.

"I know that you want the very best for me."

"Of course, I do."

"And I want to be a good daughter. I want to be appropriate, and I want to be a feather in your cap, as they say."

"Darling you are a sparkling ornament. You are the very symbol of this family. Your mother and I could not be prouder of the young woman you are becoming."

She appreciated the kind words, but did he understand that it made her feel like chattel? Like a possession whose mere existence was for show? She never questioned his love and yet she knew that women were exactly that to him. She and her mother had merely been sparkling jewels in his crown. But after all was that not their place? Would her mother have even looked at him if he had not made his fortune?

"Father, I will do whatever you ask of me for I feel that is the least of what I owe to you. You have given me a life of privilege- "

"It isn't privilege, my dear, it is only what we deserve. I have worked so hard so that we could have this *privilege*, as you call it."

"I'm sorry, father, I did not mean to sound ungrateful."

He sighed heavily.

"I know that you did not mean to, my darling daughter. I have worked so hard for this family. I have created a fortune from literally nothing. And I have used that fortune to make the best possible home life for my girls."

"I know you have, father. And I am most thankful."

She smiled warmly for she did not know any other way to proceed. The way he often spoke of her mother as if she were still in the house with them sometimes broke her heart.

What she wanted for herself was immaterial to what she wanted for her father. He had given her all and she could at least give herself to Robert Mayhew in return. If that was all he asked, then why should she not?

A knock at the door alerted Emily to answer.

Anatole stood there.

"The guests are arriving." He said and bowed.

"Thank you, Anatole." Charlotte responded.

Anatole bowed and stepped back as Emily closed the door on him. While they were all friends, they managed to maintain an air of primacy. To pretend that they had not grown up together and that they were servants to her. They all understood that doing otherwise could end in their dismissal by her father.

"Father, I should go and present myself to my guests."

"Of course, my dear." He beamed with pride.

"And you will stop by and greet everyone?"

"Yes, of course. I'll give you a bit to greet everyone first and then I will say hello."

"You know that you are welcome to stay, Papa? You know

that you are most welcome. Our friends enjoy hearing your stories."

"Your young friends humor an old man. But I know what they really want."

George McCambridge smiled and kissed his daughter on the cheek. He smelled of new leather and exotic cigars.

"Charlotte, you are everything a father could wish for. Beauty and understanding and a sense of familial duty."

She had no way of responding that was not at odds with her love for him. He turned and left the room leaving a void the shape of her unsayable words.

"Is there anything else, Miss Charlotte?" Emily asked.

"No, Emily."

Emily opened the door and held it for Charlotte. She walked out of the room with Emily staying behind to tidy the room in her absence.

Charlotte walked alone down the long wide corridor. The luxuries of her life were mostly lost on her as she had never lived another way. But she never failed to appreciate the grandeur of the entry hall as she approached from the top of the curved marble stairway with its massive crystal chandelier floating elegantly.

As she descended, she saw him. Robert Mayhew stood at the doorway giving his hat and gloves to Anatole. Charlie, the first footman stood by solemnly doing nothing. She regarded Robert Mayhew for a moment. He was unaware yet that he was being observed. She saw that he was neither solicitous nor nasty to the servants. He was just completely neutral. She felt no passion for him one way or another. She almost wished that he would do something that would make her dislike him. For it seemed that he would never do anything to make her love him.

"Miss Charlotte." He called up to her as he saw her descending the staircase.

"Robert, we're so glad you could come."

She greeted him with a warm smile, and he kissed her proffered hand.

"May I walk you in?" Robert asked.

"Please go on in without me, I have to speak to the servants about something."

"Of course."

He looked disappointed, but he nodded and took leave to the drawing room.

Anatole heard her words and stepped forward.

"Yes, Miss Charlotte?"

"Nothing." She spoke. "I just did not want to walk in on his arm. People would get the wrong idea."

"Understood." Anatole said and stepped back into place beside the door.

Charlotte waited a moment then finally entered the drawing room. The smell of banks of fresh flowers overcame her. The room had been set beautifully and everyone seemed to be mingling well. The sun was now shining beautifully, and the doors were open allowing a refreshing breeze to circulate.

She was set upon almost immediately by Beulah Sugarbaker. Beulah leaned in and kissed her on each cheek.

"So lovely to see you."

"So lovely to see you as well." Charlotte said.

"I hear that you might make an announcement this season." Beulah whispered.

Charlotte's brow furrowed for a moment.

"I cannot imagine what you mean."

"Don't worry, I can keep a secret. Your father told my father that an engagement could happen sometime this year."

Charlotte was stunned for a moment.

"Well, that is for father and Mr. Mayhew to work out."

"Of course, of course." Beulah said. "We are all just men's playthings."

She laughed her famous guffaw and Charlotte found herself involuntarily wincing.

"But please help yourself to another drink, Beulah."

Charlotte was inwardly furious that her father had discussed the matter of her engagement with Beulah's father, seemingly before he had even discussed it with her. Winston Sugarbaker was her father's solicitor, but he should not have shared that information with Beulah. Who else in the parish knew about the pending announcement? She did not know why it suddenly bothered her. She had tacitly given her approval of the engagement. But truly it was only because she knew there was no other option.

Beau and Bernadette stood in a corner chatting. They became quiet when Charlotte approached.

"How fine you both look." Charlotte said.

"Thank you, dear cousin." Bernadette smiled. "We can't wait to meet more of your friends."

"They are dying to get to know you both better after the party the other night."

Bernadette leaned into Charlotte's ear to speak.

"Will there be any eligible gentlemen here today?"

Charlotte was momentarily embarrassed but thought for a moment. Would there be a single gentleman who would be a good marriage for Bernadette and for the family that would also be ignorant or uncaring of her broken engagement? Most likely the eligible men of this parish would know nothing of whatever scandal there might be, though she thought it might be a good idea to know the exact nature of it.

Charlotte looked around the room and toward the gentleman directly across from her. He stood drinking a julep and conversing with Caroline Johnson.

"I may have someone in mind." Charlotte said aloud, but mainly to herself.

She watched as Caroline Johnson smiled uncomfortably with her intended fiancée Robert Mayhew and she imagined what it might take to make a match between the two. Tying the families together and freeing herself to make a more attractive decision when that option came along. But what if a more attractive option never came along? What if Robert Mayhew was the best man that she would ever be allowed to marry?

Chapter 8
Main Street

Anatole sat on the back of the carriage as they made their way down Royale Avenue, the Main Street of shops in Pointe Cèdre. He was accompanying Miss Charlotte and Emily to pick up a dress at Hermione Bouchard's shop. He had his own errands to run and was grateful for the ride into town.

The air was still warm, with a hint of humidity, as the summer drew to a close and autumn seemed only a breath away. The trees had not yet changed, but there was something in the air that his grandmother used to call *the plucking*. Something to do with harvest.

The top was down so that he could hear their conversation and so that they could include him in it, though having a footman in the carriage with them would have been unseemly. At least according to his own mother. It just was not done. They were able to chat the whole way about upcoming plans.

Charlotte had invited him along to carry parcels, but Anatole also suspected it was because she enjoyed the three of them together in the stolen moments where they could pretend to just be friends again. He enjoyed those moments as well. The two beautiful young women were his dearest friends. But more. If Charlotte had not been from such a superior family, he would call her his own family.

Plans were already underway for Charlotte's mother's big Christmas gala, and Charlotte found herself thrust into her mother's role as head of society. Anatole understood that Mrs. McCambridge hoped to help Charlotte to meet more suitable matches for herself. He did not know what she meant by that but had a good idea.

"So, I have to choose a fabric today for the party or it may not arrive in time!" Charlotte said.

"Then we must choose carefully. Miss Hermione already has the swatches of the newest fabrics of the season. We will know as soon as we see it, I am certain."

Anatole was never sure if Emily faked her enthusiasm for Charlotte's life events. They had all been friends for so long that they were always genuinely happy for her, but it was impossible to ignore how stilted the situation was at times. Listening to her problems and never sharing their own. Not that she would not have listened, but that she simply would not know how to respond to a problem that could not be solved with money. Or even a problem that involved a lack of money. It seemed awkward and unfair to bring her into that world which she had fortuitously avoided.

"What do you think about green for the Christmas Eve Réveillon Gala, Anatole?" Charlotte asked.

She and Emily both laughed.

"Green is a most attractive color with your skin tone, Miss Charlotte." He played along. "But honestly, I think royal blue would be more becoming."

Charlotte stopped laughing for a moment.

"You know what? I think he's right!"

The girls both laughed again, and Anatole realized how little he understood of women of any age.

The carriage lurched to a stop in front of Hermione Bouchard's dressmaking establishment.

"If you'd like to wait outside, we may be a while." Emily said to Anatole.

"If it's alright, I need to pick up a parcel for Mr. McCambridge from Mr. Bouchard's shop.

"Yes, of course, "she said, "meet us back here in an hour."

Anatole nodded to the ladies and made his way across the street to Mr. Randy's establishment. It was an overcast day but did not imminently portend rain. Still, it was a lively afternoon on the streets of Pointe Cèdre. People shopped and strolled, apparently in a good mood, as they often looked at him and smiled or nodded.

Randall Bouchard was the husband of Hermione Bouchard. He was the tailor of Pointe Cèdre, and indeed all of Terrebonne. Though he was known simply as Mr. Randy throughout the parish. He and Hermione had had a happy yet childless marriage. He had heard his mother call it a *white marriage*, though he did not yet know what that meant. And since he had only heard his mother say it in a whisper, he knew better than to ask anyone.

Mr. Randy's shop featured a sign that was merely an intricate wooden carving of thread and needle. The thread was painted violet, and the needle was silver. It swung on creaky hinges in the slight breeze. He pushed the door open and heard the bell announce his arrival.

Mr. Randy looked up from his books and smiled. He was a handsome older gentleman of about forty. He was friendly and professional and spoke to Anatole, not as a servant, but as an equal. Which was unusual.

"Good afternoon, Anatole."

"Good afternoon, sir. I am here to pick up the parcels for Mr. McCambridge."

"Yes, of course." He spoke. "Follow me."

Anatole followed Mr. Randy to the back of the store behind a curtain.

"How are your uniforms?"

"They are as fine as ever, Mr. Randy."

"It looks as though you are still growing."

"I hope not, sir." Anatole said.

"Let me see."

Mr. Randy took the tape measure from around his neck and got down on his knees. He measured Anatole's inside seam, grazing his manhood with his hand in the process.

"Quarter of an inch longer since last time. We shall have to make some alterations."

"I appreciate that, Mr. Randy."

"You really are growing into a fine lad, Anatole. Just look at these muscles you are developing from carrying parcels. And these thighs. I shall have to use more fabric next time."

Anatole blushed as he never knew what to say when Mr. Randy complimented him. He did seem to linger over his body more than necessary.

"Thank you, sir."

Mr. Randy stood and handed a few parcels, wrapped in his signature violet paper.

"Come back next week and bring your uniforms for those alterations.

"Of course."

"Oh, wait. I have one more."

"Yes, sir." Anatole smiled as Mr. Randy disappeared back behind the curtain.

The bell on the door jingled and Anatole looked up to see who had entered.

Anatole was instantly struck by how tall the man was. He was one of the few men he had seen who was as tall as he was. Dark haired and quite handsome. He was older than Anatole, but still young, perhaps 25, and impeccably groomed. He looked at Anatole quizzically.

"Are you the proprietor?" He asked. "I am in need of some new suits."

"I am not." Anatole said. "Mr. Randy is the tailor, and he is just in the back."

"That is a fine-looking coat you are wearing. He must make your suits?"

"I am merely a footman, but yes, he makes my livery for a fine household. He made this jacket for my birthday. He would take good care of you and your new suits. One moment, let me get him for you."

Anatole stepped behind the curtain and called out to Mr. Randy.

"Mr. Randy, there is a customer to see you."

Mr. Randy came out of the backroom carrying the parcels that Anatole was to carry for Mr. McCambridge.

"I am going to need a few new suits and some repairs on my uniforms.

"What sort of uniform?" Mr. Randy asked.

"Army Captain Jonathan Davies."

"Pleased to meet you sir."

Mr. Randy finished wrapping the final parcel. He handed them all to Anatole in an unwieldy stack.

"Thank you, sir."

"Do you need a hand with those?" Captain Davies asked.

"If you'd open the door for me, I would be much obliged."

Captain Davies opened the door and the bell jingled jauntily. Anatole nodded his thanks and exited the store awkwardly balancing his parcels. He made it to the carriage and deposited them neatly in the back.

Derry John, the driver waited patiently at his post on top of the carriage. His name was John but for some reason he was known as Derry John. Perhaps he was from a town called Derry. It was not that Anatole was not curious, as he was curious about almost everything, but that Derry John was a quiet man and did not seem inclined toward unnecessary conversation. A trait that probably made him a better servant and a good driver.

"Derry John," Anatole said. "I am going into the inn to have an ale. Would you care to join?"

"I shouldn't like to leave my post."

"They should be in there at least another half hour."

"Oh, alright." Derry John agreed. "Since I'm with you."

Anatole knew that he meant that he would be less likely to get into trouble if he were with him.

Before they got to the door Charlotte and Emily stepped out onto the boardwalk.

"Anatole." Emily called to him in a loud whisper.

Anatole turned to see Miss Charlotte glaring at him. She looked more sternly than he had ever seen her look before. He felt a blush of embarrassment spread over his body like a rash. He and Derry John exchanged glances and headed for the carriage.

"Beg your pardon, ma'am." Derry John said, doffing his cap and opening the door to the carriage.

"Imagine someone going into a place like that and seeing one of our staff in livery in there. It would look most improper."

Anatole bowed.

"I am sorry, Miss Charlotte. It is all my fault. Derry John did not want to go in, but I convinced him."

"He should not have been so easy to convince."

"You are quite right, Miss Charlotte." Derry John acquiesced.

Derry John gave Anatole a murderous look.

Miss Charlotte was quiet all the ride home. Anatole realized that he had almost embarrassed the House of McCambridge, which would have been difficult to recover from and could have ended his career. There was shame, but also another feeling. Loss.

The Charlotte that he had grown up with was gone. She was evolving into a young woman who would need her own as well as her familial reputation to remain unadulterated. Anatole tried to understand the pressure that his friend was under, and he realized that he was not helping.

He would need to grow up himself to meet the needs of the household. But also, to meet the needs of his friend, even if that friendship was bound to continue changing into something else. Something that he was not ready to consider.

Chapter 9
Memento Mori

Charlotte's mother had only been gone a short time. Not even a year since the fever had taken her. Each day she awoke to another chapter of the same nightmare. While the pain did not seem to ease, she did find that she was better able to hide it from her father and the people around her.

She felt unprepared for life and her father was only able to help in so many ways. For there were some things that only a mother could teach. He was so involved with his business and seemed only to care for social interactions in as much as their machinations could further his standing in the community and his business.

He had made no secret of his plan to marry her off to the son of a potential business partner. The Mayhew family were as prosperous as her own. Robert Mayhew was neither handsome nor unattractive. His countenance was unremarkable, and his personality was untroubled by charms of any kind. He was neither a good nor bad option, he was simply the option.

Option was a strange word because it implied alternatives. At present Charlotte was not aware of any alternatives to marrying

Robert Mayhew, though she had introduced him to Cousin Bernadette to create a possible interest. Right now, she only knew that her father had obviously decided her fate and she would abide by his wishes. But as she had never really known many men outside her social circle, she had no idea if she was missing anything. The only idea of romance was what she read in books and had been assured by her mother that those stories were written to stir the unseemly desires of hysterical women.

As much as she missed her mother right now, she knew that she would be in full agreement with her father. That she would also support a marriage that upheld social and financial standings was no question. Her mother loved her dearly, of that she also had no question. But she had been raised with immutable rules about social appropriateness that she had tried to pass on to Charlotte.

Charlotte had become lonely in the months since her mother's death. She had confided so much in Emily, but she needed more. She longed to have someone to talk to who understood her position. Someone from her own class, as much as she hated to admit it. Her mother had warned her about that, though she had refused to believe how friendships and needs would change.

Her mother had been raised in the stifling world of east coast society where one wrong word could destroy a girl's future. Men were immune to the machinations of high society, of course. The men usually had the money, so the women were both the queens and the chattel of that stratosphere. Charlotte had no desire to be a part of any of that, but she had no choice.

Charlotte walked out of the room and into the corridor. Charlie Mayes was walking down the hallway and stopped and stood with back against the wall, as was custom for a servant when a superior came into the hallway.

"Charlie, please get me my wrap."

Charlie nodded and stepped into the coat chamber and

quickly returned with Charlotte's favorite wrap. A long light-weight cloak of cashmere that had belonged to her mother. The scent of rosewater was only a memory now.

"Thank you."

Charlie nodded back and opened the front door. Charlotte stepped out into the cool afternoon and began her now familiar walk. For nearly a year she had worn a path between the front door of Bridlewood House and her destination. She walked up the gravel-paved driveway and up the hill a bit. She stopped just at the brick pillars and contemplated the wrought iron gate. What lay beyond was a muddle. An enigma. Everything she loved and hated all rolled into one now. Her mother, whom she loved beyond words, was there. But consumption had taken her and given Charlotte only a stone box in a mausoleum to visit. The trade was unfair, and Charlotte had spent nearly a year raging at her first experience with the inequity of this loss. And as with any child of privilege the first taste of reality had felt like a laceration across her heart.

The gate gave way easily and soundlessly. Charlotte made her way along the path she and her father had created. There had been a cemetery here before her father had bought the land for Bridlewood, and he had built a mausoleum that properly reflected their status in society and business as her father seemed equally obsessed with both.

The walk was meditative. She had done it so often. In the beginning she did it every single day. And over the months she had gotten to where she only did it two or three times a week. And in time the walk had become a time where she began her talk with her mother.

The mausoleum loomed ahead of Charlotte. Whenever she reached this point on her walk her heart always dropped into the sunken garden of loss. The priest had taught her that her mother was waiting for her just beyond the veil that separated her from this world. Still, she had died in a hospital for people with consumption. Not in her own bed. And for that Charlotte was forever angry. Her mother had wanted to die in the manner in which she had been born, in a home of great dignity.

Charlotte approached the mausoleum doors. She had still found it a dichotomy of emotions. Melancholy at her mother's resting place, but also a strange comfort at being able to sit and chat with her even in a decidedly one-sided conversation. She reached out and pushed the handle down on the door and it opened easily, as it had been well used. She pushed inside and found the antechamber lit with its skylight. There were two doors. One with what would one day be the resting place of herself and her future husband, and one with a resting place for her mother and her father.

She pushed open the door to the chamber on the right of her, the one that she would one day occupy. She stepped inside for the first time in her life. There was an eeriness to being in the room and staring at the stone box where she would spend eternity. Would her husband be buried here next to her, and would their children come and visit them here? Would her own children come here some day and mourn her? Would they mourn the grandmother they would never know? She would make certain that her spirit remained alive within them.

She was not unaware of the amount of hope she had invested in the future, nor the irony of musing over that hope while standing in her own tomb. She was literally whistling past the graveyard in her own way. But she did realize that when she did see the phantom of her future husband and children, she did not see Robert Mayhew in the picture. The face of the man was blurred, but alas it was not him. She saw this as a personal failure that she would overcome. But then she only guessed what the future held and did not yet know what would soon change.

She was young and privileged, and her mother's untimely

death was the only indication that her life would not go entirely by the strict rulebook of her class. She knew any number like herself. They all had the same upbringing, though some with more money than others. But they all had the same societal rules that they abided. They all seemed to marry the same young man to the betterment of their family fortunes. But why she, when her father's fortunes were clearly so beyond the average, why could she not find a man who pleased her and marry him no matter his rank?

She ceased the line of thinking as it seemed somehow to be ungrateful or unfaithful to her father who had done so much for her. He had given her the world and only asked for this in return. Robert Mayhew would be her husband, and they would have children and be happy and one day it would all end here in this very room when she was laid to rest. She turned and left the room and walked across to the other chamber.

She opened the door that contained the sarcophagus of her mother and the future home of her father. The Windows and the skylights filled the room with a dappled light. Light that created shadows and depth in corners and recesses. Light revealed mysteries, but it created them as well.

She stepped forward toward the stone box. And looked down upon the writing. She took a cloth from the pocket of her dress. She always secreted one away for fear that her mother's tomb would become covered in dust. She did not know why it bothered her, and she would never ask one of the servants to do it, they were all so busy.

The writing on the stone lid was still so fresh. The stone was smooth and shiny and had very little dust. Mrs. Blanchet had clearly assigned someone to regularly clean. She realized at this moment that she missed her mother as much as ever.

When the mausoleum had been built, they had built in seating. At some point one of the servants placed a chair in the chamber. They must have realized how often she came to this place. It was a chair she recognized from her father's library. A small but comfortable place to rest herself while she had her chats.

"Hello, mother." Charlotte said to the box. "I just wanted to stop in and tell you that our party went so well. You would have been proud to see what a good job Papa did, and me. I will one day be as good a hostess as you, but it may take some time. You would have been proud to see such a crowd. I hope you were able to see the party. Sometimes I fancy you floating over and seeing what all is going on.

It was an easy fantasy. Charlotte had often heard the echo of her mother's voice down an empty corridor. Merely echoes of the past, she told herself. But perhaps her mother did watch over her. Imagining it so with a mixture of horror and happiness. A guardian angel? But this was not a fairy tale, not even the darker kind of the Grimm Brothers. This was her life, and such childish ideas should be banished lest she succumb to a darker nature.

Charlotte pulled her wrap tighter around her and before she knew it, she had fallen asleep. She fell immediately into a dream. A comfort surrounded her, warm and natal. She felt a caress on her cheek and opened her eyes to see her mother standing before her. Not withered and ill as she had been at the end of her life, but as she had been before the sickness. Hearty and hale and smiling.

"My darling you have so much life to live." The voice was just as her mother's had been at its warmest. "But you must choose wisely. You must not disobey your father."

"I wouldn't." Charlotte cried. "How could I?"

"Temptations always lie on the horizon, my child. Especially for a beautiful young woman of means like yourself. But you have been raised to be above such temptations."

Charlotte woke startled and sat up in the chair. She was alone in the tomb and the light from the skylight and the

windows was fading. She did not wish to walk through the cemetery in the dwindling light. She stood up from the chair and
walked toward the door of the chamber and turned one last time
to look back at her mother's stone box.

"I love you." She said in the echo chamber.

"I love you." Echoed back to her as if it had been an answer to
what she had said. She decided to believe that it was her mother
and closed the door behind herself before setting herself on the
trail back to the house.

Chapter 10
Siblings and Rivalry

Anatole understood that as Charlotte took on the role of social head of the parish one of her most important goals was to raise money to fund the local charities that her mother had always supported. He admired that it was something that she was so involved in supporting.

The entire Bridlewood household was involved. A luncheon for the widows and orphans of the army had been planned. An organization that had long been in place, created by her own mother, but considering a possible unrest in the nation seemed like a good idea. To raise money for the widows and orphans fund, mind you, no actual widows or orphans would be invited to bring down the festive nature of such an event.

On the morning of the luncheon Anatole was summoned to Mr. Beau's rooms to prepare him for the event. He had already pressed everything for him to wear and it was hanging neatly in his armoire for Anatole to retrieve when he arrived. He brought with him a pan of hot water.

Anatole began to arrange Mr. Beau's toiletries for the day. His shaving supplies, a cup, brush, and razor were all part of a matched set. They were scratched and worn. They had obviously been well cared for but were very old. Far older than Mr. Beau himself.

He would normally lay out Mr. Beau's toiletries on the desk beside the armoire. Anatole found the desk in disarray. A case was opened and a camera, the first one that Anatole had seen this close, was nestled inside. A book about photography was next to the case. What Anatole assumed were the accoutrements of the camera lay about on the desk. Normally part of his duty was to tidy the room for his master, but he decided that it was best not to touch the array of expensive equipment.

He was startled by a quick knock at the door, and then it opened before anyone could give a response.

Bernadette Chenevert breezed into the suite of rooms as though she owned the house. She was trailed by her maid, Eunice. Eunice had the kind of pinched face where you could never decide if she was happy or tormented but working for Bernadette Anatole could only imagine that she was tormented. Anatole had formed an opinion the way that servants often did. Based entirely on the way they treated people who could do nothing for them.

"Where is my brother?"

She asked in a hurried and pointed manner.

"I beg your pardon, Mademoiselle Chenevert," Anatole bowed, "I am preparing his toilette, as Mr. Beau is expected soon."

Bernadette Chenevert stood in front of the mirror as Eunice, her lady's maid, finished pinning her hair in place from behind. Her blond hair was pulled back with curls trailing down her back.

"How is that ma'am?"

"That's quite fine, Eunice." Bernadette said. "It will do."

The door opened again and this time it was Mr. Beau himself.

The handsome, young, blond man stood before them looking quizzically.

"Whatever are you all doing in here?" He asked.

"Mr. Beau," Eunice blushed, bowed, and scraped, "I was just finishing with Miss Bernadette."

"Come in, Beau." Bernadette called.

"These are my rooms, are they not?" He enquired.

Bernadette ignored him as she beheld her own reflection in the cheval mirror. She seemed pleased with the result of the effort. Eunice had spent weeks making the gown and it fit perfectly. The velvet fabric hugged her curves perfectly. Her breasts were cradled in emerald-green satin and framed with matching lace.

Beau came in and sat in a white velvet covered chair next to the mirror.

"Ma'am, I have put aside today's jewelry already." Eunice said. "I brought them with you so that I may put them on you?"

"Yes."

Eunice retrieved the small fruitwood box from her bag and opened it to reveal the modestly sparkling set. Being twenty-three years old and still not married was not desperate, but very close.

Eunice handed Bernadette the diamond earrings first. Bernadette clipped each into place. Eunice then strung the matching necklace around her neck from behind and closed the clasp securely. She followed up with the matching bracelet.

"Perfect." Eunice admired.

"Yes, indeed." Bernadette agreed.

"Our cousin certainly has a beautiful home." Beau said.

"If you like living out in the sticks." Bernadette waved her hand around indicating the estate.

"Oh, I think I would like it for a change."

"And deal with these provincial rubes all day?" Bernadette enquired aghast. "To have your clothes made by that thinly veiled sodomite whom I was forced to smile and have a drink with at Charlotte's party? Uncle George is not from our level of society and does not know of such things, but you were raised better than that."

"I'm sure there are *thinly veiled sodomites* wherever you go." Beau replied.

"Yes, but who invites their tailor?"

"Miss Bernadette," Eunice interrupted, "I need to run down to the housekeeper's rooms to fetch something."

And with that, the dim light that was Eunice, was gone.

Beau looked at his sister.

"You look wonderful."

"I'm not sure this hairstyle is very current."

"You could have let Cousin Charlotte's hairdresser do it." Beau said.

Bernadette looked at Beau aghast, her eyes widened.

"This woman who calls herself *Queen Marie*. A *negro* woman who owns a *brothel*? I realize that we are out in the country now, but if we start lowering our standards now there will be no end to it."

"Eunice did a fine job on that gown; you could be more appreciative of her."

"I complimented her on the gown, but if you make them feel indispensable the next thing you know they will be asking for *days off*." Bernadette chided. "Did you know that *days off* is at thing they expect now? I swear, you never listen to mother."

"That much is quite true."

"How did the valet work out for you?" She asked as if Anatole were not standing right there in the room with them.

"Yes, Anatole is going to be helping me, though I can

certainly dress on my own if necessary." He gestured toward Anatole behind her.

Bernadette looked at him as if he were from another planet.

"What did I just say about standards, Beau? What has mother always said?" She was astonished. "We are the aspiration of these people. If we do not uphold the standard, then we may as well be peasants."

Beau laughed heartily.

"Sister, while I have grown used to your plutocratic tendencies, I still do not support them."

"You will," Bernadette said, "eventually you will."

Anatole found the antagonization odd in their relationship, but he had no siblings.

"Cousin Charlotte has grown into a beautiful young woman." Beau changed the subject.

"Indeed, she has." Bernadette agreed. "I hope you two will appreciate each other's charms more as time progresses."

Beau said nothing. He seemed to know what she was implying but chose to ignore it, but it was not lost on Anatole.

"I suspect Uncle George has already chosen a husband for Charlotte."

"Then you could give him a little competition. We are distant enough for marriage and you know that this would be a fine opportunity for our family."

"Yes, I am aware that the burden of this family's fortune is now upon me after what happened to you."

Bernadette cast him a look so vicious it could have cut glass.

Anatole witnessed the exchange and tried to be a good servant. One who ignores what is not meant for his ears. But Charlotte was his friend, as well as his employer. They had grown up as if as family.

"Little brother, what I lack in marital options I more than make up for in cunning."

Anatole continued to try to ignore what she said, but the tone of her voice was chilling. He could tell that she had a devious mind and a plan that involved Charlotte.

"Charlotte has an intended, even if she is not yet ready." Beau said. "Clearly the decision has been made."

"This Mayhew person?" Bernadette laughed. "This brittle little man who leaves no more of a memory of his existence than a will-o-the-wisp?"

"I know he may not meet your exacting standards, dear sister, but he does meet those of our uncle George."

"His family has money, but *we* have the name. We have always had the name. And like it or not, that is of great value in this world you were born into, my dear brother."

"Alright, I understand, and I am quite bored with talking about it. Now, please leave so that I can get ready for this damned thing."

"As you wish," Bernadette said, "but we aren't finished with this discussion."

With that she left the room in a cloud of rosewater.

"Shall we?" Beau asked.

"Yes, of course sir." Anatole replied. "Normally I would tidy the room, but I did not wish to disturb your apparatus."

"Good." Beau replied flatly.

Anatole stood by waiting for Mr. Beau to stand and begin to prepare him for the party.

"Mr. Beau?" Anatole interrupted his thought.

"What?" He snapped.

"I beg your pardon, sir." Anatole said. "Please let me know when you would like to begin."

Mr. Beau snapped out of his reverie and stood.

Unlike most men Anatole had known, Mr. Beau bathed almost every day. Perhaps the only thing they had in common. On average gentlemen of the day would bathe no more than once a week. But trends were changing among the elite, Anatole was learning.

Mr. Beau stood and unlaced his own tie and began unbuttoning his shirt. He stepped out of his trousers and left them on the floor for Anatole to retrieve, as was proper.

Anatole placed the warm water on the table next to where Mr. Beau was standing. He placed the washcloth next to the bowl.

"Do you require any assistance, sir?"

"Of course not. I'm not an invalid yet."

As Mr. Beau removed his undergarments Anatole gathered his clothes for hanging and his underthings for rinsing later. He averted his gaze as always to allow Mr. Beau his privacy.

"Would sir like the screen in place?"

"Not necessary, we are both grown men, after all."

Anatole hung up the trousers, vest, and jacket that Mr. Beau had been wearing that morning. He inspected the shirt and tie to see if they would yet need laundering. He laid out fresh undergarments for Mr. Beau, as that was what he required.

When he turned around Mr. Beau was finished bathing and awaiting the rest of his toilette. Anatole looked at the small tray of toiletries and found some things that he did not immediately recognize. Small but beautiful bottles in a travel case fit for a fastidious gentleman.

The first bottle was intricately cut glass and had a cypress branch on it.

"Open it and hand it to me."

Anatole did as he was told.

Mr. Beau took the proffered bottle and splashed an amount on his hand, handing the bottle back to Anatole. The scent of cypress and rosemary filled Anatole's nostrils. Mr. Beau took the liquid and applied it under each arm, and then lifted his own baubles and gave his manhood a going over as well. Anatole had never seen anything like this.

"Undergarments." Mr. Beau said brusquely.

Anatole held the underwear for Mr. Beau to step into, allowing Mr. Beau to button them himself. Followed by the stockings.

"Now the next bottle."

The second bottle had an orange on it. Anatole opened it and handed it to Mr. Beau. He took the bottle and splashed it on his hands as well. The scent of orange and almond pervaded the air now as Mr. Beau abluted himself with the cologne.

Next came the shirt and waistcoat. Tie and jacket. The shoes were already shined and ready for Mr. Beau to step into. The tie was tied as Mr. Beau had previously shown him.

Mr. Beau was a handsome gentleman, indeed. It was unfortunate, to Anatole, that he and his sister seemed only interested in money and position.

"Is there anything else, sir?"

"No."

Mr. Beau gave himself one last look in the mirror before heading out the door.

"I could have done this faster by myself, but well done." Mr. Beau said under his breath, as he closed the door.

Anatole felt disappointment, though he knew that he had done his best. He was determined to be a good valet and to make his mother proud. If only to save enough money to leave Bridlewood and find his own fortune.

Chapter 11
Cabinet of Curiosities

Mini trekked up the backstairs of Bridlewood carrying a load of linens up to the guest rooms. Between she and Lydia, the scullery maid, there were jobs that never ended at Bridlewood. She was constantly at the laundry and Lydia was forever at the dishes. They would often sit and talk during their lunchtime meal break, which was at ten in the morning so they could get on with preparing lunch for the family. That was also when Mini tended to change the family's bed linens. She sat the basket on the landing and then sat down on it and languished in the short five-minute break she would sometimes give herself on the backstairs.

Mini had been in Bridlewood since she moved to Point Cèdre many years ago. She had worked on a small farm with her family in Mississippi. The had been freed by a man who owned a sawmill. He had been very good to them and had treated her momma especially well.

When he died, he had tried to leave money to her momma, but she was not white enough to inherit money. Sometimes Mini would imagine what life would be like if her momma could have been rich. Living in a big house with someone else to wash the linens. But her momma said that God had a reason he didn't want them to be rich, and her daddy probably would have just drunk it all anyway.

She remembered when Miss Blanchet was first training her for the position and was taking her around the Bridlewood House on a tour. She did not imagine ever being able to clean all the beautiful things without breaking anything. But she had to and knew that she would treat each object as if it were the finest China.

One day she found herself in the library cleaning when Mr. McCambridge walked into the room. She had never met him but could tell by his presence. She had been told to quietly leave when a family member entered a room unless she was urgently doing something. Either way, they were to become invisible.

She turned to leave, but he stopped her.

"You're new here."

"Yes, sir."

"What is your name?"

"Mini, sir."

"Carry on."

"Thank you, sir."

She went on about dusting, desperate to make her escape from the large and imposing man.

"Do you know what that is?"

"No, sir." She replied honestly, "I reckon it's a kind of cabinet?"

He walked over to the ornately carved piece of furniture. There was a lock, but the key was inside. He turned the key and opened the burl wood doors. Revealed was an arrangement of drawers in different shapes and sizes. She had never seen any craftsmanship like it, but that was true for most everything at Bridlewood House.

She stood in awe.

"It's beautiful."

"Would you like to see something interesting?" He asked.

"Yes, please!"

He opened a drawer and pulled out a piece of blue-green glass.

"What is it?" She asked.

"That is a piece of sea glass." He spoke. "I have a plantation on the sea in the Caribbean. When it storms on the beach and lightning strikes the sand it makes glass."

She had never seen something so fantastical, but she had also never been to a beach.

"Let me show you something else."

There was no way that Mini could say no.

"Yes, sir!"

He opened a small drawer and pulled out a small greyish piece.

"What is it?" She asked apprehensively.

"It is a pinkie bone from a thief on my plantation in the Caribbean."

Her eyes widened in shock. She was horrified yet fascinated.

"Can I show you one more thing?" He asked.

She really did need to get on with her work, but she did not feel as though she could say no to the Master of the House.

"Yes, of course."

He pulled the handle on a long rectangular drawer.

George McCambridge pulled something out and then opened his hand and revealed white carving. As she inspected it more closely her eyes widened. It was a naked lady and a naked man. And he seemed to be thrusting himself *inside* her. She gasped.

Mr. McCambridge laughed.

"Is each drawer full of weird stuff?"

"Indeed, it is."

"Amazing." She said. "I have to get back to my work but thank you for showing me."

"Anytime, Mini." He smiled. "I have a lot more to show you, sometime."

She nodded and backed out of the room. He was a very nice man, but she could see what he wanted. She could *see* men. She knew that she would need to avoid being alone with him if she wanted to stay safe and keep her job.

Mini did not like many men. She was of a slight build and just too small to defend herself when they were aggressive. So many men had come along and taken advantage of her diminutive stature. She had spent her life defending herself against the men around her. Her father, her uncle, her brothers.

There were midnight attacks and fumblings that she sometimes could fight off and sometimes she could not. Her uncle would sometimes try to bother her when he knew she was feeding the chickens at the pen away from the house.

Their nuisance was one of the reasons she had decided to go into service at Bridlewood. A place to live and work where she might be left alone. But soon she realized that she was not even safe there.

When she was twelve her father had first come to *bother* her while she was bathing. Her mother had taught her the word *bother*, as if there were no other word for it. As if the act itself were just a nuisance to be endured and ignored.

He came and pretended like he was going to help her in the bathtub as if it was not the first time that he had ever helped with anything. What happened next, she would place into a box in her mind and never open. She learned that the mind had compartments, and some things did not ever need to be opened.

She was not a great beauty, that much she knew. That was not the reason for the attention. In fact, she imagined that it was her homeliness that made her more a target for their contempt. They would never try that with a girl like Emily. She was so pretty and so smart that no one would ever bother her. And she was Miss Charlotte's best friend. Surely that would keep her safe from the roaming hands of men.

One man she had never feared. Anatole. He was kind and helpful. And his friendship with Miss Charlotte and Miss Emily seemed to give credence to her faith in him. He always smiled and said hello to her.

Despite trusting Anatole, she did not say a lot to him. He was so tall and so handsome that he made her feel funny when she tried.

She remembered her first day at Bridlewood. Seeing Anatole and Emily talking to Miss Charlotte like an equal. She had never seen creole people treated like equals. This was before Miss Emily and Anatole worked at Bridlewood.

But Mini was not creole, she was black. And her darker skin color had always made her feel lesser than her lighter friends. And sometimes *they* made her feel that way. But Anatole never did.

She walked past the trio of friends and went about her duties as maid. She watched their interactions as if they were all born rich and white. She was fascinated but would never have spoken to them if one of them had not spoken first.

"You are new here?" She heard a voice say.

She was not used to people speaking to her except to give her orders. She turned from the fireplace and looked up at him. He was perhaps sixteen. Already tall and his future handsomeness more than apparent.

"Yes, they call me Mini."

"Is that your name?" He asked.

"No, my name is Orpha. Like in the Bible."

"Have you read the Bible?

"No, I can't read but that's what my momma told me. Have you read it?"

Anatole sat down next to her.

"I have." He said, "Mrs. McCambridge made sure that Emily and I learned along with Charlotte."

"Oh, that's fancy. Y'all are kinda fancy, like Queen Marie herself."

"Who?"

Mini was astonished.

"You don't know who Queen Marie is?"

"Tell us."

"Yes, tell us!" Emily and Charlotte chimed in.

"Queen Marie is a creole woman in New Orleans. She is the most important woman in the quarter."

"Why is that?" Emily asked.

"Because her daddy is the mayor of New Orleans."

There was a slight gasp.

"But he's white, surely!" Miss Charlotte had said, in her naiveté.

"Yes, ma'am. He is." Mini agreed. "They have what they call an out of wedlock situation. I think they call her a *bastard*."

More gasps.

"That's when a man and woman who ain't married have a baby."

"I don't think we should be talking about this." Charlotte said.

"I'm so sorry, Miss Charlotte."

"It's alright, Mini." Emily said. "Seems like a lot of things we aren't supposed to know about."

"Emily, you know what mother would say."

"I sure do, that's why I wouldn't repeat it in front of her."

Emily laughed and Charlotte could not help but join in. Anatole looked at Mini and they followed.

But Mini could tell from the way Miss Charlotte looked at her that she had said something inappropriate and felt immediately out of place. Emily and Anatole laughed it off, but they weren't her employers.

"Excuse me, ma'am, I best be getting back to the laundry."

The next day Anatole had seen her in the laundry area and said hello to her. His own momma was her boss. She said hello back, and right away she understood that he didn't want a thing from her. One of the first men she ever met who didn't want nothing.

"Mini, can I ask you a question?"

"Sure."

"Does it bother you? I mean, not being able to read?"

"Oh, no sir. Not at all. Not really."

"Don't you think it might make life a little easier if you did know how?"

"I don't put on no airs, Mr. Anatole."

He laughed.

"Neither do I, Mini, I'm just Anatole. I'm going to work here, just like you."

"Not *just* like me, I hope. You'd hate doin' laundry."

He looked at her and then she started laughing and he smiled along with her.

"Well, no. I'm going to be the new hall boy."

"That's wonderful, Anatole. It'll be good to see you every day. Oh, I hope that's not inappropriate to say."

"It is not, and I agree. It will be good to see you too. And maybe, if you want to, we could do a few lessons on reading?"

"I'll sure think about it."

Mini often thought of his offer. He never mentioned it again, but she knew she would only have to ask. The idea of spending time with Anatole made her smile.

Mini was startled from her reverie by the door opening into

the stairwell. She stood up immediately and picked up her laundry basket. It was Anatole himself. He had a strange look on his face. *A face full of clouds*, she could hear her momma saying.

"You alright, Anatole?"

He seemed startled to see anyone there disturbing him from some thoughts.

"I'm fine, Mini." He said. "Do you need some help with those sheets?"

"No, I got it but thank you."

He walked down the stairs like he didn't know where he was going.

"Hey, wait a minute." She called after him.

"Yes?"

"I still haven't forgot about those reading lessons you promised me."

He smiled.

"Anytime, Mini. Anytime."

She smiled back. It meant the world to her that he cared about her reading. He thought she had a choice to read or not. She did not have a choice, and she did not have a voice. Choices were for people with freedom.

People without voices or choices had to hide all these little things away inside little boxes in their minds. Like her experiences with men, she found that eventually she locked it all away inside her mind, like the *cabinet of curiosities* that Mr. McCambridge had shown her that day.

Chapter 12
No Good Deed

Anatole had been raised with the only children of his age in Point Cèdre, Emily Delphin and Charlotte McCambridge. His mother was employed at Bridlewood House, as was Emily's father. His friendship with her and Charlotte had just happened. Mrs. McCambridge seemed to embrace it, and even encourage it, while his own mother did not.

Anatole's mother, Fabienne Blanchet, was a maid at Bridlewood House at that time. She brought Anatole to work with her on her first day and put him outside to play under the massive oak trees between the house and the chapel.

He saw two little girls playing with their dolls. He walked up to them and said hello. He was too young to care that one was white, and one was creole. He did notice that one was wearing an expensive dress, and the other was dressed in pretty but plain patterned cotton. He still had the innocence of his age.

They were playing a game of pat-a-cake and laughing and clapping each other's hands.

"Hi, I'm Anatole."

They stopped and giggled and looked at him.

"I'm Emily, and this is Charlotte."

"Hello, Anatole." Charlotte said. "It is very nice to meet you."

"My mother works here now." Anatole said. "She's a maid."

"My father works here too." Emily shrugged. "But I don't know what he does."

"My father used to work here." Anatole said. "He helped build this house."

"Oh, that is amazing." Emily said.

He looked at Charlotte.

"Do your parents work here?"

"I don't think so." Charlotte said. "But we do live here."

Anatole was confused at first. He did not really understand what Bridlewood House was. It seemed far too large to be just a home. He had thought it was some kind of business or institution. The way people spoke of it reverentially it could have been a church, for all he knew.

"What a fancy place to live."

Charlotte shrugged.

While Bridlewood House was fancy to Anatole, it was merely home for Charlotte. Neither had known anything different before this day and neither seemed to care about their differences at the time. They were all around eight years old and those differences were far from their concerns. But they would reveal themselves eventually.

Mrs. McCambridge soon took Emily and Anatole under her wing. She insisted that they sit in on Georganne's classes with the governess and learn to read. That part seemed to make Fabienne happy. Being able to read was a great advantage for a servant.

Fabienne even suggested that the only reason she did it was for the prestige of having servants who could read.

Anatole was twelve years old when he realized the difference between him and Emily and Charlotte. Not just the differences in their sexes, for that had been largely ignored for most of their friendship. But there was something else about Charlotte that soon became clear. Something that he had maybe always known, but suddenly had become impossible to ignore.

Just a simple game in the woods.

Anatole was small for his age and his father mocked him as a runt. None of them knew that he was about to have a massive growth spurt. Emily and Charlotte were the only children around close to his age and they bonded as siblings.

His father had worked on building Bridlewood House, and his mother was still in service inside the house. She was still a maid at that time before she became Housekeeper.

They often played games in the woods. Hide and seek and tag.

He ran through the woods, and it opened into a glade. The small clearing in the woods was awash in yellow. A thick carpet of daffodils spread across the entire glade. The wet spring air was sweet with the vanillin scent of daffodil.

He stood deadly silent for a moment and listened for a clue. After a moment he heard one. The snap of a branch. His hearing was excellent, so he knew instantly which direction the snap came from. He stepped back into the woods and walked around the perimeter of the glade, staying behind the tree line. He came upon young Charlotte hunkering down beside a tree. Her head covered by a hood of cornflower blue velvet. She looked up and the hood fell backward revealing her mane of copper curls.

"I'll tell my father." She said quietly as she looked up defiantly with her innocent yet piercing blue eyes that matched her hood.

He had never thought of it before. It was a concept that meant nothing to him until this point. His mother was a maid at Bridlewood. Suddenly a connection was made in his young brain that angering the daughter of his mother's employer could have consequences. She did not say it, but she did not need to say it. He realized that she had already made this connection herself.

Though she never again in their relationship made him feel that way again, the thought of her as a sibling was forever altered. She did not need to say it again for once the feeling was imprinted on his brain, he was never quite able to shake it completely. How could he ever be completely himself again with someone who held his entire family's wellbeing in her hand? Perhaps that had been his mother's concern.

Anatole did not prescribe to his mother's feelings about Mrs. McCambridge. He thought she was a kind lady and a decent one as well. And before she died, Mrs. McCambridge asked to see him. He went to her bed, and she lay there wasted away to nothing. She was as pale and white as her linens. She was to be taken to the sanitarium to recover, but even his young mind knew that he would not see her again.

"I wanted to thank you for your service to the family." She said, weak, but alert. "For your friendship with Charlotte."

His friendship with Charlotte had never been anything that he had considered before. Nothing that had any preconceived intention. They had just met and liked each other. It was purely organic.

He nodded to her, unsure how or if to answer.

"Please, watch over her after I am gone. She won't be able to handle this without her friends and her family."

While Anatole prided himself on knowing his place in the household, he also carried with him the words of Mrs. McCambridge. Anatole mustered his courage and knocked on the door before entering. Charlotte sat on the divan with her needlepoint. She seemed to be forever at the task and never finishing it.

"Anatole." She spoke. "How are you today?"

"Very well, Miss Charlotte."

Unlike Emily, he had never forgotten again to say *Miss* Charlotte.

"I have to go into town tomorrow to pick up some parcels. I wanted to see if you require anything from me?"

"No, I think I have everything I need. Thank you."

"Miss Charlotte—" he stammered.

"Yes?"

Anatole found his voice again.

"Before I was employed here, we were raised as friends, were we not?"

Her eyebrow arched, but she continued at her work.

"Yes, of course."

"And while I am your devoted servant, I have a further dedication to you as a friend."

"I appreciate that, Anatole." Charlotte replied. "And I also value your friendship."

"I have overheard some talk, and I would normally be the soul of discretion. But in this case, it is about you."

He could sense an immediate tensing of the muscles of her face. Charlotte put her things to the side and began to pay closer attention.

"I have heard your cousins speaking of you in a way that suggests his intention to woo you perhaps to marry you for your financial situation."

Charlotte sat speechless for a moment. Anatole suddenly felt more vulnerable than ever. He knew he had stepped over an invisible boundary that had been in place since the day he began to work in the household. Perhaps it had always been there, but after employment things had changed. And especially since Charlotte had become the lady of the manor, so to speak.

"Thank you, Anatole. I appreciate you sharing that with me."

She picked up her needlework and continued her work. Her look was not the look of someone working on needlepoint. Not the look he had seen when he had first walked into the room. This was not the look of leisurely pursuit. She stared hard at her work while not seeming too actually be regarding it.

"You're excused."

The words were like a stab in the heart. He knew this was a mistake. His mother would be furious, and he might well lose his position here. He knew she would be upset by the news, but now he realized that the person that she would be upset with was him.

"I am sorry if I have offended you, Miss Charlotte."

"You have not offended me. But I think you have misunderstood, as I happen to know that my cousin Beau is already likely to wed a wealthy socialite in North Carolina."

"My apologies, Miss Charlotte. I obviously misunderstood the conversation. My concern was entirely for your wellbeing."

"I understand, Anatole, and I appreciate that. But despite what you and my father may think I have a good head on my shoulders."

"Again, apologies, ma'am."

The even more formal *ma'am* came out of his mouth before he could stop it. His blunder had so weakened him that he did not know what to do. He suddenly felt a feeling of dread that he could not explain. But one thing he knew was that no real friend or family member would ever make him feel that way.

As he bowed and backed out of the room, he realized that he had not prepared himself for her reaction. Perhaps she already knew but had chosen to ignore it. Perhaps she did not wish for her cousins to appear to be the schemers they appeared to be. The only thing he knew was that he had not misunderstood the words of her cousin Bernadette. She had made her point clear.

He had seen hurt in her eyes. He had prepared himself for her to angrily reject his news, but he had not expected the hurt. He had hurt her, and he had never meant to.

Anatole returned to his position at the front door. Charlie Mayes stood silently by.

"Where the Hell have you been?" Charlie spat.

"Mind your own goddamned business."

Charlie seemed too stunned to speak. He may have been Anatole's superior, but he had no authority over him.

Anatole stood at the door as they awaited Mr. McCambridge's guest to arrive. A deadly silence between he and Charlie lay like a dense and poisonous fog. Anatole's body was tense and ready. He would gladly tear Charlie Mayes' head off with the slightest provocation. Charlie's rare silence implied that he was keenly aware of this.

This is what his mother had warned him about. This was why she had discouraged their friendship. Because the complications of their differences in class would one day occlude their friendship. He could not tell if he was exaggerating, but he could not help but feel that his actions had made his employment at Bridlewood House untenable.

He cleared his mind and calmed himself with thoughts of his own freedom. To make his way on the land until he could find work in carpentry or building. He was big and strong. He was capable and knowledgeable. There was no need for him to remain a housecat for Bridlewood. To be treated as an ornament for the over-privileged.

He had been saving money. He had not quite saved enough, but he now saw his purpose renewed. He would leave Bridlewood and everything he knew behind. His dream of freedom would become reality. He would never again be beholden to another person. He might have a meager existence, but he would never be cowed or owned again.

Chapter 13
Tea for Two

Charlotte walked down the stairs with the clack of her footsteps on marble echoing behind her. The house seemed empty, which was funny because there were never fewer than twenty people in the house. The servants were below stairs and her father was in town with Cousin Beau. When the house was like this, she felt a strange loneliness. At times like this she would have gone to her mother and talked with her while she knitted or painted.

Her mother remained omnipresent in this house. In her rooms. Where winter months she would have set up her easel or a chair for her knitting. Charlotte could sense her presence and smell her perfume. She knew, or at least hoped, that she was watching over her. But at the same time, she feared the specter of her mother. That she might somehow be disappointing to her.

Her mother enjoyed the arts and crafts and felt they were essential to being well-bred. And they were the only acceptable endeavors for such a young lady. Charlotte had learned crewelwork and knitting and flower arranging all entirely because she enjoyed spending time with her often-distant mother. Charlotte could not imagine wanting anything more now than she wanted to sit and talk and crochet with her mother.

She was heartened when Cousin Bernadette had kindly sent a note to her room asking her if she would have tea with her today. She had no plans for the day. She was suddenly free and looked forward to having a little tea with her cousin. Missing her mother had made her crave the kind of girl talk that she could not have with Emily.

Charlotte walked into the conservatory where Bernadette had requested the tea. She loved the room in winter. The walls and ceiling were glass and made the most of the scant sunlight of autumn and winter. The wrought iron buttresses soared up thirty feet. There was a strangely warm and humid feeling, almost as if they were perpetually in summer. But the cold would come soon.

She found her cousin sitting at a small marble table which she often used for tea when she was alone. She liked the fact that her cousin had chosen that spot, amongst the unseasonably greenery of the conservatory. Surrounded by the brief light of midwinter, but still protected from the elements.

Bernadette stood up when she saw Charlotte. She was dressed in a mauve gown with gray piping. Charlotte chastised herself for thinking it dated. Then, with some horror, she recognized it as one of her own from a few years ago. She was embarrassed and she did not know why. She knew that her cousins were not well to do. Their father had squandered their money on bad investments and that her mother had often sent her old gowns to Bernadette. But seeing it in person seemed unexpectedly awkward.

"Cousin!" Bernadette said, as she leaned in for a kiss. Charlotte met her kiss and reciprocated as their lips met each other's cheeks.

"I'm so glad you were able to join me for tea today."

"I'm so glad you invited me!"

"Well, it is *your* home, but you made me feel so welcome."

"I am so pleased that you feel welcomed here at Bridlewood House."

Bernadette seemed so cheerful that Charlotte forgot all about the gown.

"It has been a long time since I was at your home in New Orleans, but you and your family have always made us feel most welcome."

"I am ashamed that we have not invited you to the city in the past few years, but you understand our situation."

"You don't think that I would ever judge-"

"No, no of course not." Bernadette said, with a downcast look. "But I would be embarrassed for you to see us living in those conditions."

"What do you mean?" Charlotte asked. "What conditions?"

Bernadette brought her gaze back up to meet Charlotte's sympathetic stare.

"Mother and I..." Bernadette paused before continuing.

"Go on, you can tell me."

"Mother and I are having to share a lady's maid now."

Charlotte's eyes widened in surprise. It was simply not done. Their financial situation must have been far more dire than she had previously understood.

"I'm so sorry, Bernadette. I had no idea."

"Mother would not want you to know. Please never repeat this to another living soul."

Charlotte shook her head, the well-pinned curls placed by her own personal maid stayed in place.

"Mothers have great pride," Charlotte said, "I know mine certainly did. And since they were cousins and were practically raised together, I can well understand how your mother must feel."

"It is a disgrace to our entire family, which is why she would not want anyone to know. We would never want your name to be tarnished as well by our circumstances."

"Oh, don't worry about that."

"Our mothers understood one thing," Bernadette said. "They understood the importance of maintaining standards."

"Yes, they did. Or rather still do, in your case."

They were interrupted by the sound of the tea cart rolling into the room. Mini appeared around the corner pushing the cart gently, attempting to make very little noise. That was the most important part of training a servant. Be invisible. Disappear. But the jingle of silver and China was impossible to silence.

Mini brought tea into the room and placed the silver tea tray on the small table.

"Mother always says that a good servant is invisible."

Charlotte nodded, smiling.

"Invisible and yet always seeming to know what you need at all times. You can tell that our mothers were raised together."

"Mini could probably use a little more work in that area, but I guess it isn't hurting anyone."

"She'll probably learn." Bernadette said. "But you do have to be firm with them and I'm afraid not everyone has the stomach for that."

Charlotte was concerned for a moment. Was she saying that her servants were not well trained? Her quizzical look quickly transmitted to Bernadette.

"I'm sorry, I didn't mean to imply-"

"No, you're quite right. I really do not have my mother's hand at all. I don't know how to be firm when necessary."

"I have noticed, if I may, how familiar some of your servants are with you. Particularly your maid."

"Oh yes, Emily and I were raised together."

"Yes, I have close relationships with my nanny and a few other servants. But ultimately you must learn to separate your feelings from them. You must learn to treat them like servants, even though you love them. Otherwise, they have a tendency toward the lazy."

"Oh, Emily is anything but lazy."

"Of course, now. But as time goes on and she realizes that you are too emotionally invested to fire her. Then who knows? Then you might have to fire her."

"I guess I had not thought of it that way."

"So, you see, keeping them in their place is doing them a favor. It will keep her from losing her job. And without a good reference, could she ever hope to find a job as good as this one?"

"I see what you mean."

Charlotte had never considered that she might be making life harder for Emily and even Anatole by holding them too close. By allowing them to overstep.

"I suppose you're right. I never looked at it that way."

"It really isn't my place to say, of course, but I know that is what my mother, and indeed your mother, would say."

She realized that Bernadette was right. Her mother would probably say exactly that. In fact, she could remember her mother telling her at some point to train her help better. She did not like referring to Emily or Anatole as *help*. Perhaps that is when her mother realized that she had made a mistake raising her with children who would one day become her servants. It made her sad to think about it.

"I'm sorry." Bernadette said. "I realize now that I should not have said anything.

"No, no." Charlotte insisted. "You are correct and saying so made me realize what my mother had been saying to me."

"Well. Anyway. Tell me about your plans for the Christmas party. Beau and I intend to return for it, of course."

"I am so excited about the Christmas party." Charlotte said, thrilled to change the subject. "We have an orchestra coming in from New Orleans and our chef has been working on some very special creations from his own Christmases in France."

"How delightful." Bernadette replied. "You know Beau loves Christmas more than anything."

"He does seem to be a most agreeable person."

"I'm glad you think so. In fact, I know he has a special place in his heart for you."

"How lovely. It is certainly reciprocated."

"I have often thought what a good marriage you two might make. Your relation is just distant enough to make it feasible."

"Indeed. However, alas my father has other plans."

"Does he, indeed?"

"Yes. A Robert Mayhew. His family is long a friend of our family. They are also in the sugar business, on the refinery side."

"I see. And do you also find him agreeable?"

Charlotte paused, unsure of how to answer.

"Cousin, may I share a confidence with you?"

"Of course." Bernadette replied.

"The fact is that Robert Mayhew is neither agreeable nor disagreeable. He is neither attractive nor is he repulsive."

"I understand." Bernadette nodded.

"I want more, but it is the duty of the daughter who has been given much to return the favors requested by her family. And he is not a bad person. His father is as rich as my own. By all indications he is a decent man and will make a very good husband."

"Is decent what you are looking for? Good? Do you not also wish to have your heart burst when he walks into a room?"

"Of course," Charlotte said, "but how can I, of all people, ask for more? Look at this house and my gowns and my servants. What kind of entitlement would I display to ask for more than that? When so many have nothing. I cannot bring myself to be that person."

"You are a good woman, Charlotte. You never ask for more for yourself."

"I do not, but only because I have been so blessed. Look what God has bestowed upon me. To ask for more would be obscene."

"To ask for love would never be obscene." Bernadette insisted. "To ask for romance would be asking for the stars, but who is to say that you do not deserve the entire firmament?"

"I've already been given a firmament. Heaven itself right here in Terrebonne Parish."

"As long as you are happy."

Bernadette sipped her tea and investigated the middle distance.

"I am, my dear cousin, I promise you that I am."

"And if the opportunity for more should ever arise, please promise me that you will consider it."

"I promise you that I will."

There was an awkward quiet for a moment.

"Tell me, cousin," Charlotte began, "what of your romantic options in New Orleans?"

"I was, as you know, engaged for a time."

"Yes, I was sorry to hear of its dissolution."

"But I am currently seeking another connection, dear cousin."

"Let me think if I know of any such single gentlemen."

"I would appreciate that." Bernadette said, looking down at her lap, "I feel most outclassed by the gentlemen of New Orleans since I was taken advantage of by Mr. Weston."

"Would you care to tell me what happened?"

"It is a difficult story, I'm afraid."

"Then don't tell the story." Georganne assured her. "But I will personally find what gentlemen are available and you can meet a few of them at a tea."

"You would do that for me?"

"A tea in your honor?" Georganne said, "Of course, I would be most pleased to do that for you!"

A look of relief spread across Bernadette's face.

"I cannot thank you enough."

"You do not need to thank me." Georganne said. "You can thank me by finding happiness."

Chapter 14
Father Figure

The next morning Anatole took a break from his duties. He had been working steadily since dawn and was due a tea break but decided to spend it seeking advice from a friend who had long been someone he looked up to.

Anatole knocked briefly and entered the chapel. He was greeted by the warm and familiar scents of the chapel. Candle wax, incense, and something even more familiar; wood oil. His childhood home and Bridlewood always smelled of the same wood oil. Though this particular combination only seemed to exist in the chapel. It smelled of Sundays and confessions.

"Hello?" He called out.

A figure stepped out of a doorway at the rear.

"Yes?" The familiar voice of Father Del Danvers responded.

"Hello, Father Del."

"Anatole. So good to see you, my son. It has been a while. Please come in."

Anatole had not realized that it had been a while since he had come to the church just to talk to Father Del. His family had been catholic, but when he went to work for the McCambridge's he had basically become an Anglican by default. But Father Del was still happy to hear your problems, no matter your religion. He had been a clear voice of reason in his life.

"What can I do for you?"

"Thank you, Father. I just wanted to talk to you about something."

"Of course, my son. Would you like to step into the confessional like the old days, or my office?"

"Right here is fine."

Father Del gestured to a seat on a pew. Anatole sat and Father Del followed. The pew had that familiar discomfort of all churches he had been in.

"What would you like to talk to me about?"

Anatole did not know how to begin, then hoped that the best way to begin was to state the truth.

"I know how lucky I am to be in service here at Bridlewood House. I don't want to sound ungrateful. I have known the McCambridge family my entire life and they are almost as family to me."

"Of course."

"But ever since I was a boy I have longed to travel. I have wanted to go out into the world and make my own fortune. To find my own destiny."

Father Del seemed to take this in stride, as if he had expected this.

"Why can't your destiny be right here at Bridlewood?"

"Maybe it is. But why should I not go out into the world and find out for sure?"

"Where would you go? What would you do?"

"I have a lot of skills in carpentry. I had to do everything around our house when I was growing up, so I can build anything or work on anything. I'm not afraid of hard work. Perhaps I would go out into the wild and try to settle my own land, even."

"I don't know if you understand what a massive challenge you are talking about. Do you know how vast this country is or how desperate so many of the men are out there in that wilderness?"

"You are right that I do not yet understand the vastness of this land. And I am not saying that I think it would be easy."

"I'm sorry, I know you are not, but I have known you your entire life. You'll forgive me for being protective."

"I appreciate that, Father. I have not always been able to turn to my own father for understanding or support."

"I know. There are things in your father's past that have changed him. Maybe one day he will return to Christ and to his family."

"It's too late."

Father Del nodded, and his eyes showed an understanding that did not need to be spoken.

"Besides, don't you think it's time for you to settle down and get married?"

"I am constantly being told that I am of an age where I should meet a girl and make her my wife."

"Often young men your age do just that," Father Del nodded.

"But I have not met such a young woman."

"That is also not unusual, my son. You are a busy young man."

"Then how am I supposed to meet such a young woman and how will I know that it is a good match?"

"Often young men such as yourself are matched by their mothers or by women of standing in the community."

"And what if they are not a person that I want to be married to?"

"My son, marriage is your duty because procreation is your duty."

"But what about love?"

"Love comes to those who share common desires. Consider it a dividend of making the correct choice in a mate."

"But Father, I have no idea how to choose a mate."

"Start with attraction. Is there a young woman whom you feel an attraction to?"

"Not really. I think that is why I feel drawn to travel. I want to see other worlds and other peoples. I don't see how I could be ready to settle down when my desire to see the world is so great.

"Anatole." He paused. "Your future is here in Terrebonne Parish. And most likely so is the woman who will become your wife."

"What are you saying?"

"Merely that you should be considering options around you."

Anatole laughed.

"You're not saying-"

"Yes, I am saying that you and Emily have grown up together and are both in service at Bridlewood. It only makes sense."

"She is like my sister; I can't even imagine that."

"Good relationships often start with a friendship. But marriage, no matter your rank in society, is a partnership. Each bringing something to the table."

"But a lady's maid can't be married."

"That was true back in England. But this is America. Things are different here. We no longer need to hold to their traditions. There are opportunities for change. I came here for a different way of life. I took the ship from Southampton to New Orleans with the intention of heading west to start up a church. My father had funded my journey and the church that I had intended to start. But coming from England I had no idea, as indeed none of us did, how massive this country would be, or how few people would be out west. But I found English and Scottish men who were looking to make their fortunes. Men like Mr. McCambridge who wanted to take that fortune and live like aristocracy. They often married women like Mrs. McCambridge whose family had a prestigious name, but little money left. So, the trade was made. He gained some level of respect in the community and her family gained access to his fortune.

Anatole merely nodded his head, not wanting to say that his mother had told him something similar. Father Del did not need to know that his mother knew or spoke of such things.

"That is what I mean when I say that marriage is ultimately a partnership.

"I see." Anatole said.

"There is more." Father Del said. "When I failed at starting the church that my father wanted, I fell into some bad habits. I began to drink and gamble. I lost all the money that my father had given me."

Anatole was astonished to hear Father Del share this story.

"That is when Mr. McCambridge offered me the opportunity to create a small vicarage here on his estate."

"That was generous."

"Not really. He was the person I lost all my money to."

Anatole stared blankly, unable to know how to respond appropriately.

Father Del broke the awkward silence by laughing first, then Anatole joined.

"He built this chapel with the money I lost to him and installed me as the rector of his little parish. He introduced me to the woman who would be become Mrs. Danvers."

Anatole smiled, then seemed to have a second thought.

"But do you not harbor any resentment at the man who took your money?"

"Not at all, my son. He saved me and gave me this opportunity not to have to turn back to my father in shame. My father thinks this chapel is mine, built with his money. And he is not wrong."

"May I ask a personal question?"

"Of course."

"Do you love Mrs. Danvers?"

"I do. She is a very good woman."

"And were you instantly...attracted to her?"

Father Del laughed good naturedly at the question.

"There is another kind of attraction that the young do not yet understand. The attraction that is not driven by impulses of the flesh. I knew that she was a strong woman who would help keep me on the path. The desires of the flesh have never really shown themselves in our bedroom."

"Sir, I am confused. Are you saying that *those* kinds of desires have not materialized and yet it is still a good marriage?"

"Some men do not experience desires of that nature for women."

"Do they not?"

Anatole felt a momentary relief.

Father Del placed his hand on Anatole's long and toned thigh and gave the fabric a long stroke.

"No, many don't."

"I see."

Anatole felt more confused than ever, but at the same time he understood. The hand on his thigh was reminiscent of what he felt when he was alone with Mr. Randy. While he did not feel a *romantic* attraction to either man, he now realized that there was another type of attraction. Something base. Was this tension that he felt now, was this the desire that some men feel for...other men? Was this the desire that he was supposed to feel for women?

If so, was that not an even more important reason to leave Bridlewood before he made a mistake that cast aspersions onto his family?

That was when Anatole realized that Bridlewood House was

a trap. George McCambridge had set a trap for Father Del, and he had fallen into it. He had created a gilded cage for the man. But a cage is a cage no matter what it is made of. His parents had also fallen into the pitfall. His father had wanted to go into business for himself. To become a carpenter, but Bridlewood House had changed that. Perhaps all of Terrebonne Parish was a trap. But he still had an able body and a way to pull himself out of it.

"Thank you, Father Del., I appreciate your time and your thoughtfulness."

"I hope I was able to help you make a clear decision."

"I will let you know. I have a lot to think about, but I really appreciated your wisdom on the subject."

"That is all I can hope to do."

Anatole stood up and nodded one last time at Father Del before heading out of the Chapel. He felt more confused than ever about his choice, but no less determined to do something with his life. He knew that a change was coming. He could feel it. While he did not know what he wanted in life, he knew that Father Del's description of a marriage convenience was not the answer he wanted for himself. There was something more that existed for him outside Bridlewood House. Freedom. Adventure. Love?

Chapter 15
Michaelmas

The past few days had been hinting at a resurgence of summer in the mid fall. Anatole's grandmother had called it Old Woman Summer. The days were far warmer than normal for October. The days were shortening and there had been a tease of cooler temperatures, but then the heat had returned for one last visit. At least the evenings were cool.

Anatole's brow and every crease of his body seemed constantly damp. He found his clothes sodden with sweat before he even got started. He took great pride in his appearance, but no amount of grooming could keep him cool or dry. He wished for a storm to blow in and cool things off, perhaps even bring the proper beginning of autumn with it.

As he finished polishing the silver, he realized that he had the afternoon to himself. With Mister McCambridge and Charlotte having gone to New Orleans for a party with Miss Bernadette and Mr. Beau he would not need to serve anyone but himself for a change. And he knew exactly what he wanted to do with his free time.

Anatole went back to his rooms and changed out of his footman's livery and into his own clothes for a hike through the woods. Light muslin trousers and shirting. He laced up his shoes and headed out of his modest room. On his way out of Bridle-wood House, he grabbed a book from the library, as that was a privilege of the house. He treated them as if they were his own for it was a privilege he did not wish to lose. After a brief search, he settled on a copy of Swinburne's newest Poems and Ballads. Purchased, no doubt, by Charlotte. She was also a great admirer of the poets of nature.

Anatole strolled until he reached the edge of the manicured property and entered the woods of Bridlewood estate. An immense forest surrounded by water. With many pools fed by springs and creeks that flowed down to the swamps of Lake Marchant.

Since childhood he remembered loving being outdoors. Amongst the trees and the water and the green ground cover of the primeval woods of Terrebonne parish. His mother had always had to fight to keep him indoors. Especially at this time of year when the rainy skies of late summer had given way to the normally cool afternoons of late fall. He would leave with Charlotte and Emily and be gone for most of the day. They would return for lunch at Bridlewood and be gone again until nightfall.

He entered his favorite glade and the sound of water running over rocks thrilled his ears. He had discovered this place as a child. When he and Emily and Charlotte were merely friends. Things were simpler. The glade was his cathedral. His worship of God was entirely in his appreciation of the nature that God had created, but without man's interference.

He followed the creek to the edge of an embankment. A pool of fresh spring water greeted him like an old friend. The creek pushed a constant torrent of water through the pool, keeping it fresh and discouraging any creatures from setting up home there.

Thus, creating a perfect bathing pool in the summer. Every year he celebrated bathing in the pool like a holiday.

He removed his clothing and sat himself down on the edge of the pool with his feet in the icy spring water. His shiny black hair, normally bound by a ribbon, was unleashed, and hung around his face and neck in loose waves that framed his strong jawline and neck. He leaned back and opened his book. Reading the poems of these fellow lovers of nature. He had only just finished Leaves of Grass.

The heat of the sun warmed him all over, but the sun was too bright and sweat stung his eyes when he opened them to try to read. He rolled over onto his stomach and read the first stanza in the shadow of his own head and glorious mane of hair. He imagined himself looking like a wild man of nature. Like the natives that these writers of nature would often encounter. He could not help but smile at his own comparison.

A shadow crossed his book other than his own. He turned and looked up to see Beau Chenevert standing over him.

He was too startled at first, but then remembered his own nakedness. He had seen Mr. Beau naked enough, as it was his job, but he was not expecting to ever display himself in such a manner.

"Beg your pardon, sir. I thought you had gone with the family."

Anatole could scarcely stand up without revealing more, so he chose to stay in place.

"No, I could not face another tea at the moment."

Beau regarded Anatole's book, and an unreadable look crossed his face.

"From too much love of living,
From hope and fear set free,
We thank with brief thanksgiving
Whatever gods may be

That no life lives forever;
That dead men rise up never;
That even the weariest river
Winds somewhere safe to sea.
Glory to Man in the highest!
For Man is the master of things."

Anatole looked puzzled.

"I beg your pardon, sir?"

"Swinburne." Beau said. "I see you're also a reader."

Anatole was merely surprised that Mr. Beau had quoted a rare and almost scandalous quote that placed Man as his own master.

"I enjoy nature and those poets who love it, sir."

Beau laughed, though Anatole did not understand what was quite so funny.

"You don't have to call me sir when you're naked."

"Alright." Anatole said, perplexed. Honorary titles were reflexive to him.

"Would you mind if I joined you for bathing this afternoon? I would not normally intrude on your idyll, but it looks so inviting and I am hot and cannot get comfortable in the house."

"Of course. It has been my little oasis in the forest since I was a child. However, did you find it?"

"I got lost and just stumbled into the glade."

"It seemed like a good place to be on this warm afternoon."

"St. Michael's Summer."

"I beg your pardon?" Anatole said.

"When you have a hot spell following Michaelmas. My father used to call it St. Michael's Summer."

"Interesting. I am named for St. Michael. Michael Anatole Blanchet."

"Then please enjoy this extended summer in your honor."

Anatole was eager to change the subject.

"I see you have your camera with you."

"Oh this." Beau gestured toward the apparatus. "Yes. I'm afraid I'm a bit of a nuisance with it. I scour every location for a worthy tableau."

"And have you found one here? Anatole asked.

"I may have."

Beau set his camera on the grass and began to disrobe. He loosened his tie and began to remove his shirt. Anatole was momentarily confused because that would normally be his job, but this situation was different.

"Sir, should I- "

"No, I have it."

He thought for a moment how it would look if someone came into the glad and found them face to face naked as Anatole was helping him disrobe.

Anatole looked back down at his book. Having been relieved of his duty and allowed to enjoy his reverie. He returned to his book, but the only passage he could concentrate on was the one that Beau had quoted. A poem that he had not yet read, but clearly Beau had saved as one of his favorites.

He did not dare move his head again until he heard the splash of Mr. Beau jumping into the pool. *His pool,* he thought with some peevishness, that he now had to share with this inter-loper from the city. He had seen him naked dozens of times, but somehow this was different. This was not work, this was almost social in its setting.

"Come in, the water is most quickening."

Anatole rolled over and sat up. He was neither modest nor immodest. He was not ashamed of his body nor his manhood. He simply did not know how to act casually around his social superi-ors. Beau was swimming across the pool and back and not paying attention to Anatole. This seemed the perfect opportunity to slide into the water.

The water was more than quickening, it was an invigorating explosion throughout his body. The heat of the day clashed with the cold of the spring fed pool caused a riot of sensations, yet he resisted the urge to cry out. Everything in his system seemed to come alive at once, even the follicles of his hair seemed activated by the plunge.

When he resurfaced, he was face to face with Beau. They were equalized in a way. Their eyes locked in a strange way. He had never noticed how green Mr. Beau's eyes were. As he had been instructed not to look at a gentleman while he was dressing him as it could seem awkward.

Beau winked and his eyes sparkled in the sunshine. He, like Anatole, was underwater from the neck down. They tread water in the small but deep pool feeling the water from the underground spring rushing past torsos and legs. Caressing their body. Thrilling and breathtaking in its chill.

"Permit me to make an observation."

"Of course." Anatole responded.

"A servant who reads is not likely to remain a servant forever."

Anatole was astonished.

"I am a humble servant who is happy with his station."

"Of course." Beau said.

Anatole felt as though he were being patronized by this man of wealth and station. Whether or not he was patronizing him did not matter for he had no recourse. He could say nothing back to the man without fear of losing his coveted position. He merely nodded in acquiescence.

Anatole swam across to the other side of the pool then back to where he had first entered. He pulled himself out of the water and stood for a moment dripping dry. He decided to forgo his false modesty and turned toward Beau.

"I do not mind if you mock my station, sir. For I am exactly who I want to be, and I know that you only jest."

"Indeed." Beau said, gazing at him. "How could I mock you when you are so beautiful and your eyes so deep."

"Deep?"

"Yes, like this pool. Has no one ever told you?"

"That is quite a thing to say."

"Is it?" Beau asked. "Beauty is merely nature. Would Swinburne not say as much?"

Anatole sat on the ground and began to gather his things around him.

"Quite a decadent read for a man so enamored with servitude."

"I beg your pardon, sir?" Anatole's brow furrowed.

"Oh, just that love of nature is considered fashionable and decadent. Perverse, in some circles."

"Perverse?"

"And slightly heathen in tone. In that it is often a luxury only the wealthy can enjoy. But mainly because many see it as taking away from the worship of God. Those circles."

"Circles in which I do not move, sir. I appreciate the beauty of nature because it has never called upon me to live by society's standards, or indeed any standards."

"Society would have it that you worship God through the rules of man." Mr. Beau said. "You love nature as others love God, yet you do not see that they are one in the same?"

"I do see that."

"And do you see a God who loves you for appreciating his creation?"

Anatole was silent, for he had not considered this.

"I hope that you do. You are one of his beautiful creations and society's standards are not God's standards. They are merely the rules of control by which we all seem bound to live."

Anatole was not sure how to respond. What Beau had said was very close to something he himself believed. Fine for a person of Beau Chenevert's status, but that kind of talk could get a person in Anatole's position in trouble.

Beau swam to the bank of the pool and pulled himself out. He rolled over and lay down next to Anatole, but at a respectable distance.

Anatole sat up and began to dress. He pulled on his trousers and his shirt. He found himself suddenly quite irritated that this man had invaded his *idyll* and forced him to discuss matter that could easily leave him without a job. With his trousers and his shoes on he gathered his shirt and his book.

"I hope you find something worth photographing here in these woods." Anatole said.

"Perhaps I will show you when I return for the Christmas holidays."

With that Anatole turned and walked back into the forest toward Bridlewood leaving Beau behind. Anatole wondered if he had been somehow caught in a trap. He felt as though he had been called out for something, and yet he was too simple to comprehend what Mr. Beau was alluding to. Or perhaps he knew but his mind was not ready to tarry there.

Chapter 16

The Friendship

E mily stood behind Charlotte as she did multiple times a day. Her job, it seemed, consisted entirely of standing behind her mistress. Either styling hair, lacing garments, or latching jewelry that could fund her families' lives for a hundred years.

She instantly regretted the thought and chastised herself. She had never had a feeling our thought like it before. Where did it come from? The McCambridge family had been like family to her.

She was content with her job, though it was not always as she had thought it would be. But the pressures on Charlotte were different than they had been, and Emily tried her best to understand.

"I think it has been good having my cousins visit."

"You seem to have very much enjoyed their companionship."

"I truly have."

Emily imagined that what she meant was that she enjoyed having someone she could talk to about *rich white lady* things with. It seemed Emily that Charlotte's life was taking a turn in the direction of high society that had always been destined. It made sense that her own cousin would be the one to usher her toward that now that her mother had passed.

"Remember when we were children and would braid each other's hair?"

"I do." Charlotte smiled.

"We would sit in the woods and talk for hours."

"Life was so simple then."

There was a knock at the door.

"Yes." Charlotte called.

The door opened revealing the face of Miss Bernadette.

"If I may pop in for a moment?"

"Please do, cousin." Charlotte said warmly.

Miss Bernadette entered, followed closely by her maid Eunice. Eunice closed the door behind them and stood by the fireplace.

It was not lost on Emily how different Miss Bernadette's face was when Charlotte was in the room versus when she was not. She smiled and was overly demure and unctuous. But in the face of mere servants, she was cold.

But she also noticed how Charlotte's expressions had changed. There was a time when Charlotte held herself in perfect pose until her mother left the room. Later, when it was just she and Emily, she would relax and laugh. But that seemed to have changed as well. Now she would find herself alone with Charlotte with an air of mild tension over the room. As if they had not spent a lifetime together. As if they did not know each other's deepest secrets.

Charlotte gestured toward the chair next to her. Bernadette gathered her skirts and sat. There were four women in the room, but two of them were servants so she focused herself on Charlotte.

"As you know Beau and I are returning to our home soon."

"Yes, of course." Charlotte said, her tone one of genuine regret.

"I know that you have much to do here at Bridlewood House, but I wonder if you might like to join me in New Orleans for Lina Belvedere's engagement party. I know that you have been invited and I think it would be a wonderful opportunity to take part in real New Orleans society."

"Oh, that sounds marvelous, but I don't know if I should?"

"You are not yet engaged. It is perfectly respectable to attend if you are accompanied by family. Besides, if you truly want to make Bridlewood House a center of society you will need to have more experience in New Orleans at some point."

"I suppose you are right, cousin."

Bernadette smiled and patted her on the knee.

"Also, Governor and Mrs. Walker will be there, and I would like to suggest that you invite them to your Christmas Réveillon gala this year."

Charlotte gasped and broke out into a great smile. Emily could see the change taking place in her.

"Oh, my. He has been here before, but do you really think he would come to Réveillon?"

Réveillon was a Christmas Eve celebration of untold excess. The wealthy enjoying their wealth in a ludicrous display of exotic food and drink. It was always a tremendous amount of work. More than any regular party they had. Though the staff seemed to consider it a personal triumph

Emily listened as she worked and was excited at the prospect of a trip to New Orleans for the engagement party, however. She would be able to see her parents.

Another knock came to the door.

"Yes." Called Charlotte.

Mini entered. Her head was down, as always. Her small dark

hands held tightly to a stack of white bathing linens. She deposited them into the linen cupboard near the bathtub.

Emily pushed pins into place in Charlotte's hairstyle as everyone in the room seemed to ignore the presence of a *lesser* servant. The hierarchy of servitude was a constant source of discussion amongst the servants. Emily refused to engage in the nonsense.

Mini gathered up the discarded linens from earlier into a ball in her arms and carried them toward the door. She balanced them on her hip to open the door, but Eunice stepped forward and opened it for her. They nodded to each other.

"Creoles really are the best servants." Bernadette said. "But it is not most unsettling to have actual negroes living inside your house?"

Emily felt a shock throughout her body but tried hard to look unfazed. She resisted every urge in her body. She instead focused on Charlotte's hair, but in the mirror, she could see the look of confusion on Charlotte's face.

"What do you mean, cousin?" Charlotte asked.

"They are too wild of spirit. I have heard tales of horror about slave uprisings on plantations here and in the Caribbean. They rise up in the night and slash your throat and burn your house down!"

Charlotte laughed.

"Surely you are not worried our dear Mini will attack you."

"It isn't just that, of course. You understand that negroes have different diseases that they can spread to us."

"Bernadette, I assure you that we take all the proper precautions.

Emily looked up and saw Eunice. Eunice continued working with the same tight-lipped expression on her face that she always had. Her face was inscrutable, but her mouth was ringed with wrinkles from being tightly closed to stop unutterable words escaping. Their eyes met and telegraphed instantly all the thoughts that each had on Miss Bernadette. The way that all creole women, indeed all women of color had learned to communicate with each other across a room. Not telepathy, merely with brows and the set of a mouth.

Emily was not a stranger to this. Trying to create a social hierarchy of skin color. She understood the true divisive nature of the caste system.

"I am merely thinking of The Governor and Mrs. Walker. I just want them to feel most welcome here at your Bridlewood House."

"Thank you, cousin, you do think of everything."

Bernadette nodded humbly.

"Well, I must be on my way to get prepared for the day."

"Thank you, cousin." Charlotte said.

Miss Bernadette rose and patted Charlotte on the shoulder. She turned and headed for the door. Eunice opened the door and followed Miss Bernadette from the room with her eyes cast down to avoid accidentally revealing any more opinions on her employer.

As soon as they were gone Emily turned to face Charlotte in the mirror.

"You know that is not true."

"What is not true?" Charlotte asked.

"Negroes do not wish to murder you all in your sleep."

It tumbled out of Emily's mouth before she could think to stop herself.

Charlotte looked suddenly anxious. Just as she had back when her mother was watching her and expecting her to do better. Her smiling veneer replaced by a pensive expression.

"I have heard of uprisings at my father's plantation in the Caribbean." Charlotte said. "Workers rebelling in the dead of night."

"But that is not our Mini."

Emily said, impassioned. Though what she really yearned to say was that *they are not workers they are slaves, enslaved in their own homeland.*

"Oh, I know. But Cousin Bernadette is from a different level of society than we are here. They are very formal there in their customs. She will learn how we do things here."

Emily kept her eyes on her work. She looked up into the mirror and saw Charlottes beautiful face. Then she saw her own and realized that her own mouth was tightly shut and drawn as Eunice's. Tightly closed but full of words that must not be said. Words that could end her employment.

She realized that she was now more concerned with losing her job than her friendship. It was then that Emily truly began to understand that her friendship with Charlotte was never going to be the same again. When words must be metered to save oneself then there is no freedom.

"You said that life was so simple then." Emily said.

"It was." Charlotte replied.

"It still is for you."

"That isn't fair, Emily. So much has changed since my mother died. For you too."

Emily felt a surprising sting in her heart.

"Of course, it has. I loved that woman almost as my *own* mother."

"So, you understand why I need to take her place in society as she wanted me to."

"Yes, I understand. But I don't see any of Mrs. McCambridge in Miss Bernadette. And I would hate to see her disappear from you too."

There was a shocked silence after her words. She knew that she had said too much to her friend and her employer. She saw the look of hurt on Charlotte's face.

"I am most sorry, Miss Charlotte. I did not mean—"

"Thank you, Emily." Charlotte said. "I would rather not talk now."

Emily composed herself and quietly finished dressing Charlotte. Whatever shift in their relationship had started had now been made clear.

She would always love Charlotte. She now realized that the feelings of confusion and hopelessness lately were merely grief at a staggering loss. First Mrs. McCambridge and now Charlotte. Unlike with Mrs. McCambridge it was a sudden loss that she had not seen coming. There was no cancer or tuberculosis to warn of an impending and drawn-out demise. This was more like a knife through the heart.

Chapter 17
Exposure

Anatole walked briskly down the corridor. He had been told on so many occasions not to run that, like most of the household servants, he had learned to walk as quickly as possible that somehow still felt like an awkward run. Even when in a desperate hurry. But once you were in the family areas of the home you had to keep a certain pace. You could never be seen rushing unless there was an emergency.

Anatole had managed all his morning footman tasks. He had lit fires in the drawing room, the morning room, and the library. He had assisted Mini in moving the drawing room furniture for cleaning underneath.

He had been to Mister Beau's rooms to do his valet duties, though Mister Beau had not yet risen for his ablutions. Anatole had still tidied his rooms and laid a fire. He was finally going to have a break for a cup of tea.

"Anatole!" He turned when he heard the familiar voice.

Mister Beau stood in the corridor just outside his rooms. He was wearing his more casual clothes, not dressed for tea. He was holding a box. Anatole wished he had been quicker making his way down the hall, he could already be enjoying his tea.

"Sorry to trouble you."

"No trouble at all, sir."

Anatole looked down and recognized the photography materials that Mister Beau had arrived with, plus some new things.

"Could you help me move these things into the empty airing closet?"

"Of course, sir."

Mister Beau gestured over his shoulder.

"There is another box that just arrived on the table."

Anatole picked up the box and followed Mister Beau into the small and dark room. A table had already been placed and small metal dishes full of liquid.

"You can set that box right there."

Anatole set the box down on the table.

"Just take those bottles out and set them over there, please."

Anatole removed various brown bottles and set them on the table against the wall where they would not be knocked over. The bottles reminded him of the bottles he had seen in the laundry room that contained astringents and surfactants.

"Is this alright, sir?"

"Yes, that's fine, Anatole. Now rinse your hands in the basin. One of those bottles is arsenic."

Anatole used the basin to rinse his hands, though he did not think the bottle had been breached yet. But he would rather be safe.

"Are you worried about rats, sir?"

Anatole asked, having been familiar with arsenic only as rat poison.

"No, not at all. It is used as a fixative."

Anatole somehow felt like he knew less than before he asked.

There was a knock at the jamb of the open door. Mini stood there holding a tea tray.

"Just over there." He gestured to the small table in the corner without ever taking his eyes off whatever he was studying.

She placed it quietly on the table and backed out of the room.

Anatole was curious watching him. He had been taught never to ask questions while serving unless directly related to the task at hand, but his curiosity got the better of him.

"May I ask what you are doing, sir?"

He answered without ever taking his eyes off the object in his hands.

"I am temporarily turning this room into my development room for my daguerreotypes."

"I have heard very little about them, but they seem fascinating."

"An image is captured on this copper plate and then it can be fixed and viewed."

"Yes, I have seen one of Mr. McCambridge in the study."

"I would have loved to have gone to Paris to study with Louis Daguerre."

Anatole was puzzled, was it a name he should have known?

"I'm sorry, who?"

"Oh, he's the man who invented the daguerreotype. He is the father of photography. Forgive me, his name is not well known except among those of us who are interested in the craft."

Anatole appreciated that Beau tried to make him feel better, though he still felt like it was a name he should have known.

"Is it too late?"

"Too late?" Beau asked.

"Too late to go work with him in Paris?"

"Rather. He is aged and not well."

"I am sorry to hear that, sir."

"Would you like to see something I think you will find interesting?"

Anatole could not say no, but he also found himself genuinely interested.

"Yes, I think I would."

Mister Beau closed the door. The room was lit only by a small candle inside a red shade. The room was suddenly awash in red. It was like nothing Anatole had ever seen before. Mister Beau turned back to him and Anatole was struck by how different his features appeared in the red glow.

"What I am about to show you takes the daguerreotype to a new level. You will be able to expose that plate to light and put a copy of that picture onto paper."

Mister Beau stepped past him, unable to do so without touching him. The familiar scent of his shaving tonic filled the room. It suddenly seemed warm.

Beau opened a small box and placed a small and highly polished piece of metal and a blank paper inside. He closed the box and slid a lever in place.

"Would you like some tea?"

"Of course, sir, I'll get it."

"No, I can pour."

"Milk or sugar?"

"Neither thank you."

Beau poured the tea and handed him the cup. Anatole was not used to being served, certainly not by one of his betters. The situation was almost too awkward to appreciate.

Beau added cream to the other cup then poured his own tea. He leaned against the wall and sipped his tea. Anatole could not help but notice the arrow cufflinks.

"Those are interesting cufflinks, sir."

"Thank you. You can call me Beau. In here, we are equals, if you like."

"That's very kind of you, but I don't think I could."

"You can try."

"Alright. Beau."

Anatole felt himself blushing a bit and grateful for the dim light of the room.

"Thank you, Anatole. The cufflinks were a gift from my father when I turned eighteen."

"Arrows?"

"Yes, I am named after Saint Sebastian. Sebastian Beau Chenevert."

"Ah, then there is a thing that we have in common. I am also named after a saint."

"Shall I guess which one?"

"If you like."

"Saint Michael?"

Anatole laughed in surprise.

"Yes Saint Michael. Michael Anatole Blanchet. How did you guess."

"You are so tall and strong and handsome. It's hard to imagine any other saint that you might be."

Anatole blushed again. What a curious manner of conversation the upper class had.

"And you are a fitting Saint Sebastian, though I hope you avoid the slings and arrows."

"Of outrageous fortune?" Beau asked, smiling.

Anatole understood the reference.

"Yes, I have read Shakespeare."

"While lying in the glade by the water?"

"On many occasions."

"You are a curiosity, Saint Michael Anatole."

"You don't think a man of my class can read Shakespeare?"

"Don't be silly. In general reading Shakespeare is rare enough in any class."

"Beg your pardon."

"I am saying," Beau said, "that I am not a classist snob, rather I am an intellectual snob. I hate stupid people."

Anatole laughed; he did not know what to say.

"Charlie. The other footman? Is he a friend of yours?"

"He is not."

"He is an imbecile." Beau said flatly. "That isn't classism, that is just a fact."

"Perhaps you think me an imbecile because I did not know the name Louis Daguerre?

"Ignorance can be forgiven, but intellectual incuriosity is a sign of a weak mind."

Anatole shrugged and sipped his tea.

"I cannot argue with that."

Beau opened the box and removed the paper. He placed the paper into the liquid of the first tray.

The image was captured on this piece of copper.

"This is the first step of development process."

Anatole looked but did not see anything yet. Beau took tongs and removed the paper and placed it into the next bath. Still nothing. But then something began to take shape. Anatole could see the lines begin to form on the paper.

"Now for the third bath. This will fix the image onto the paper so that it will remain even after it is exposed to light."

Beau placed the paper into the fixative and now Anatole could almost make out the image. Beau took it out and hung it to dry in front of Anatole.

His eyes widened as he realized what he was looking at.

The photograph that developed before his eyes was of a young man laying naked in grass next to the water. His body looked toned, and it looked good. His buttocks round, firm, and muscular. His dark hair long and wet.

Beau stood behind him and leaned in.

"Do you remember?"

Anatole was speechless as it began to crystallize in his mind that this was a photograph of himself lying in the glade that day. He was somehow both embarrassed and proud at the same time. He had never seen himself like this and never imagined that he would.

"What do you think?"

"I don't know what to think." Anatole said.

"Look how beautiful you are."

"Sir, you forget yourself. Do not tease a naïve servant."

Beau laughed.

"There is absolutely nothing naïve about you, Anatole. Saint Michael."

"Why did you invite me into your little dark room? Was it to tease me? I warn you that I am immune to that nature of teasing."

"Who is teasing?" Beau asked. "I am an aesthete, and I always have been. When I was a boy, I would walk through the streets and the parks and the mansions of New Orleans and I would ache to be able to describe the cobblestones, the blossoms, and the cornices of my gorgeous city.

I see beauty everywhere, even in the decay of that city. And when I do I catalogue it with my mind. However, I always lacked the words to describe it in the way I wanted. But now, with the camera, I can capture it for prosperity. Beauty that is no longer locked inside my mind, but visible to others who wish to see it too."

Anatole sat blankly looking at Beau's face in the red light. A thin bead of sweat was developing on his upper lip.

"Wait, are you going to show this to people?"

"Not if you do not want me to. But I wanted to celebrate this beauty for myself. Would you like me to keep it to myself?"

Anatole looked at the paper. The image was somehow magnetic. The lines and the curves of his body amounted to more than the sum of his parts. There was a mysterious geometry of appeal at work here that he had never seen of himself. A way that he could never have seen himself before.

"I am sorry." Beau said. "I know I should have asked you first. But there is a beauty in this composition that others will appreciate. Surely you see it?"

Anatole was quiet again.

"I don't think I mind if others," he said, "at least people who do not know me, see this."

Beau smiled, his teeth glittering in the red-washed darkness.

"Thank you for the tea, Mister Beau. It is time to return to reality."

"My pleasure."

Anatole stood and set his teacup down on the table. He gave Beau one last look before turning and opening the door.

"See." Beau said.

Anatole turned and saw the paper with his image one last time. And indeed, it remained even as exposed to the light. He had been frozen in time. He began to think that his previous perceptions of Sebastian Beau Chenevert had been hasty. He immediately thought of Charlotte and what he had said to her. She had been right, and he had been overprotective. He was glad to have been proven wrong.

Chapter 18
Blood Ties

Charlotte had the sensation of being in another world. Familiar, yet new. New Orleans was, in a way, a different world. The fashions were more current. The people had a different attitude that one might call *haughty*; something that truly did not exist in the provinces. Weeks had passed since cousins Bernadette and Beau had returned to New Orleans and she found she missed their company and while she did not always understand her cousin, she was glad to be back with them.

New Orleans society had a formality, as well, even more so than at Bridlewood House. She stood by as her name was announced. She stepped out to a round of light applause. Every eye in the room was upon her. Cousin Beau appeared from the side to take her arm and escort her across the room toward a table of refreshments. It was something like she had read about from old world Europe.

"Thank you, cousin."

"It is my pleasure." Beau smiled.

He handed her a glass of champagne.

"Thank you, cousin. You are so obliging; I understand there is a lucky young woman to whom you may be betrothed."

"We have yet to make the announcement, but yes, it is true."

"I am so happy for you both."

"Thank you, cousin."

"I hope marriage is everything you want it to be. I myself may be announcing soon."

"I understand that your father may have someone intended for you?"

"He does indeed, and he is a fine man. Though I would not mind marrying for love since *I* do not need to marry for wealth or position."

Charlotte gasped when she realized what she had said and how it sounded.

"I am sorry, I should not have said it in that way. I did not mean to imply-"

"It is alright, cousin. Please do not apologize. You are quite correct. Mine is a marriage of importance to our family's fortunes. There is no shame in this for me, only shame for what my father did with our own fortune."

A young man approached them and broke the tension of the moment.

"Cedric," Beau smiled, "may I introduce you to my cousin Miss Charlotte McCambridge."

"Miss Charlotte, if I may. I am Cedric du Pointe, and I believe I have the first dance with you."

"A pleasure to meet you, Mr. du Pointe."

She said before turning back to her cousin Beau.

"Never mind what we were talking about," Beau said, "it was all just nonsense which we will laugh about later."

"Thank you for understanding, dear cousin."

Charlotte smiled an awkward smile and nodded. She made her way to the dance floor escorted by Mr. du Pointe. An evening of the privileged class enjoying their privileges began in earnest. She danced with the most eligible men of New Orleans for an entire whirlwind of an evening.

The party for Lina Belvedere's engagement had gone particularly well. Charlotte, Beau, and Bernadette had enjoyed a fine time. The Belvedere home was legendary in the Garden District. It was as fine a home as you would see in New Orleans. Not a town home, it was fully a mansion, and it sat on a large plot of land.

Unlike most of the local society the McCambridge's had decided against having a town home in New Orleans. Charlotte's father insisted that they exist entirely at Bridlewood House, and society was more than willing to come to them. When in New Orleans they would often stay with their cousins. But when George McCambridge was in New Orleans on business, she knew that he stayed at his club. She suspected that was code for something else, but she did not ever ask.

Charlotte was well known among the social circle of New Orleans. She was not often seen at New Orleans parties, which seemed to make her appearance even more of a social event. She found herself in this strange new position. Being the center of attention even at events where she was neither the host nor the guest of honor. The way that the young women of New Orleans, and the young men as well, would attend her as they had not in previous years. Her position was becoming clear to her; and apparently had already become clear to everyone else.

After the party she and Bernadette enjoyed a quiet ride home in the carriage. Beau had stayed behind at the party to catch up with friends who had been traveling. When they arrived at the Chenevert townhouse on Rue Royale, they stepped out of the carriage and into the chilly autumn air.

"Would you care for a drink to settle your mind before bed?" Bernadette asked.

It seemed like such a sophisticated invitation, like one her mother would have accepted, that she immediately said yes. Though she instantly wished she had been coyer about it to not sound desperate. She realized that she had been studying Cousin Bernadette's moves and responses. She seemed so much more sophisticated. Like the sort of person, she herself should be.

The footman took their wraps, and the two ladies settled into the drawing room. The same footman reappeared and poured their sherries and delivered them on a small silver tray.

"I suppose you have noticed the effect you are having on New Orleans society."

"It is all so confusing, to be honest."

"When your dear mother died you immediately became a major fixture of the social set of Louisiana. But since you are also of age to come out you are an even more prominent star in the firmament."

"I feel completely unprepared."

"It is alright, cousin." Bernadette said. "I will gladly help you navigate these rocky waters."

A look of relief passed over Charlotte's face.

"Thank you so much. And thank you for having me here at your home." Charlotte began.

Bernadette winced and recovered with a wan smile.

"It is almost embarrassing to have you here, dear cousin. Our standards are no longer what they used to be."

"Everything seems to be running smoothly." Charlotte assured her.

Bernadette sat down; her eyes cast to the floor.

"Mother would not want you to know this. Perhaps I should not say."

"Say what?"

"Mother hired extra staff just for your stay so that you would not be inconvenienced."

Charlotte gasped.

"Please, do not say a word to her about this. To anyone!"

"Cousin, I would never!"

"She is just such a proud woman and would never wish for you to know. I can't- "

Bernadette stopped herself and dabbed her eye.

"What?" Charlotte leaned into her cousin. "What more?"

"We've lost our box at the opera."

Charlotte had no idea it had gotten as bad as all this.

"Please, mother would never want you to know how far we've fallen."

"But you have not fallen in dignity or in society, dear cousin."

Charlotte tried to assure her, but she knew of the icy chill of a society who has turned their back. She herself had not experienced it, nor was she in danger of it. But she had certainly heard her mother's stern warnings about behaviors that could lead to social ruin.

Charlotte's mind began to turn with machinations that were altruistic, yet also selfish. Perhaps she could use her own social clout to assist cousin. Perhaps her cousin could even return the favor.

Charlotte's mind began to run wild with ideas.

If she were able to broker a match between her cousin Bernadette and Robert Mayhew then perhaps, she would be allowed to meet a man that she might love. It was a long shot, but the only way that could be guaranteed was if there were no alternative. What if she introduced Robert Mayhew to Cousin Bernadette and they fell in love? If they met and fell in love and married, then was it not still a marriage of convenience for the family? Then how could her father be angry with her?

"I will come down to Bridlewood and help you plan the next event."

"Oh, I hate to ask so much of you!"

"It is no bother at all." Bernadette said. "I am of little use to Mother here. I would be glad to get out of the house and help you."

"Cousin, your family have been so hospitable and selfless with me lately and I fear I may have spoiled things with your brother Beau. I made a comment about marriages of convenience that came out wrong. I feel like I can say nothing right. This is why I need your help."

"Beau is significantly less fragile than you think, I assure you."

"I am glad to hear that. Your visit was so enjoyed by father and me. I confess that I had quite a laugh at what a fuss it caused in the household."

Charlotte noticed Bernadette's head turn and eyebrow arch almost imperceptibly.

"Fuss?"

"Just something overheard by my footman Anatole about you wanting your brother Beau to marry me."

Bernadette laughed. She leaned in and grasped Charlotte's still-gloved hand.

"Well, I did tell you that servants are not your friends. But more importantly, they can never be your family. Not your blood. Like Beau and me."

"I know they mean well." Charlotte smiled. "They are merely looking after me."

"Well now you have me to help with that."

"I am indebted to you, Bernadette. We are already working on arrangements for Christmas Réveillon. Would you be prepared to come and spend all of December with us at Bridle-wood House?"

A smile spread across Bernadette's handsome face.

"Indeed, I would, and Beau would join us before the party."

"Then it is all set."

Réveillon was the Christmas Eve affair that all New Orleans and Louisiana society waited for all year. Beginning after Christmas Eve mass at midnight and well into the small hours of the morning. It was always the most decadent event of the year. The food, the wine, the clothes. This would be her first Réveillon, and it would be the best.

Charlotte imagined at least one tea or luncheon before Réveillon where she could insinuate Bernadette into Robert Mayhew's field of vision. She was most comely, and he would be bound to notice her again.

Charlotte began to realize that something she had been missing was a friend of her own class who was an ally, not a competitor. They were of the same blood and therefore they were aligned and allied. She could now see what her mother had been saying all along. Many things were becoming clear.

Charlotte McCambridge had been brought up in the kind of wealth that drew a great curtain across the inequities of other lives. As it was meant to be, a curtain that blinded her from reality, but also a palisade that protected her from the knowledge of other people's struggles. Charlotte was aware that impoverished people existed but was shielded from the cause and to her own role in it. This was all as had been intended for her and for her mother before her.

Her family and her friends were all from the same social set. While she had been raised with Anatole and Emily, she was not sure if she had ever been to their homes. She had never lived a moment in their lives, they had merely been guests in hers.

As a child she and her mother would frequently come to New Orleans to stay with her mother's cousin who was the mother of Beau and Bernadette. But she had not been back in many years. She had not seen their reversal of fortunes for herself, or if she had she had not been aware. Had that great curtain of wealth kept her from seeing the difficulties of her own family?

"Cousin, I feel like my mother is drawing us tother."

Bernadette brightened.

"Oh, I agree, cousin. I can feel her presence. She wants me to help you get acclimated to society. *This* is what she would have wanted."

"Thank you, dear Bernadette. I don't know how I can thank you."

Chapter 19

The Great Loss

Anatole walked along the wooded path from Bridlewood House to his own meager childhood home. The light was dappled with the shade of innumerable leaves and branches. He now lived and worked at Bridlewood House, but his home would always be down the short and often muddy lane in the small wood house with thatched roof. He always felt a mix of the warmth of remembrance. But when he approached the house that was tempered by an echo of fear of his father's wrath repeated down the corridors of his memory.

Growing up he never knew what way his father's volatile moods might swing. Some days he would get that loving father figure that his mother often assured him existed hidden deep within the layers of bourbon and regret. But most days he got the father who was hard and angry. Even when he was not drunk, he was a miserable bastard.

Anatole pushed the door open and stepped inside to the familiar smells of home cooking. His mother immediately embraced him and gave him a kiss as though they did not see each other at Bridlewood House every day. Though they kept their relationship there professional to not raise any suspicions of favoritism.

Anatole turned and watched as the rain began to fall in earnest. The large window was quite a luxury for a family of their means.

"How is everything?" Fabienne asked.

"It's going well, mama. Thank you."

"You seem a little melancholy."

"It's just all the rain, I guess."

"Your father has been asking about you."

"I doubt that."

"Now, none of that." She scolded. "This is Sunday supper and the only time we really have together."

"I'm sorry mama."

He looked out and saw a fawn running through the woods, then its mother followed closely after. They seemed to be playing in the rain.

"Do you know the story of these windows?" Fabienne asked.

Anatole nodded; of course, he had heard the story over and over through the years.

"They were a gift from Mr. McCambridge back when father was helping build Bridlewood House."

Anatole had always been surprised that Mr. McCambridge gifted anything. He was certainly not known for his generosity to his servants or workers.

"Yes, I remember. They were part of an outbuilding that ended up not being built."

He wondered why she was telling this story yet again.

"Yes. Because of the accident. They were up there installing the windows in the cupola at the very top. They say it is a stunning view up there and your father is one of the few people who have ever seen it. He used to brag about that...before the accident."

Now Anatole was intrigued. He had not been told or had long since forgotten about an accident.

"Accident?"

"What you don't know about your father." She began, and he could see that it was difficult for her. "What you don't know is that he was there when his friend Abel Spall fell from the top of Bridlewood House. He and Abel were friends. Best friends. They had shared a room together in town before we met and decided to settle down together here. Then he built us this cottage with left-over scraps from Bridlewood House on this land which had been given to us by my family. You may not think it is much, but it is a symbol of his love for you and me."

Anatole had a hard time imagining the person she was describing as the person he knew today.

"But then the day came that Abel fell to his death at Bridlewood."

His mother gazed into the distance as if she were reliving the memory.

"Their friendship was the most important relationship to your father, besides mine and yours."

"Mother, I don't recognize the man you are speaking of." Anatole said flatly.

Her expression changed to a look of sadness that he did not recognize.

"That is because *that* man disappeared. First, he was over-come with grief. But then by anger, bitterness, and guilt. And maybe even something else that I cannot express. But the anger and the bitterness and the guilt...they do not leave room for anything else. I watched him slip under the waves. Eventually they overtook him like a *lespri mal*."

"A what?"

"An evil spirit.

"You think father was possessed?"

"Not exactly, son, but I think grief can be a kind of possession. They derange your very person."

Anatole listened intently. He had never heard his mother be so candid about his father. He began to feel a twinge of sympathy for the old man. He at least could feel that his father had once been a decent person, and that gave him a peculiar pleasure. A hope. But because of his own mercurial nature it also gave him pause about the monster that may lay dormant inside of himself.

He and his father were so different. But what if they were really two sides of the same coin? What if he was only one great loss away from slipping under the waves of despair? It was enough to make a person long for solitude.

The front door shut hard, startling them both. His father stood there shaking the rain off himself. He did not acknowledge either of them. He was disheveled as usual. Finally, he looked up at Anatole.

"We're going to need some firewood soon." He grumbled.

Then he made his way back to his bedroom where he closed the door loudly behind himself.

"I'll get the firewood cut on my next dry day off." Anatole said to his mother, though his gaze was still fixed on the area.

"Thank you, son."

Anatole began to set the table for Sunday supper. He took the plates down from the cabinet. His father came back into the living room and sat down in his chair by the unlit fireplace.

"Why don't you go and try to have a conversation with him?"

Anatole set the plates on the table.

"Alright."

Anatole went into the living room and sat down in the chair opposite his father. His father had aged a great deal more than his actual age. Drink and smoke and laziness had ruined him, and he smelled of all three.

"How are you doing, papa?"

"The same as the last time you asked, I guess."

"I've been working as both valet and second footman. Carstairs reckons I might make first footman when Charlie Mayes moves up to valet for Mr. McCambridge."

"You give your life to those people, and they won't ever give you anything back."

"They give me money and a place to live."

"You gotta place to live right here and we could use the help around the house."

The circular nature of their discussions was one of the main reasons he had a hard time engaging with his father. There was nothing in common and nothing to talk about. His father did not care to hear about his work, probably because it made him consider his own shiftlessness. And Anatole did not care to hear about whatever uselessness his father would discuss. But he intended to make an effort for his mother.

"I have the opportunity to learn a trade that I can take to any fine home that I may wish to work in."

His father finally turned his eyes to him and held his gaze.

"Then do it and get out of that house."

His voice was low and gravelly.

"That house is evil, and you will fall to its curse, I have already seen it."

Anatole was used to his father's drunken tirades, but while he sounded crazy. Also, he seemed quite sober, which was almost more terrifying. The look in his eyes sent a chill through Anatole. He grabbed Anatole by the arm in a vice-like grip.

"It's the reason I left Bridlewood House. It's the reason I never returned. He was my truest friend, and I let him down. Literally."

His father laughed at the play on words. More like a grunt than a laugh.

Anatole was confused and attempted in vain to pull away.

"What are you talking about?"

"I went back to work immediately after Abel died. I had no choice. The *gift* of these windows and the lumber for this home *had* been made and I had to return because it was no gift. There are no gifts from the man who owns you."

Anatole was not surprised to hear this part, as it was much more closely aligned with what he knew of Mr. McCambridge.

"The funeral was the next day, and I returned directly afterward. There were deadlines to meet because parties had been planned. I went immediately back to installing the windows in the cupola. I looked out to find the other workers scrubbing his blood from the stone veranda below. That's when I first saw him."

"Saw who?"

Anatole's father looked him directly in the eye and Anatole understood that he was completely sober.

"Abel Spall."

Anatole had a chill for a moment.

"What?"

"He stood on the edge of the veranda in the same overalls he had been wearing when he fell. He stood there confused with his shirt stained through with his own blood. And then he was just... gone."

Anatole listened carefully to his father's story. He had never had such an honest discussion with the old man. Was he so full of despair that he had imagined the ghost of his friend? Followed by anger and hatred at Mr. McCambridge?

"I don't expect you to understand." His father said.

His father let go of his arm and Anatole felt a pain as the blood rushed back.

"Perhaps in your grief-"

"Don't you dare!" His father thundered back.

"Please, keep it civil." Fabienne called from the kitchen.

"That wasn't the only time I saw him." He continued. "A

week later as I was leaving the property, I heard his footsteps following me along the path. I recognized the sounds of those steps as we had traveled together for years. I recognized his steps as I would recognize my own.

"I stopped and I said aloud without turning *why are you doing this to me?* But he did not answer, so I turned, and I saw him standing so close behind me that I could have felt his breath if he had any. He was slowly shaking his head, and I could tell that he wanted to tell me something, but he could not for his head was ruined from the fall and his jaw was disconnected in a most gruesome way.

"I began screaming and I could not stop. Someone came and dragged me away to home and gave me a whisky to calm me down and your mother tried to console the inconsolable."

"Papa, I'm so sorry."

Anatole was astonished and confused. He felt tears come to his own eyes.

His father's voice softened.

"The final time I saw him was the final time I set foot on the Bridlewood Estate. I was eating my lunch in the newly finished chapel, and he came to me. But this time I was not startled, as I had been expecting it. Every single day I had been expecting it. But now I looked upon his ruined countenance and I no longer saw my Abel. I saw the dregs of his existence. And he said to me only *do not tarry here, for you or yours may die here and never rest.*

"He showed me a vision of the house filled with ghostly beings engaged in a never-ending dance. A vision of the Indians being slaughtered on this land. The Indians cursed that land. Not just the house, but the whole land. I can't explain but they cursed that land and now we're all paying for the white man's sins. That's what he showed me.

"He turned from me and left me with the image of his destroyed head and brain matter oozing down his back. I dropped my sandwich and stood up. My mouth agape in horror. I ran from the chapel and down the road and back to our little shack which had just been finished. I crawled into a bottle of whisky, and I never returned."

Anatole stared into his father's wild eyes and swore that he saw no trace of himself.

Chapter 20
Le Corbeau

Anatole's boots clacked on the warped slats as he sauntered down the boardwalk of Point Cèdre. The unseasonable warmth had finally given abruptly away when a cold front moved in announcing the arrival of November. He was headed to Mr. Randy's again to pick up his newly tailored uniforms.

Ladies looked up to him as he walked and he tipped his hat when they were near, as he had been taught. As usual, women often offered him a smile, which always confused him. They were all well above his station and did have any real idea what to do if they had been at his station. Although, if Charlie Mayes was to be believed, he could have his way with a variety of women. But he did not put much stock in the stories of Charlie Mayes.

Not that he had ever tried to. He was far too afraid of losing his job and he did not feel any particular interest in being homeless and hungry. Charlie clearly had no such compunctions. One word from a lady of proper society and he could be fired immediately and never work in service again. Not to say that Charlotte would not be sad to see him go, but her father would not stand for that kind of nonsense. No one dared sully the McCambridge name.

Anatole pushed the door open to Mr. Randy's and the bell jingled announcing him.

"Be right there!" Mr. Randy called from the back room.

Anatole perused the various haberdashery that he could not afford. He came upon a table of cufflinks and tie pins. One set of cufflinks was crafted of silver and had a sword and an elegantly etched wing upon it. Anatole picked one up and turned it over, admiring it in his hand.

"It's very expensive."

A voice from behind startled him. It was Mr. Randy, standing closer than was seemly.

"I was just admiring it." Anatole said. "Far too expensive for me."

"Saint Michael." Mr. Randy said. "His sword and wing."

"Yes, of course." Anatole said. "I am named after Saint Michael."

"You are?"

"Yes, Michael Anatole Blanchet."

"A beautiful name for a beautiful young man." Mr. Randy added.

"Thank you, kind sir." Anatole said, blushing slightly.

"Since it is your name, perhaps you should have it."

"No, sir." Anatole said, "I could never afford such luxuries."

Mr. Randy placed his hand on Anatole's forearm.

"I'm sure we could work something out."

It was not that Anatole had not noticed Mr. Randy's attentions in the past. He had simply chosen to ignore them. He was not an uncomely man. He was probably twenty years older and married. Mr. Randy clearly had an affection for him and Anatole knew it. But he was not interested in playing with the affections of the older man. Mr. Randy and Miss Hermione were unable to have children, so he probably looked at Anatole as a son. Anatole thought it would be cruel to lead him on in that way. But to merely say no could be offensive.

"I am beholden to my employer, and Mr. McCambridge does not allow us to wear jewelry, and I would have nowhere else to wear it."

"I understand." Mr. Randy said.

"Thank you for the very generous offer. Mr. McCambridge often speaks of what a good gentleman you are, and I see that he is correct."

Anatole lied, but he could see the effect of such charms on Mr. Randy. He practically blushed.

"My pleasure."

Mr. Randy smiled and stroked Anatole's arm. Anatole allowed him the pleasure of the closeness as no one else was there and it did not bother him at all.

"Are my livery uniforms ready, by any chance?" Anatole asked.

"Yes, of course. Would you like to try them on?"

"No, thank you. I don't have the time today."

Another lie. Anatole had the time but did not wish to press his luck by having Mr. Randy within groping distance of his wedding tackle again so soon.

Mr. Randy disappeared into the back and reappeared with his parcels in a bag. He knew that he was afoot and would be carrying them back to Bridlewood.

"Thank you, sir. And thank you for all the fine work you do for us at Bridlewood."

It was Mr. Randy's turn to blush crimson.

Anatole nodded and tipped his hat to Mr. Randy and exited his shop with a jingle of the bell.

Anatole was unsure of what to do with a free afternoon. The

concept of *free time* was so foreign to him as to make the exercise seem almost exotic.

He had just gotten paid. He had been saving every cent since he was hired at Bridlewood. He was living on the estate and did not have to worry about room or board expenses. Why should he not enjoy a small extravagance?

Ahead hung the sign for Le Corbeau, the local inn of Point Cèdre. The sign swung in the slight afternoon breeze. Painted red with gold lettering, it stood out among the other more subdued signs on the street, some that had never been painted and some that had faded that the paint colors were a mere memory. But Le Corbeau had been maintained like a well-kept lady.

Anatole had been inside once with his mother. That day came rushing back to him, as the present fell away in an instant.

He was young, perhaps ten. His mother walked ahead of him swiftly and with purpose. He could not tell if she was more angry or fearful. But he followed dutifully behind as she strode up to the doors of the inn. She turned to Anatole and looked down at him. Her face stern and her eyes set in a confused set of expressions that were battling between motherly love and some desperate anger.

"Stay out here while I take care of this." She said sternly. "Do you understand?"

Anatole nodded, though he did not understand, and his curiosity prevailed, as it often would in his life. He pushed open the doors to the inn and followed his mother into the saloon's gambling hall. There he found his mother stood in front of a table of card players. He could tell, even at this young age, that something big was happening. She was taking a stand about something, but he did not understand what. He walked closer to the table, secreting himself behind a column.

"My husband is taking the food out of the mouth of his child to be here right now!" She had said, strong but not screaming. Then she focused her rage directly at his father.

"This child needs food, and shoes, and a roof. I don't care if I starve to death, but I will kill you and every one of these assholes as well before I allow you to destroy our child too."

And with that she pulled every dollar and coin off that table. The men were silent as she stormed out of the gambling hall. No one followed or tried to regain the lost monies.

Her position as housekeeper of Bridlewood had not been achieved yet, she was still only a maid. She had so little to lose and so much to gain. A secondary lesson that never eluded Anatole; that the more you achieved the more you had to lose.

He stepped into the luxuriously dark atmosphere of the inn. The darkness afforded anonymity to those who sought it. The air was perfumed with camellias. He found banks of them in various pots and vases as he walked through the place. But otherwise, it did not seem much altered since his last visit in childhood.

"Can I help you, mister?" A woman asked.

"I just wanted to have something to eat and a drink." Anatole said.

"Come this way," she said.

She bade him to follow and made sure to wiggle her assets in a way meant to grab his attention. And it succeeded. He felt a stirring in his loins and a reminder that he had not found release in some time. But he was not interested in relieving his tensions in a house of ill repute. Though he did not mind having food and drink there. He would take matters in hand when he returned home.

The lady seated him in a booth to himself. He ordered the steak pie and ale. He felt like a great land baron, being able to order what he wanted to eat. Surely this must be how they felt. To have the luxury of choice. He had worked hard for the opportunity to have what he wanted. His mother would be furious if she knew that he was wasting money at an establishment like this when there was food at home. But he needed this. He *wanted* this. To, for one moment, have the illusion of mastery.

He sensed the voice before he really heard it. It was a booming, whispering lady's voice. Somehow familiar, yet strange. A person who had never learned to moderate her tone.

"...and she won't even care." The voice said. "She's inheriting a fortune, and she won't even know what to do with it. She wears the simplest clothes and she only counsels with maids and negroes."

He recognized the voice. Its gritty voluminousness grated his eardrums the more he heard it. It was none other than Miss Beulah Sugarbaker.

"I know for a fact that she doesn't want to marry the man her father wants her to marry. He wants her to marry this man Mayhew. He's going to inherit the Mayhew Processing Factory fortune."

Anatole paused a moment. The son of the Mayhew sugar magnate. That could only be Robert Mayhew. He was Charlotte's intended. Suddenly, and for the first time in his life, he was very interested in Beulah's conversation.

"You could come between them so easily." She said.

"And what makes you think that I could?" A deep male voice answered.

"With your handsome countenance and charm, you'd have her easily. Not just her virtue, which trades easily enough these days, but also her heart."

"It sounds like my kind of challenge."

"More importantly, she doesn't need Mayhew's fortune. She has a larger one of her own.

He could not see the face, but the voice conveyed an oiliness. The man's voice again seemed impossibly deep. Businesslike, and yet somehow full of charm. Short and simple, but potent enough to wake up thoughts in Anatole that he had not entertained in some time.

"She will bend to my will," he said. "But how will you introduce me? I am certainly not from your social strata."

"I'll introduce you as my distant cousin at her Christmas party. She need never know about your social standing in great detail. Not if you *dew her lily* properly."

"Alright then. Challenge accepted."

"I must be going." Beulah replied.

"Do you need a hand with those?" The male voice said.

That was when it occurred to Anatole. The voice. The man's voice. He had heard it before. The man in the shops. The army captain who had come to Mr. Randy's establishment the last time he had been there. The tall and handsome stranger.

Anatole attempted to lean over in a clandestine manner to affirm his suspicions. In the process he knocked a spoon off the table and made a jangling noise onto the stone floor. He shrank back, but no one seemed to notice. As Anatole leaned to the left, he caught a glimpse of the man's face. He was engaged in conversation. It was the same gentleman. The army captain with the handsome face and alluring eyes. He sat there with a disembodied voice that he knew belonged to Beulah Sugarbaker and conspired against someone. And that someone could only be his lifelong friend Charlotte McCambridge. But he had already made the mistake of telling her that Beau Chenevert was after her money. It had angered her, and she would certainly not be receptive to another announcement. He had no idea what to do. Perhaps he could tell Emily and hope that she would share the message.

But what if she did not? What if she had her own agenda or was angry that he had been out flaunting his higher pay by eating at an inn? He would have to deal with that when it happened.

His instinct was to get up and leave. But his food came at this very moment. The wench set down a cold mug of brew at the same time she set down a plate of rabbit pie. He decided to stay and enjoy his meal and think about what he had heard and how to handle the situation, though he now found himself without an appetite.

Chapter 21
Miss Bernadette

A week later December had arrived, and the long warm autumn was finally over. Cool days and nights came but blue skies still prevailed for at least a while longer before the gray skies rolled in for their months long stay. Chimneys were being swept and fires were being lit. The smell of wood burning fires pervaded the air again, overtaking autumn's cool, damp, and earthy scent. The *mushroomy* loam of earth that never truly dried.

Eunice and Bernadette had arrived the week previous. It was as if they were arriving for the very first time. Something in the air was different. Eunice had found the staff cold at first, but they were beginning to warm to her again. They seemed to dislike her mistress, which she understood. Her mistress had particularly high expectations.

Miss Bernadette was clearly settling into her role as mistress of the house that she had apparently given herself. The staff could not help but notice that she already seemed to be a new force in the household. Gossip was that she was meant as a guiding force to teach Charlotte the ways of running a household.

She was a little older and had more experience in these things. Eunice was concerned that this morning's announcement would create another glacial shift in the staff's treatment of her. It was not uncommon to take a dislike of a superior out on their immediate help. She dreaded the meeting of staff, but hoped the other announcement would temper their irritation.

Today there would be a tea in honor of Bernadette Chenevert given by her dear cousin Charlotte McCambridge. The unspeakable scandal that had darkened her opportunities in New Orleans did not seem to penetrate the heavy veil of Spanish moss of the bayou country.

Bernadette walked down the corridor toward her rooms when she spotted Anatole with the bronze bucket that he used to carry ashes from the fireplaces. Upon seeing them he stopped and stepped back against the wall, as was customary for servants.

Miss Bernadette stopped to address him in her crisp manner.

"My brother is arriving next week."

"Yes ma'am. I will be prepared to take care of him."

"He has decided that he will not need a valet this time, so don't bother. I just wanted you to know so that you would not go out of your way when you will be needed elsewhere."

Did she notice a wrinkle of a smile from her mistress? Did she enjoy saying this to Anatole? Her mistress's cruelty seemed more obvious here at Bridlewood House. At home perhaps it had grown so commonplace, and yet here she was able to see how Miss Charlotte treated her servants. She spoke with authority but also with kindness. Perhaps her own mistress would learn something.

And did he wince? Did he seem injured by the interaction? Eunice watched him closely and saw clouds cross his handsome face. He was known to be the comeliest of all the footmen and yet he did not seem cocky, unlike the other one. Merely disappointed.

"I am sorry, I hope I did my best to serve him when he was here before."

"Who can say, my brother has his own mind." She said bluntly before turning and continuing down the corridor.

Eunice knew why Mr. Beau would not be requiring a valet this time. Miss Bernadette had freely shared the gossip with her. Apparently, Anatole had broken the key rule of not sharing opinions with your betters and had shared an opinion about Mr. Beau with Miss Charlotte. In most households he would have been fired.

Eunice followed Miss Bernadette to her rooms. She had moved into the suite of rooms formerly occupied by Charlotte's mother, the late Mrs. McCambridge. A tremendous step up from the guest suite she had previously occupied. Her own mother's dear cousin.

The rooms were sumptuous with yards of ivory colored silk moiré and plush chocolate brown velvet. Braided swags and beaded pillows. Ancient artifacts and object d'art. It was the room of an empress.

Once they entered, she wasted no time. She walked directly to the fireplace and stood as if she were an actress about to do a monologue.

Eunice had much to do and went immediately to heating the water for Miss Bernadette's bath. She was a forced audience for the show, but she still had work to do.

"Today is very special, I don't think I need to tell you that."

"I understand, Miss Bernadette."

"If I am able to take off socially here then I may just be able to set our finances and then I can actually keep you on."

"Of course, ma'am."

"So, you have to do your best work today."

"Yes, ma'am."

Eunice did not feel a particular fear for the loss of her job.

She knew that Miss Bernadette would rather die than change her own clothes or brush her own hair. Also, she would not find anyone who would work for what Eunice worked for. And frankly she knew too much.

Bernadette sat down on an ornately carved gilt chair upholstered in a fine chocolate colored satin with burgundy piping. She stuck out her right foot and Eunice began unlacing and removing the boot. Then Bernadette stuck out her left and they continued the movements that had become rote to them each after so many years together.

Bernadette stood and Eunice followed suit and began unlacing the gown Bernadette had been wearing that morning. A knock at the door broke the silent ballet.

"Yes?"

Eunice moved over to the bathtub to add the final bucket of water that had been heating over the fire.

Bernadette stood finally fully nude in front of the cheval mirror. She admired herself, as she often did. Taking stock of the merchandise that she had hoped would help her save her own fortunes. Those hopes had been dashed, but today they had been renewed by her cousin.

Bernadette turned and walked toward the tub. She stepped in carefully. The water was hotter than she had ever felt. Water this hot was a luxury so she embraced it and stepped in with both feet and lowered herself down. The water was so hot it sent chills over her body. Her skin would be bright red for a while after getting out, but for now she just enjoyed the sheer indulgence.

"Would you like me to scrub?" Eunice asked.

"No, I can manage this myself. Just prepare everything."

Eunice nodded and went to the dressing table. She had already laid out all the styling instruments. She had brought everything she would need to take care of Bernadette, as always, but once ensconced in the rooms of the late Mrs. McCambridge she discovered a beautiful set of silver and bone combs and a boar's bristle brush. Handmade bejeweled hair pins. She was not sure about using them, but Bernadette had insisted.

After the dressing ablutions had finished and the hair and gown were immaculately styled, Miss Bernadette headed downstairs alone for a meeting with Miss Charlotte. Eunice followed later, knowing that a meeting and an announcement were coming.

The staff gathered in the ballroom as they had been instructed by the housekeeper, Fabienne Blanchet. The instruction had been clear while the household was preparing for the day. They would meet after breakfast in the ballroom for an announcement from Miss Charlotte herself. A rare enough occasion to set the entire staff to talking.

Eunice waited quietly at the front of the line, having arrived earlier with her mistress Miss Bernadette. Mini was always the last to arrive, she seemed to have the most to do and often being the last to hear. She walked hurriedly into the ballroom to the sounds of all the other staff murmuring whispered ideas of what the unconventional meeting could be about. She rushed up next to Eunice and stood still and quiet for a moment.

She then leaned over to Eunice.

"What is this about?"

Eunice knew but was afraid to say that she knew.

"Has there been a death? Or worse?"

Eunice turned to her quizzically.

"What would be worse than a death?"

"Scandal. Theft. Stealing is way worse than a death around here. One time Mrs. McCambridge lost an earring. Everyone had to have their homes searched until they found it in her own chamber pot. Then the hall boy got fired for not emptying her chamber pot in a timely manner."

The gilt doors to the ballroom opened and Miss Charlotte and Miss Bernadette entered followed by Fabienne Blanchet. The crowd fell silent as the trio walked in and made their way to the front of the small crowd. Charlotte displayed her much-practiced benevolent expression which she had learned from her mother, while Fabienne was expressionless. Bernadette smiled like a magician who was about to perform a trick that they were confident would confuse you. A look that Eunice was familiar with.

Charlotte spoke first.

"Thank you all for joining us for this brief announcement this morning."

No one recalled having a choice.

"As you all know this has been a difficult year for us here at Bridlewood House. Having my dear mother being ill for so long and then her tragic death. It has been an insurmountable loss. Or at least it would be without my dear friends and family and this wonderful staff who make everything run so smoothly.

"However, it has come to my attention that we are not operating at the same level as many of the finer homes in New Orleans. We have a mission to give back to the town and the state of Louisiana. We do that with service to the community and that service starts right here at home.

"Fortunately for us, we have my dear cousin Miss Bernadette Chenevert who has generously offered her time to help me get through my first Réveillon here at Bridlewood. As you know, Réveillon is our grandest affair of the year. Absolutely everyone will be here for the most coveted invitation in the state. I would like to announce that thanks to our dear cousins, Governor and Mrs. Walker will be here."

Small gasps of surprise could be heard throughout the room.

The energy in the room changed instantly, with a frisson of excitement. Charlotte nodded toward Bernadette.

"You will give Miss Bernadette the same attention that you give myself and my father. She is a part of this family, and she will instruct you when she sees fit, and you will take that instruction as if it had come from myself. I believe that Bridlewood House will become a force in society that my mother always hoped it would. And with the help of Miss Bernadette, I am even more convinced."

There was a smattering of polite applause. Bernadette stepped forward. Her face was resolute.

"Good morning, everyone. I am so pleased to be here. My only hope is to serve Bridlewood House and my family to make this year's Réveillon the best that it can be. As you know Réveillon is the traditional celebration of Christmas Day that starts at midnight on Christmas Eve. We have so much to do to prepare for this year's gala. It will not be easy, but with perseverance and hard work I know that we can do it.

The staff seemed energized and excited by the news. The governor had never been to Bridlewood before. And Mrs. Walker was a serious social asset. She was one of the Thibodeaux triplets who had dominated society thirty years previous. Daughters of a robber baron.

The announcement of the addition of Miss Bernadette might have been insulting to the staff who had run Bridlewood House smoothly since it was completed, but the news of the governor's visit seemed to soften the blow. The staff seemed to understand their task, now. The need for the addition of Miss Bernadette's assistance to achieve this lofty goal that some would argue they had already achieved.

Fabienne Blanchet stood one step behind the women, her lips tight. Whatever she thought about the arrangement would never pass through those lips, at least not while she was on Bridlewood property. Her face, however, told its own story that anyone who knew her could read.

"Thank you all for coming," Charlotte said, "you may now all return to your work."

Eunice was pleased to see that the chatter that followed as everyone filed out of the room and back to their work seemed more about the excitement of the governor's visit than anything else. That meant that they would not be giving her a difficult time because of her mistress. At least not yet.

Chapter 22
The Manbo

Queen Marie was a robust woman who wore colors and jewelry unlike anything Emily had seen before. Layers of multicolored silks wrapped and pinned with bejeweled brooches. Her curly hair was pinned up into a wrap of vibrant yellow silk.

She imagined that this must be how creole women of means dressed in the city of New Orleans. The social strata were different there, according to her mother. She spoke of creole women who owned businesses and homes! Like Queen Marie herself, a legend that everyone knew.

Emily had been raised in Terrebonne Parish, though her parents lived in New Orleans now. She rarely had the opportunity to visit since becoming Charlotte's maid. Her father worked at a foundry and her mother worked in a fine home there.

She had often been in the presence of Queen Marie over the years and had heard many stories about her. She was a legend. She was half white, illegitimate daughter of the mayor. She ran a brothel, a hairstyling business, and a parlor of healing. She was a known *manbo*, a voodoo priestess.

She was an incredibly charismatic person even when she said nothing. Emily had never had the courage to speak to her. She had the sensation of understanding her thoughts as they were transmitted entirely through glances. Though she was sure that was merely the power of suggestion.

She watched as Queen Marie gathered Charlotte's hair and pinned each curl in place. Emily noticed that she tended to work in silence until Miss Charlotte or Mrs. McCambridge started a conversation. Charlotte was too young yet to make idle conversation with a woman older than herself. Emily watched and learned as styling Charlotte's hair was her own everyday job.

Emily began to realize that Queen Marie was the first woman of her own kind that she could look up to. She loved her mother dearly, and she had followed her example in the life of service. She had always looked up to Mrs. McCambridge, but that was not reality. Emily knew that she would never be a rich man's wife. She would never lead society, and she was not sure that she would ever want to.

But Queen Marie was a creole, just like Emily. She had come from meager circumstances but had the sense to pull herself out of it. She used her connections and her wit, and she became a success story. Not only by creole standards, but by any standards applied to women. While Emily did not have any connections, she knew that she had the wit to do it if she could just meet the right people. Perhaps it was time to truly meet Queen Marie.

After Queen Marie finished Emily walked with her down the corridor to the stairs. She tried to work up the courage to speak to her.

Queen Marie looked over at her and kept walking.

"Spit it out, chile."

Emily was caught off guard.

"Ma'am, my name is Emily, and I have watched you do your

work for a long time, and I think that you are the best that I have seen. You are a legend among the creole."

Queen Marie looked at her again, but this time she stopped.

"Mmm hmm."

"Everyone knows how you have different businesses. I want to know how you became a woman who handles her own affairs?"

Queen Marie paused and turned to look at Emily. Not just look at her, rather she seemed to truly appraise her. She looked into her eyes and Emily felt as though her very soul was being assayed. And after a few moments of this she spoke.

"I became a businesswoman because I had no other choice. God had given me wit and connections. They will tell you that a woman is nothing in this world without a man, especially a woman of color. And I said that this will not stand. Not for me. I knew that I would make my own way.

I see in your heart that you are wondering if you can make your own way. And I am telling you that you can."

"I can?"

"Is that *all* you want to know?"

Emily looked at her quizzically.

"I don't know what else there is to know?"

"When you figure it out, you are welcome to come to me again. I can see that you are at a turning point. I see that there is a snake in the garden, and you are going to get bit if you're not careful."

With that she turned and left Emily standing confused in the corridor.

That evening, as she took down all of Queen Marie's hard work, she memorized the placement of every curl so that she might reproduce the look one day and impress Miss Charlotte. She then removed the parure and put the jewels back into their glossy fruitwood box.

She had never heard the word *parure* before. How could she?

The word she learned after becoming Miss Charlotte's maid referred to the set of emeralds that was famous in the parish. The emeralds that Mr. McCambridge had famously won for Mrs. McCambridge in Europe so long ago and then had been made into a necklace, earrings, bracelet, and tiara.

The idea of wearing an entire fortune on one's body was so strange to Emily. A man's need to show off his wife and his fortune like trophies. To make your neighbor jealous of what you had was considered mischance or *move chans*. Bragging before God could bring his wrath.

The people of wealth and privilege, her employers, were so different than her own. People who had never experienced hardship, so wrath was something that happened to other people. Lesser people. They seemed to think it a way to show off what God had given them. Both the wife and the jewels were trophies that could be put away until needed.

She stepped outside the room into the corridor. She was so inside her own thoughts that she was startled to see Carstairs standing there, as he always was after a party. His final task of the evening was to take the jewels down to the safe and lock them behind the steel doors.

Emily had her own small room near Charlotte's. She returned to that room and undressed herself for bed. She used a basin and cloth to give herself a wash before bed as she always did. She crawled into her bed and curled up under the covers. She drifted off into a fitful sleep of troubling images.

She found herself walking through a sunken dream of Bridle-wood House. She padded barefoot silently down empty corridors almost as if she were in a foggy altered reality. Plaster cracked and crumbling. Draperies were merely moth-eaten shreds of fabric. Furniture collapsed. Chandeliers shattered on the floor. She felt the crystals cut into her feet as she stepped upon them, but there was no pain, just the sensation.

But in the middle of it all she found Queen Marie standing regally in the drawing room. Her hands were clasped at her waist as though she had been expecting to see her there.

"I'm glad you came. It took you long enough."

"I don't understand." Emily said. "What is this place?"

"I don't always understand it either, chile. I just find myself in places where *He* sends me."

"Who is *He?*"

"You know."

"Then why has He sent me here too?"

Queen Marie seemed to ignore the question.

"I have a gift called *astral projection*. I have studied it for many years. I lay in bed and I ask Him what it is he wants to tell me. Then I meditate."

"Meditate?"

"Yes, chile, it means to quiet your mind. The emptiness allows room for things to reveal themselves to you. I empty my mind of all thoughts until the visions or messages come to me. There is no point in asking the questions if you haven't made room for the answers."

Emily tried to understand.

"Earlier when I saw you at Bridlewood House. I looked into your eyes, and I saw something. I did not know what it meant at the time, but it was revealed in my meditations that there was a message for you. And therefore, you and I were both summoned to this place, and you were smart enough to come."

Emily felt confusion and she knew that that confusion was reflected on her face. She had not known that she had a choice in coming.

"Who is the message from?" Emily asked.

"I don't always understand the messages or who they are from. He projects me to other places and when I wake up, I don't

175

always remember any of it. Sometimes I have a foggy memory, but often nothing at all."

"What is the message?" Emily found herself asking again.

Emily heard a voice, not unlike that of Mrs. McCambridge speaking in her refined, but hurried tone.

The power. Surely by now you have felt it. You have grown up seeing them and you have placed them around my darling Charlotte's head and neck so many times. Have you not felt the power?

The emeralds floated in front of her, but they were not part of the parure. They were part of one great cluster. They were unrecognizable and yet she knew exactly what they were. One large stone with many emeralds embedded. The stone began to dissolve before her eyes the emeralds separated from it. They were uncut and unpolished. They were as raw as when they had been dug up from the earth. They were green, but not yet sparkling. She had a sense that they had a value beyond money. Was this the power that Mrs. McCambridge had been talking about?

A man appeared before her. He had skin not unlike her own, yet he was not Creole. He had a turban with jewels and a feather. He wore a silk gown with miles of jeweled necklaces.

He spoke and his accent was not known to her.

"Green is the color of envy, desire, and greed. It is the color of poison and danger. Lust. Green is the color of the snake of temptation. You must be aware that the emeralds have a power. A power greater than diamonds."

Emily awoke with a start. She looked around the room, disoriented. The room was dark, it was the middle of the night. She sat up and lit the candle on the table beside her bed. She threw back the covers and stood up to walk to get her robe. A stinging in her feet made her sit immediately back down. She lifted her left foot and saw that it was bleeding, a red smear stained the floor. She had somehow cut it without knowing. Her mind flashed back to the dream. She could barely remember, only glimpses. All she remembered from the dream was a vague feeling of unease, of portent. Like something was looming; something was going to happen. Like something was *coming*.

Emily stood again and winced as she hobbled to the window. The cut was superficial and would be healed soon. But the memory of it and the cause would haunt her. Out the window she looked toward the bayou. The landscape was lighted by what her mother used to call black moonlight. The moon was not entirely visible, but it still cast light across the landscape creating shadows even in the night.

Emily had an unnamed dread of what was out there. But before she finished the thought, she realized that her dread was more about what was inside Bridlewood House than out. A chill spread throughout her body. She pulled her arms around herself as she shuddered.

Chapter 23
Réveillon

"Wait!"

Anatole turned when he heard his mother's voice. She was in the corridor outside his small room.

Fabienne ran up to him full of excitement, smiling with a small box in her hands.

"What is this? It's not Christmas until midnight."

"I want you to have this now."

Anatole had never had such a beautifully wrapped gift. He quickly pulled the wrapping cloth off the box. He opened the box and gasped. The St. Michael cufflinks with the flaming swords. The ones he had seen at Mr. Randy's shop.

"Do you like them?"

Anatole realized that he had not made a sound and that his face was frozen in surprise. He broke out into a broad smile, his eyes wet with love.

"I love them, but you really should not have."

He embraced her and all the warm scents of mother and comfort washed over him.

"This is your first Réveillon party here at Bridlewood House. Soon you will be surrounded by all this finery, and I wanted you to have something fine of your *own*."

He quickly took out his old cufflinks and Fabienne helped him put the new cufflinks in place. He stared at them with a pride he had not felt before.

"Thank you so much."

"Now, go on with you before Charlie comes looking for you."

Anatole smiled and started walking down the corridor toward the main vestibule. He slid the old cufflinks out and slid the new cufflinks in, depositing the old ones into the box.

He saw Charlie Mayes and quickly fell into line and stayed several steps behind him. Charlie always seemed intent on squeezing every particle of importance out of the difference between their positions. He was one year older, but in his mind he had thirty more years of knowledge.

"Once the guests have all arrived, we will take trays of champagne throughout the crowd."

Anatole nodded intently as if this were not the exact plan that they had in place for all parties.

"Yes, of course."

When the guests were all inside Anatole followed Charlie up to the table in the butler's pantry where wines were being poured and carefully took a tray. He walked into the ballroom and felt the heat of the crowd. Even in December the room warmed quickly with so many people. The noise hit him next. The chattering and laughter of the hundreds of people in the ballroom.

He saw Mr. McCambridge immediately. He did not have a drink in his hand, so he returned to the makeshift bar and requested a scotch. The *good* scotch, the twenty-year-old Macallan. He stepped back out into the ballroom and made his way to Mr. McCambridge. He stood in front of him with the tray of champagne and the scotch.

"Thank you, Anatole." Mr. McCambridge said, taking the proffered scotch.

Anatole nodded then backed away. He entered the crowd of people and watched as flutes of champagne were lifted from his tray without a word. The room was overwhelmed with a fragrance of scented candles and perfume. Fortunately, it was winter. Truly the rich stink as much as the poor, but good "breeding" had imbued them with the ability to ignore it.

By the time he reached the other side of the room his tray was empty, and he was ready to return for a refill. Along the way he picked up empty glasses and any refuse that had been dropped by merry makers.

"Anatole!" He turned as he heard his name from a familiar voice. It was Charlotte.

"Yes, Miss Charlotte."

"Would you be a dear and get me a glass of champagne?"

"I will see to it."

He did not need to ask to know what she meant. She did not want the champagne that the rest of the guests were drinking. She wanted the sparkling rosé.

Anatole nodded and left the ballroom once again, pushing open the doors into the kitchen. He saw Charlie Mayes filling his tray.

"Miss Charlotte would like to have the sparkling rosé."

"In the cellar at the back. I took it out and set it in ice. Why are you asking me, you know where it is."

Anatole had always hated the cellar. It was so dark and there was never anyone else down there. He grabbed a candle and opened the door. He descended into the dankness of the vast wine cellar. The merriment upstairs was still audible but muted now. The dimmest sounds of music and laughter filtered down. It almost made it somehow more eerie.

There was some light, hurricane lanterns had been set along

the path. The vast room was cold. He was in a basement in December, so of course it was cold. But the chill had a preternatural quality. The stones seemed more mossy than usual. The air more stale than before. He had always had a fear of the massive wine cellar basement. The rows of tall wine racks seemed to go on forever and hide the true size of the room. In the darkness it seemed like it could go on infinitely.

Anatole's footsteps echoed off the walls and low ceiling. He mustered his courage and walked quickly to the end of the row where he knew the champagne had been set out in ice to chill. A candelabra sat next to the champagne bucket. It flickered in a draft coming from somewhere. Anatole picked up two bottles of sparkling rosé. He knew that Charlotte would not drink much, but he certainly did not wish to make another trip down here.

"A fine vintage, to be sure." A voice in the darkness.

Anatole nearly dropped the bottles as he spun to see where the voice was coming from. Anatole felt the bottles slip out of his hands but quickly and narrowly saved a catastrophe that would probably end up coming out of his pay.

"You can hear me?" The voice said.

"Who's there?" Anatole called out.

He attempted to make his voice even deeper than it normally was, but fear had stretched his vocal cords to the point of sounding an octave higher. No one answered back and he was not sure whether or not he was relieved by this. He looked down the impossibly long row of wine racks. So far was the row that he could not see the end. He began walking toward along the row and gripped each bottle tightly. His heart raced beneath his shirt. He was a big man. A strong healthy young man. But his fear was of something that his youth and strength could not fight.

At that moment *he* appeared. He could not make out features, just that a figure in workman's clothes; a man in trousers and work shirt. Anatole's heart raced beneath his shirt. He could feel it and hear it pounding like waves slamming into the shore-line of the bayou in a hurricane. He stood completely still, but the figure neither moved forward nor retreated.

"So, you can see me too." The figure said.

Anatole mustered his courage.

"I can and I do not fear you." Anatole lied.

The figure disappeared completely.

Not knowing what to do, Anatole broke out into a run toward the exit. Just as he was nearing the end of the row, he heard the voice again and turned to look behind him. He lost his balance and fell to the ground. He cradled each bottle of champagne and rolled across the stone floor of the cellar.

"Shit!" He exclaimed.

He looked up and saw no one. He scrambled up quickly to his feet and staggered backward to the stairs. His breathing was ragged, and his chest was tight. He backed up the stairs to the kitchen.

As the shock wore off, he began to feel the pain of the fall.

"What in Hell happened to you?" Carstairs bellowed.

"I fell."

"Did you meet Abel?" Charlie Mayes asked.

The entire kitchen broke out into laughter.

"Who?"

"Abel Spall. He haunts the cellar. Sometimes he gets a notion to spook the new boys."

Again, the kitchen erupted in laughter.

"Your livery is a mess!" Carstairs was furious. "Go and change immediately. And have those clothes mended and it is coming out of your wages."

"Yes sir." Anatole said. He placed the bottles of champagne in the ice bucket with the others and headed to his quarters for a quick change. He knew it was his mother's job to decide what came out of his wages, so he would not worry about it at the moment.

Anatole returned within minutes and had Charlottes sparkling rosé in her hand without too much delay. He could feel the sweat of anxiety still beading up on his neck and running down his back, his pulse still racing from the adrenaline.

"Thank you so much, Anatole." She said.

"You're very welcome, Charlotte." He said.

"Surely you mean *Miss* Charlotte." Miss Margaret Heatherwood, with her most disagreeable countenance, laughed.

In his rush Anatole had forgotten his manners. He blushed hot red.

"Begging your pardon. Yes, Miss Charlotte."

Charlotte smiled and sipped her champagne. She was clearly distracted by something. He followed her eyeline and realized what it was. The man, the object of her fascination, stood across the room. He was chatting with a group of girls who appeared enthralled with his story telling ability. He was tall and rakishly handsome. His features were chiseled, like a marble statue. Anatole could immediately see why she was fascinated. He cut a striking and strangely familiar figure, wearing an army uniform and standing several inches above the girls gathered around him.

Anatole recognized the grifter immediately. He was none other than Captain Jonathan Davies. It was too late. Charlotte's gaze never strayed.

Anatole also noticed that everyone else was watching him too. In the way that society does, the way all social engagements seem to unfold. Most standing on the sideline paying close attention to every single movement of the eye or hand. Watching the way that Charlotte was drawn to him. Or at least that is the way it seemed to him.

This evening, like all parties, would be exhaustively

discussed at teas and dinners over the following weeks. He had seen how it unfolded in the Bridlewood House drawing room at many teas before. Privileged guests would gather and gossip about what had gone wrong and what had gone right at the previous week's parties. He could not say that he did not enjoy some of the gossip. Having grown up with Charlotte he had known most of the debutantes their entire lives.

But it was only Charlotte who still treated him like a human being. The rest either looked at him as an object of amusement, or of contempt. Or they ignored his existence completely, which was sometimes preferable.

Anatole knew the inner working of class and society and that he would never move beyond his own. He knew his place, but his unusual upbringing and job ensured that he would have a hard time getting to know the culture of the people from which he came. He would only know as much about creole culture as his mother and father could teach him at home. And his father only drank and beat and did not revel in the culture of his heritage, he especially did not teach it.

As he eyed the darkly handsome army captain across the room, he realized that so many eyes were locked on the same location. How many esteemed guests long to know more about this captain?

Like a whirlwind of silk and perfume, Beulah Sugarbaker appeared out of nowhere.

"Darling, what a splendid party tonight."

"Thank you so much, Beulah." Charlotte said.

"I have taken the liberty of filling out your dance card for you."

"Oh?"

"Well, the truth is." Beulah lowered her voice conspiratorially, "my cousin from out of town came with me and he would love to meet you."

"Oh really?" Charlotte failed to sound excited.

Beulah waved her hand and suddenly a man appeared at Charlotte's side. It was him! The very man of the hour, the army captain. Anatole realized that it was not just any army captain, but the man that Beulah Sugarbaker had been conspiring with at Le Corbeau.

"You are Miss McCambridge, I assume?"

"Captain Jonathan Davies, I would like you to meet the Belle of Terrebonne Parish, Miss Charlotte McCambridge."

His face was handsome and angular. His dark wavy hair was brushed back to control the curls. His smile instantly hypnotized those around him in a way that Anatole did not instantly trust. So much power with very little skill. Anatole immediately admonished himself for thinking such things. While it may sound like jealousy, Anatole knew that he only had the best intentions for his friend. But he had heard this man's plans for Charlotte.

"Captain Davies, it seems that you are the first dance on my card."

"It would be my greatest pleasure."

"Beulah, be a dear and get us some punch for after."

And with that they swirled off to the strains of the orchestra dancing around in their newly found romance. Anatole could not help but look in the general direction of Robert Mayhew to see if he was noticing this moment. And once again it seems that his eyes followed everyone else's. Robert Mayhew stood surrounded by several young women who would gladly take Charlotte's place as the wife of this wealthy and seemingly decent young man.

By the time the party concluded, and the guests had all be escorted to their carriages or to their rooms as some were staying as overnight guests, Anatole was exhausted. He fell into his bed, barely getting his livery off, and was immediately asleep. Though his sleep was fitful and full of dispiriting dreams. The voice he had heard in the cellar came back to him and it seemed to want something. A connection of some kind? A warning?

When Anatole woke in the morning, he was still tired, but much needed to be done. And a servant did not have the luxury of being tired. He got up from his bed and looked at his naked body in the mirror. Reflected back was the body of perfect youth. Except for the scratch on his thigh from the fall.

Chapter 24
A Woman of Means

Palm House
Charleston South Carolina

Allison Banfield was a handsome young woman. *Handsome* was a word often used to describe her as it alluded to her good skin and bone structure that was not fine enough to be considered beautiful by the standards of society. She was tall and kept her body toned and healthy with exercise of sport and hiking.

Handsome was in no way a diminishment of her beauty. She was just simply not one of the porcelain-skinned, fine-boned dolls of society. Though it was universally understood that she did not strive to achieve those standards that so plagued women of the day. As it was equally understood that she did not need to do so.

She was the only child of the scions of a banking dynasty and a railway barony. She had been born with the curse of intelligence in a day when it alone was not appreciated in a person of the fairer sex. Her wit matched her intelligence and could be considered either cutting or dark by people who did not meet her level.

Her father had inherited his own father's genius for banking business. Her mother had inherited none of the interest in her own family's fortunes, as was considered correct for a woman of means of the day.

But Allison was different. She had inherited a knack for both. She had a keen understanding of numbers but would never be allowed to involve herself in banking. She had an interest in and an understanding of the railroad business, though she would never be allowed to plan growth or utilize any of the ideas she had already drafted in copious notes.

Her father and her grandfather had each let her spend a great deal of time in their offices. They had fostered her interest in the family business while knowing that she would not be allowed contribution. They hoped perhaps that her knowledge would help her understand the need to marry well. Though they had been thus far disappointed in her lack of interest.

Palm House was a grand affair built by her grandfather decades before. The estate named for the majestic palmettos that lined its drive and its perimeter, it echoed the Italianate palaces of the Mediterranean. A house like those seen by her grandparents on the riviera on their *grand tour* honeymoon. The house was built of stone and plaster with marble and artwork culled from their journeys.

Her mother had filled the house with artwork from her travels as well. The neoclassicists seemed to reflect the life she wanted to live. She had a Tiepolo and a Fragonard in her bedroom. She had even had a portrait of herself done by Ingres, commissioned by her parents when she was a young girl.

Allison had been born and raised there in this gilded museum. Though there were so many rooms that she had probably never even seen before. The rooms she had been given as a child were still hers today, though there was no longer a governess in the room next door. Rather there was Giselle, her personal secretary.

Allison sat at her burled fruit wood desk in an antechamber that existed between her and Giselle's room. She pored over the dates in her social calendar. Each entry was written in Giselle's neat and crisp handwriting.

A puzzled look crossed Allison's face.

"I cannot understand this entry on the nineteenth."

Giselle looked down and scrutinized the page.

"WSMM." She answered. "Yes, that is my new abbreviation for Women's Suffrage Movement Meeting. I did not think it wise to spell it out on your personal calendar."

"Ah, yes. I suppose you are right, but what could they really do?"

"Probably nothing to you. But me, they would make an example out of me."

"You come from a fine family, Giselle."

"I come from a fine family with no money. I failed to make a marriage, so now I am what you are trying to avoid becoming."

Allison nodded tacit understanding then changed the subject.

"We must clear some time to make a trip to New Orleans. I think it is time to meet my prospective intended and his family."

"Should he not come here first?" Giselle asked.

"Traditionally, perhaps yes. But I do not wish to waste any more time."

"Would it change your mind?"

"I think not," Allison replied, "unless he does not turn out to be the person that he has purported himself to be in his letters."

"What is it exactly that you wish from these people?"

"I only wish to have a husband, as I will not be given peace until I have one. Beau Chenevert is socially appropriate and through our correspondence I have reason to believe that he would be an *understanding* husband."

"Understanding?"

"You know what I mean."

"I suppose I do. I am not keen to share you with anyone, but I do not see that I have a choice."

"Neither of us have a choice, Giselle, having been born women."

"I understand, I just wish you did not have to marry."

"A woman in my position has no choice but to marry. As a single woman I will be the suspicion of every woman in society. I will be snubbed."

Giselle laughed.

"You do not care about that."

"*I* do not, but my mother does. What I really care about is that if I get married to the *right* man, I will be able to do as I please."

"And what is it you please?"

"My father and his father before him built a business empire. My mother's family have done the same. I know each of these businesses intimately, thanks largely to my grandfathers. I want to have say in how these businesses are managed."

"But even married you would-"

"I still would not be able to run a business. But my husband would. And I would be running it right there beside him. Especially if that husband had other hobbies."

"Such as?"

"Mr. Beau Chenevert is terribly fond of photography."

"What in the world is that?"

"It is the art of photographing. Surely you are familiar."

"I really am not, actually."

"Anyway, it's terribly new and he is quite a lot more interested in that than in making a living."

Giselle raised an eyebrow.

"I see. An *artist*."

"Exactly. And one who would allow me my own interests, as I would allow him his."

"And you are not just speaking of vocations and avocations."

"No, indeed. Mr. Beau Chenevert and I appear to be like-minded on several things. Including the love that dare not speak its name."

"I assumed as much."

"Ultimately there are only two things that would stop me from marrying Beau Chenevert."

"What are they?"

"If he is unwilling to relocate to Charleston, and I do not see that as a likely problem. His family is in ruin in New Orleans and my family prospers here."

"And what is the other thing?"

"It is something that I would not dare put in writing. Something that I would only ask him at the right moment upon meeting him in person. The only other thing that interests me, as you well know, women's suffrage."

Giselle raised a brow.

"You would not marry him if he were not in favor of a woman's right to vote?"

"Giselle, you know me better than perhaps anyone. And you know that I would not give up my independence to a man. Not now, not ever. I would remain unmarried and spend my life and my fortune securing the right for women to have a say in the country they helped create."

"Now I understand."

"I had hoped that you would, Giselle. My mother, whom I love dearly, is content to enjoy what she sees as the privileges of her class and her sex. To never want or need for anything, but also to never have the choice. That is a prison that I do not choose to accept and that is why my choice of husband must be well considered."

"Is that going to be acceptable to your mother?"

"I have made my wishes known to her. That is why she hopes that this arrangement with Beau Chenevert will work."

"Also, she wants grandchildren."

"Of course she does." Allison said. "This marriage will allow her to keep that dream alive a little longer."

"Would you like to have children?"

"I might." Allison looked ahead, lost in thought for a moment. "I actually might."

"At least you have a choice."

"Choice is a luxury that I have because of family money and station. Do not think that I underestimate the entitlement of my position, Giselle. It would be a sin not to use these assets for good. Sin in the truest understanding of the word. And perhaps if I were able to bring children into this world who could make it a better place that would be enough for me."

Allison turned at the knock on the door.

"Yes?"

An aged butler appeared with several envelopes on a silver salver. He walked over to where she sat at her desk and placed the tray on the desk.

"Today's correspondence, ma'am."

"Thank you, Jameson."

Giselle picked up the mail and sifted through the day's invitations to various lunches and teas with little interest.

"Anything worth attending?"

"You will probably want to attend the gala for the opera on the eighteenth."

"I enjoy the opera, not the galas."

"Yes, but this one is hosted by Marjorie and Jackson Pickett-

Burnside." Giselle said, referring to the man Allison's father was working with on a European banking merger.

Allison's eyebrow arched up imperceptibly to anyone but Giselle, as it often did when she was reconsidering something.

"Ah, yes. That does change things."

Giselle picked up one envelope and opened it. Her eyebrows raised perceptibly.

"Oh."

"What is it?"

"It is an unexpected invitation."

"Oh, I do love a surprise."

Giselle smiled wanly, knowing otherwise, and handed Allison the letter. Crisp paper of highest quality. The engraved top of the stationery said simply *Bridlewood House.*

"Oh." She said, "it seems we are to have the pleasure sooner rather than later."

"What does it say?"

Allison began to read aloud.

"Dear Miss Banfield,

I hope this note finds you well and that you do not find it presumptuous. I am Charlotte McCambridge, and I understand that you and my cousin Beau Chenevert are acquainted, and I would love to extend an invitation to you to come and visit us at Bridlewood House. From what cousin Beau has told me about you I feel you would greatly enjoy some time here in the country getting to know our family. I am planning a tea for my cousin Bernadette, Beau's sister, and we would love for you to be a special guest. Please let me know what dates you might be free, and we will choose one that works for all involved."

Allison raised an eyebrow.

"Presumptuous, indeed."

Allison placed the note back on the desk and leaned back.

"Yes, I suppose it is a little. But I almost find it refreshing. She

195

is just getting to the point, and you know how I adore getting to the point."

"No one knows better than I do."

"Then I suppose we need to find some dates for this visit. Cancel my attendance for the botanical gardens gala if you must."

"I can't do that; you know Mrs. Danvers—"

"I know that Mrs. Danvers enjoys our healthy donation, and I know that she will do what you tell her."

Giselle rolled her eyes discreetly and nodded her head.

"Did you just pull a face at me?" Allison gasped. "I know you were raised better than that."

"I'm not sure I was."

Chapter 25
Sweet Revelations

Anatole stood on the stone doorstep of Bridlewood House and surveyed the dark landscape of the winter's evening. The water of the bayou was still, and the moon reflected its fullness through a lace of light cloud cover. The cold air was still and bracing. Refreshing after being inside serving the group of the evening dinner guests.

As usual, he stayed after the last of the guests had gone, so he could sweep the front hall and the doorstep behind them. He stepped inside and finished tidying the front corridor. It had always given him a sense of purpose and pride in ending the day as cleanly as it had begun.

As he turned to go inside, he saw Beau walking through the corridor. Their eye contact was brief, yet immediately stopped. Clearly Beau did not want to interact, and he did not know why. The fickle ways of the wealthy and prominent were not unknown to Anatole. He just wished he had known what he had done. He decided to forget it best he could.

"Are you finally done?"

He turned to see Emily; her lovely face partially obscured by hair that had fallen from its tie. Her face brought a smile to his own.

"Yes, I am done."

She nodded.

"Then come downstairs and join me for a piece of the pie that your mother made."

"Alright, I would like that."

Anatole followed Emily down the corridor and down the backstairs to the kitchens.

Downstairs was dark. All the day's work was finally over, and the lamps extinguished. His mother Fabienne, the housekeeper, was long since home and the rest of the staff were in bed.

Emily lit one of the lanterns in the kitchen and she retrieved the pie from the pie safe.

"What kind did she make?" Anatole asked.

"Mincemeat."

He smiled. He had many memories of his mother making mincemeat pies in winter. A luxury and a treat.

"That sounds perfect."

Emily got down the plates while Anatole set down cups for milk. He filled the cups and placed the jug back in the larder. He pulled out a chair for Emily on the side of the table and then sat at the head of the table. Emily cut the pie and served them each up a generous slice.

The smell of brandy and figs and a hint of lemon zest brought back a moment from childhood when he had stood in his mother's kitchen at home when he had helped her gather ingredients for this same pie.

His mother grew lemons in the conservatory of Bridlewood House and preserved them for the winter. The luxury of living near the estate was never lost on him. His mother always wanted him to understand how blessed they were. To never forget that Bridlewood came with many advantages. He understood that what she really wanted him to know was that her sacrifices for her job were for something. The pie was wonderful, but his education was something he would not have had without Bridle-wood. He was not sure why he was having this realization at that moment.

Emily took a bite of the pie. Her eyes closed and she savored the flavors.

"Oh God, your mother knows how to make a fine crust."

"That she does."

"Don't ever tell Mrs. Paddington that I said this, but she makes a better pie crust than the cook."

Anatole smiled.

"She has a secret, but I'm not supposed to tell."

"You and I don't have secrets." Emily gave him a conspiratorial look.

Anatole smiled.

"She only makes pies in the winter. And she puts the pie crust outside in the cold overnight before baking. She says it makes the crust flakier."

"Oh, my! I am going to steal that, but I promise not to tell Mrs. Paddington."

They both laughed.

Anatole took a bite of the pie and memories filled his mind. Memories of every holiday and celebration of his life. The rich and nutty flavors were the flavors of his life. A life that had been sweet and rich, with or without money. He looked over at Emily and saw her staring off into the distance, her smile now gone like when the sun is obscured by a cloud.

"What is going on? You don't seem entirely yourself lately."

She jerked her head back into reality.

"I am sorry, I didn't realize I had gone off into my mind for a moment."

"So, tell me," Anatole asked, "what is wrong?"

She shook her head.

"Nothing, really."

Anatole sat back and looked at her more intently.

"No. Really. Tell me."

She turned and looked at her lifelong friend.

"Alright." She began slowly. "I just feel lately that *she* has changed. That *she* is changing."

She did not have to explain who *she* was. Their lives revolved around one *she*.

"What do you mean?"

"I'm sorry, I should not have said anything.

"Mon cher, you can tell me anything."

She shook her head.

"I know I can, but this feels wrong or disrespectful for me to say it. I can't explain it. I just feel like things are different now. I feel like our friendship is over and now I am just her maid."

Anatole put a comforting hand on her shoulder.

"You two have been too close for too long for your friendship to be over."

"I can just see such a change in her since her since Big Maman died."

Emily invoked the name they had always called Mrs. McCambridge when they were kids.

"Of course, she has changed." Anatole replied. "Look at all the responsibility she is taking on."

"I know that is true."

"And Miss Bernadette has come to help her with the burden."

"You don't really believe that do you?"

"What else could she want?"

"A woman like her could want a lot of things."

Anatole knew that Emily was privy to so much that he was not. The things that she heard in the confines of the mistress' suite were usually never discussed. He dared not repeat what he himself had heard.

"She is looking for a husband. She is using Bridlewood House as a hunting ground because she has ruined herself in New Orleans."

Anatole's shock was visible on his face.

"What did she do?"

"No one seems to know, and Charlotte does not seem to want to know."

"I see."

"So now she has come to Bridlewood House to make a marriage. And I think that Miss Charlotte is trying to push her onto Robert Mayhew so that she can fall in love with someone she wants to marry."

"What have you heard?"

"I heard Miss Charlotte and Miss Bernadette conspiring to have Robert Mayhew sit next to Miss Bernadette at her tea."

Anatole was enjoying the gossip. It was almost as delicious as the pie.

"But there is more, and you must swear to never repeat it to anyone because I would be likely fired."

Anatole's eyes grew wide.

"What is it?"

"I have been passing messages between Miss Charlotte and this gentleman caller. They have been meeting secretly after dark out at the folly."

Anatole sat in silence for a moment. Stunned. This was not like the Charlotte he knew at all. Big Maman would never approve. He had a good idea who it was, but he dared not tell her or anyone else what he knew about Captain John Davies and Beulah Sugarbaker after he had told Miss Charlotte about his suspicions of Mr. Beau. That had been a disaster.

"There is something else you should know."

Anatole braced himself, not sure he was ready for more news.

"You have noticed that Mr. Beau has requested not to have a valet on this visit?"

Anatole suddenly felt very warm.

"Yes, of course."

"That is because Charlotte told Miss Bernadette that you warned her about the pair of them."

Anatole's blood ran cold. He only thought it had been a disaster before, but now it was beginning to affect his work.

"What do you mean?"

"She told her that you warned her that they were gold diggers. Did you?"

He just shook his head.

"I did."

Emily laughed.

"I wish I had your gall, because you are absolutely right."

"I don't know." Anatole replied, the wind still knocked out of him. "There is so much going on right now and I don't know. I feel like I should apologize to him, because now I am not sure that he was even the problem."

"But she is. His sister Bernadette definitely is an obayifo."

Now it was his turn to laugh.

"You think she is an obayifo? Like some sort of vampire?"

Her laugh finally returned.

"Well, a kind of vampire."

They sat for a moment in silence and contemplated the pie and their thoughts.

"Perhaps I should apologize to him." Anatole mused.

Emily shrugged.

"You do what feels right to you, but I'm not sure that an apology would mean anything to those people."

"I know, I just feel terrible. And now with Miss Bernadette practically running the house..."

"Perhaps I should not have told you."

"No," he put his hand on her hand, "you were right for telling me. I don't ever want you to not be able to tell me."

"That goes for you to." Emily replied, squeezing his hand in return. "You know that you can tell me too."

"Tell you what?"

"Whatever it is that you are keeping locked up inside there like a treasure."

"I'm not hiding anything."

"Honey, I have known you most of your life. And you know me, I don't pry into anybody's personal business. I only want the best for you."

Emily leaned forward and looked directly into his eyes.

"You can tell me whenever you are ready to tell me," She said, "and I will still be right here on your side afterward."

Something about the way she looked at him made him feel like she knew more than she could have known. Something made him feel like there was something he did not even have to say but hoped one day that he would be able to.

"I love you." He said.

"I love you too." She smiled.

"I will tidy up these dishes," he said, "get to bed."

And with that she pushed her chair back with a scrape and stood up. She leaned over and kissed Anatole on the forehead and left the room. Their love for each other had always been and would always be like siblings.

Anatole stood up and cleaned the dishes in the sink as he promised. His mind was awhirl with things that he could not yet say to anyone, and how could he? How could he say the things that must never be said? How could he tell anyone what he had overheard from Captain John Davies and Beulah Sugarbaker after he had foolishly opened his mouth about Mr. Beau?

There was much to think about, but the only thing on his

mind was an ill-conceived apology to Mr. Beau. He would figure out in the morning what he would say and when.

Anatole turned down the oil lamp and walked toward the stairs in the darkness.

"Soon."

The voice came out of nowhere. But he recognized it immediately. The voice of the ghost of Abel Spall.

Chapter 26
Tête-à-tête

"I'll be out taking some of the night air." Charlotte announced to Emily, who already knew where she would be.

"Yes, ma'am." Emily replied.

Charlotte looked in the mirror and was pleased with how the burgundy gown contrasted beautifully with her copper hair. She wore simple gold jewelry. Simple by her standards, though still far above what any other person in the parish could afford. Her eyes seemed to sparkle even more in her current exultant mood. Emily handed her the fur wrap that she tended to wear out on cool evenings.

Charlotte left her room and walked down the corridor. Her mind was fully on her meeting with Captain Jonathan Davies at the folly. Just a few stolen moments in private in their covert hideaway.

She could not help but notice how the servants were behaving since Cousin Bernadette had arrived. Each one of them seemed to be working harder. They were more prompt, more attentive, more *servile*. Perhaps Cousin Bernadette had been right. Her methods certainly seemed to be working.

As she made her way down the corridor an open doorway caught her attention. The small room that Cousin Beau had been using for his hobby that she did not quite understand. He had tried to explain the process of *photography*, but she found little interest in the subject.

She looked inside the room lit only by a small candle inside a red lantern. The glass photographs were arranged on his table along with various bottles of chemicals she imagined were needed for the process, including a large one marked *arsenic*. She stepped inside for a moment to peruse his work. The landscapes of Bridlewood and the surrounding Terrebonne Parish were quite unexpectedly beautiful.

On another table was a box with what seemed paper versions of those same pieces. She picked one up and inspected it. It was a photograph of Bridlewood House itself. She had to admit that it looked even more stately and grand in the rendering. He had caught the whimsical Italianate nature of the home. It looked somehow more charming than imposing.

She looked at each of the photographs in the stack one at a time. So many taken on the estate, and a few taken in town. Each one was more beautiful than the last and told the story of Pointe Cèdre.

Until she saw it. A shock went through her body. Her heart seemed to stop and then to race. Her eyes widened in the dim light as she looked at it again. A naked man lying on his stomach outside by the water. Was this taken by the spring pond in the glad in the woods? But who was this man? He had long, dark, wavy hair. Then the realization. Could it be? Anatole?

She heard steps in the corridor and placed the photograph on the bottom of the stack and placed it back in their box. She turned back around to look at the landscape photographs on the other table.

Beau appeared with a look of genuine surprise on his face.

"Oh, hello."

She tried to muster surprise as well.

"Hello, cousin." She smiled.

"I see you are looking at my photography."

"Yes, I must admit that I had not understood the true nature of your hobby until I saw these landscapes. Cousin, you are truly an artist."

Did she sense relief cross his face?

"I do hope that one day this craft is considered an art." He replied.

"To be honest, when you first described this passion of yours, I did not think much of it. I only had in mind the one photograph I had ever seen. Just a portrait of the president on glass."

"Yes, they say that it is how the next war will be covered by the press. Photographers will be memorializing the battles as they go."

"Does the subject not have to be very still during the photograph?"

"A battlefield is nothing but stillness after a battle."

Charlotte did not wish to tarry there.

"Do you think there will be a war?" She asked.

"Truly I do not know. I hope that we come together as a nation and avoid the scourge of war."

Charlotte nodded; she did not want to think of Captain Jonathan Davies being sent back off to war. Dark thoughts dwelled there then changed the subject.

"The way you have captured Bridlewood House is grand." She gestured. "Indeed, the way you have captured all of Terrebonne Parish is impressive."

"Thank you, cousin. I do hope you will allow me to take your portrait one day."

"You would like to photograph me? But I am not a river or important landscape."

"I would. And your father, George, as well. You two are the great lady and gentleman of a great house. You are the center of society here. You two are the most important people of this parish."

"But I have already agreed to sit for a painter in New Orleans for my portrait."

"Painted portraits are works of art that tell the story of the artist's gifts. But photographs tell the *truth*. And one day photographs will be all that is left of us. They will be the real ghosts long after we are gone."

Charlotte was bewildered for a moment.

"And father and I will be the ghosts of Bridlewood?"

"I am sorry, that sounded morose." He spoke. "But truly, photography is the future. People will read about you in one hundred years, and they will read descriptions of you and see paintings of you. Those would all be the artist's rendering of you. They would not be seeing you, rather the artist's interpretation of you. A photograph *is* you."

Charlotte nodded.

"I see."

"I would like my photographs to be a long-lasting testament to the grandeur of this estate and to the beauty of my cousin and the strength of her father."

There was something about the idea that she liked, even as it made her realize that painted portraits were all that she would ever have of her own mother.

"I would like that, cousin."

He smiled broadly in appreciation.

"Now, if you will excuse me, I am going to have a walk outside."

"Would you like me to accompany you?"

"No, thank you dear cousin, but I want to be alone with my thoughts for a bit."

He nodded.

"Goodnight, cousin."

Charlotte left the room and continued down the corridor and down the stairs. The photograph of the naked Anatole was not forgotten. What was it about Anatole that was important enough to capture for posterity? Her only thought was of leaving behind a legacy. What would it be?

Charlie Mayes stood by the front door and opened it for her as she approached.

"Thank you." She nodded.

The cool evening air was refreshing. She often had a walk after dinner, especially if they were not entertaining. This evening, she had enjoyed dinner with only her father. They had not had a moment alone in a while, since cousins Beau and Bernadette had arrived, and only once did he bring up the subject of marriage to Robert Mayhew.

"Robert Mayhew is coming to the tea for your cousin Bernadette?" he had asked from across the long table.

"Yes, of course." She replied, though she did not tell him that she was seating him next to Cousin Bernadette.

Her father took a moment as he cut his steak. He had steak almost every night. He liked it cooked far past what her mother deemed appropriate. She watched him cut the leathery meat. Mrs. Paddington had made her favorite fish, but she had just pushed it around on the plate.

"I feel like this spring might be a wonderful time to announce your engagement."

"As you wish, father."

"Are you not excited to be betrothed, my sweet girl?"

Charlotte chose her words carefully.

"I am happy to do my duty for my father and my family that has given me so much."

She did not lie, for she was willing to do whatever was needed of her. But if she could possibly tempt Robert Mayhew with her cousin Bernadette, then the family connection would be solid, and she would be free to marry whomever she chose.

Charlotte continued her walk across the park. Her memory of the evening promise was still fresh in her mind. If things did not work out with Cousin Bernadette, she would indeed marry Robert Mayhew.

Charlotte traipsed through the brown grass of winter. There was a satisfying crunch underfoot. The edge of the grass came up to the dark line of the forest. She was not afraid, for she knew that Captain Jonathan Davies awaited her in the folly.

She stepped into the woods and turned to look back. The golden glow of the house warmed her heart. It was safety and it was her destiny. But she would not let it be her prison.

The woods were frightening to some, but to Charlotte they were safety. The woods had been her playground as a child. Where she and Emily and Anatole would run and hide and play for hours until Anatole's mother would call for them.

The folly stood in darkness, save for a shaft of moonlight. It was far enough into the woods to not be seen from the house. It was a perfect place for a midnight rendezvous with Captain Davies. She was surprised by her own excitement. All day she had anticipated the meeting to an embarrassing extent. She had found herself playing the scenario over and over in her head. Each time she allowed him to go further and further. Even now as she thought of him, she found a heat rising to her face, and other destinations to the south.

"I'm glad you could make it."

Charlotte gasped. She knew he would be there, but she was still caught off guard.

"I am sorry." She laughed.

He stepped out of the shadows so that she could see his handsome face in the silvery light of the moon. He continued toward her and reached out to touch her cheek. He ran his hand down her neck.

He had not been so forward before, except in her dreams. She knew that she should object, and yet she had never felt a thrill like this. For the first time she understood why girls sometimes went astray.

He leaned down and pressed his lips to hers. She could not stop herself from returning his kiss. His hands found their way down her sides to her backside, caressing every inch of her along the way.

The chemistry between the two of them was palpable. She had never felt this way with anyone before. No schoolboy crush or dancing partner at a party had ever made her feel this way.

That was when she realized that this was what she wanted. This was the feeling that she had read about in novels, and probably why her mother did not want her reading novels. This was what she would never have with Robert Mayhew, no matter how noble a gentleman he might be.

Chapter 27
Mariage Blanc

Anatole had no intentions of causing ill ease in the McCambridge household, and yet that was just what he had done. He had decided to apologize to Beau, and with any luck he would forgive him. But he had created this mess and no one else could fix it. His mother had taught him to face his mistakes and pray for forgiveness. He feared her disappointment more than anything he could imagine. His heart began to beat faster and his palms to sweat.

Anatole knocked gently then walked in to find Beau reclined on the recamier with his long legs crossed at the ankles and his eyes glued firmly to his book. A blond forelock had fallen forward and made his expression seem intense, yet slightly rakish. Anatole got the impression that he was focused on the book but not the words. That he was escaping from the moment and not reading. This moment was eerily reminiscent of when he had told Charlotte about his concern about Beau, and that had turned out terribly.

Beau's head was deep in his book and that would have been a clue to any good servant to leave him be. Everything his mother had taught him about a life in service was out the window. Anatole was past being a good servant. He was now desperate to be understood and to break that wall of servitude. He had to speak freely to this man, and he had to do it now.

Anatole had often seen him in this position, and it usually meant that he did not wish to be disturbed. No good valet would disturb their master when involved in a book or other pursuit, no matter how trivial. *A good servant is invisible,* he could hear his mother's words, *a good servant anticipates.*

"I have to tell you something."

"I already know." Beau said quietly, eyes never leaving his book.

"You may know what I did, sir, but do you know why I did it?"

Beau did not respond.

"When I heard you and your sister discussing Miss Charlotte's wealth and standing, I could not help but hate you a little bit. Now I know that I was wrong and that it was someone else all along who intended a scheme upon Miss Charlotte."

Beau's deportment remained unchanged.

That was it for Anatole. This man could have him dismissed in an instant and he would not have an easy time finding another job, especially since he and Charlotte had had their disagreement. He hoped she would forgive him, but there was no certainty. None of that mattered right now. He was so incensed with this man that he had to say something.

"What is it that you want?" Anatole finally asked, he had had enough, and his tone was pointed. "I don't mean to be rude, but I see you looking at me like you hate me, and I want to know what the problem is. I have done nothing to you. All I did was try to warn my friend and employer about what I had heard. And despite what I have since learned, there is no way I misheard your sister and her vile comments."

Beau slammed his book shut and threw it across the room. He stared Anatole down with a look so intense that he recoiled.

"That wasn't my plan, and I think you know it. That was a fantasy brewing in my sister's head all along." Beau said. "You are no doubt aware that I have another intended for me in North Carolina."

"I have heard that."

Anatole stood stone faced, unsure what to do.

"In fact, I think you know exactly what is going on here."

"I don't."

"You think I hate you? I don't hate you," Beau spat, "I wish I could."

"What does that mean? I have been an excellent servant."

Beau's eyes and his voice both softened.

"I wish I could hate you, Anatole." He repeated.

Anatole was now more confused than ever.

"I merely wanted to apologize."

"There is no need."

"Yes, sir, there is."

"We cannot have an argument as equals if you keep calling me sir." Beau smirked.

Anatole began to get agitated. While what he had done had been a mistake, he did not appreciate being made to look like a fool because of it. He would gladly drop the pretense to make the point.

"We may be having an argument, but we sure as hell aren't equals, *cher*. I did it because I was raised alongside Charlotte like family. And I *love* her as family. Even if she is angry with me."

"She or her father, could dismiss you from your position in an instant if you displease them." Beau said. "That is not a familial relationship."

"Are you trying to make light of my situation?"

"Of course not."

"As you sit here being treated like a king in their castle with all your family wealth and prestige.

"My family has no wealth left," Beau said, "we have only a name. And I am not dismissing its value because that is certainly a commodity in these strange times."

Beau put his book down and stood up. He crossed the few steps until he was directly in front of Anatole. They could hear each other breathing.

"Strike me if you like," Anatole said, "but I will strike you down if you do. What would I have to lose."

Beau looked confused. He sighed heavily and stepped forward. He was only inches away from Anatole. He leaned forward and spoke quietly into Anatole's ear.

"I do not wish to strike you any more than you wish to strike me. For not only do we both know that you are physically superior, but also that there is something that we both want far more."

Anatole felt the hot breath on his ear. Beau's chin nearly brushed his neck. He was shocked at the unexpected exhilaration.

"What are you talking about?"

"I'm talking about the thing for which men have turned to violence as a refuge from for centuries."

Again, Anatole felt an unexpected thrill at the heat and the intensity of the moment. He stepped back.

With that, Beau put his hand up to Anatole's head and caressed it gently. Anatole bristled for a moment, not understanding his intention. Beau pulled Anatole's head toward him. Their lips met and Anatole could not summon the desire to pull back. It was as if he was feeling something that he had always been meant to feel. Then Beau's tongue entered his mouth and everything that Anatole had ever wanted seemed to have suddenly become a possibility. Desires that he had refused to acknowledge were suddenly unstoppable. A connection had been made. Charges and pulses were detonating all over his body. And behind his closed eyes was an explosion of fireworks the likes of which he had never seen.

They could feel each other's heartbeats. They seemed to be synchronizing. Anatole stepped back from Beau's embrace and realized that he had changed. Not changed, rather he had been *revealed*. Everything he had ever known about himself but had ignored had now come brilliantly to light. His heart raced and his brain could not keep up. He would have feared passing out if he had the presence of mind to think.

He fell back into Beau's embrace and their lips met again. This time less gentle and more passionate. Gone was the feeling of bewilderment because he was who he had always been. The revelation was merely a pulling back of the curtain. At that moment he did not want anything else but what he was right then. Nothing but what was right in front of him. How was everything he ever wanted suddenly so clear? Where he was, what he was, what he believed in...was all in front of him.

The kiss ended and they separated for a moment and Anatole was suddenly overcome with fear and anger.

"Are you insane, I could die for this."

"We could, yes."

"No, just me." Anatole said. "I am merely a servant, and I would surely hang. You and your class have your transgressions swept under a rug."

Beau looked hurt for a moment.

"I am sorry. I know that you are right, and I should not have done this. It was impulsive and impetuous."

Beau was quiet for a moment.

"Actually," he said, "it was not impetuous. I have wanted to kiss you since I first met you. You are not only a beautiful man, but you are also a beautiful person. Inside and out. And innocent and un-jaded in so many ways. You see the curse of my class is to be jaded by everything. I am sorry."

Beau's brow and mouth dropped into the shape of misery.

"I am sorry. I did not mean to put you in this situation. I did not think. But even as I was furious with you for thinking I would marry my cousin for her money, I admired you for standing up for someone you loved."

Anatole stood quietly for a moment. His fear and his anger seemed to dissipate as he looked into Beau's brilliant green eyes.

"No." Anatole said. "Please do not apologize. It is very much what I wanted; I just would never have done it."

Relief spread across Beau's face as it relaxed into a smile.

"You do not hate me?"

"How could I?" Anatole asked, "And yet how could it make me happy when I know that it damns us both?"

Beau smiled wide.

"Why do you smile like a fool when you know the same?"

"I smile because I now know that the one with whom I am smitten requites my feelings?"

Beau's eyes beamed with happiness that Anatole could not understand.

"You are from a different world." Anatole explained. "One where they ignore certain behaviors because of status or money. Well, I have neither."

Beau's smile waned as he seemed to consider the effect this could have on Anatole.

"If I am to marry this girl, it will be for her money, and she will be marrying me for my position. It will not be for love, for either of us. Then why could you not come with me? Why could you not become a part of our household?"

Anatole was incredulous.

"As your servant?"

"What options are there for us?" Beau asked.

Anatole was silent a moment as he considered the possibility. Could he allow himself the possibility of happiness? Could he move across the country to be with this household of wealth and position and be the valet of the man that he now realized he was attracted to?

"I have to think."

Anatole looked down and regarded his shoes for a moment.

"I think I love you." Beau said.

"Don't say that." Anatole said. "Say *anything* but that."

"I can only say the truth." Beau said. "And you are *my* truth."

"My mind is filled with confusion." Anatole said. "I don't understand how something that feels so natural can be wrong?"

"What we are feeling," Beau said, "is mutual. We have a love for each other that is only now blossoming."

Anatole's head swam in a sea of a thousand thoughts. For a moment Anatole was lost in the possibility of what could happen next. And for all his mind's confusion, his sex did not seem to have the same concerns. His member seemed to have instantly become engorged with all the blood that had should have been in his brain.

Anatole came to his senses long enough to push back from him.

"It is all fine for you. You will be tolerated as an eccentric in polite society. You will still be able to marry. But me? I could lose my job and be forced to leave the entire territory, if I am lucky. Much worse awaits the average person. I could be hanged for this."

"It does not have to be this way."

"There is nothing else for us. Not for me, anyway."

"As I mentioned, I have been offered a marriage opportunity. My family has a great name and is well respected in the social register. I never held this in great value until now."

"Why now?"

"Because a family of great wealth has offered a betrothal to its only daughter. She and I have written to each other, and we understand each other in a most unique way. She is not interested in me, nor in any other men. And she understood that the feeling is mutual. A connection of our families would mutually benefit each side. And Allison and I, for that is her name, would be free to live our lives as ourselves."

"Wonderful." Anatole said flatly. "I hope you'll be very happy."

"But I would be." Beau said. "Because you would be there. By my side. As my valet."

Anatole was too stunned to comment for a moment and then found his voice.

"You think I am going to move across the country to South Carolina to be your servant?"

"Much more than my servant." Beau looked hurt.

"Yes, a servant who puts your cock in my mouth." Anatole shouted. "I am not a whore, Beau. No matter what you may think of the serving class."

"I never thought you were. I thought this would be the perfect way, indeed the only way, that we can be together. I swear I meant nothing more by it."

Anatole settled for a moment. His hair had bristled like a cat in a fight, but he calmed.

"How long have you been planning this?"

"For the matter of it—I consent to much—I regret much—I blame or reject nothing. I should as soon think of finding fault with you as with a thundercloud or a nightshade blossom. All I can say of you or them—is that God made you, and that you are very wonderful and beautiful."

"You quote poetry like it will save us from this *damnation*."

"It isn't poetry. It's a love letter, which I guess is what a lot of poetry is. From John Ruskin to Swinburne. Regardless, I do not intend to be damned by God, the one who made me this way. The one who gave *us* this feeling between us."

"How long have you felt this way." Anatole repeated.

"Since that afternoon at your swimming hole. Perhaps before, but when I finally got a chance to talk to you about books and nature, I knew."

Anatole looked into Beau's eyes and thought he could see his future. He could live the rest of his life and never had the opportunity to find this feeling again. Or he could stay behind and become old and embittered like Carstairs. He needed time to think about the consequences of each option.

Chapter 28
Folly a Deux

Emily laid out the brushes, cold creams, and the box of pins she would need to prepare Miss Charlotte for bed. Her routine rarely varied. She would disassemble Miss Charlotte's hairstyle, putting pins back in the box. Brushing the hair out and braiding it so that her long copper locks would not get tangled in the night. Miss Charlotte would wash her face in the basin that Emily had brought in and then she would apply the creams to ensure that Miss Charlotte's skin was as soft and supple as possible.

Charlotte came in and sat down without a word.

"I'm sorry, Charlotte, I-"

"*Miss.*" Charlotte insisted. "I've told you to call me Miss Charlotte so we don't have an awkward situation in public."

The comment stung Emily, though she tried not to let it show on her face. She knew that Bernadette's influence was finally taking hold.

"I'm sorry, ma'am."

Charlotte looked even more exasperated.

"You don't have to call me ma'am." Charlotte said. "But I am constantly being judged in society and how does it look that my maid calls me by my first name without an honorific? Every day I am trying and failing at replacing my mother in society."

"I'm sorry, Miss Charlotte."

Charlotte looked down at her dressing table.

"I'm sorry, Emily. I just feel like I can't do anything right."

"It's alright, Miss Charlotte. I know how you feel."

"I need you to do me a favor."

"Yes, Miss Charlotte."

"I was supposed to meet our Captain Davies out at the folly. Now I can't go. I've had a disagreement with father and now I've gotten myself all upset and now I need you to go tell him."

"Yes, ma'am. I can do that for you."

Emily finished preparing Charlotte for bed and instead of getting herself ready for bed she went downstairs and retrieved her own coat. She left through the back door of Bridlewood and made her way past the chapel and into the woods. She knew the path well and did not worry. She had grown up here and nothing frightened her about Bridlewood. Except for the cemetery and the mausoleum that Mr. McCambridge had built as a monument. At times the entirety of Bridlewood Estate seemed like a monument to his wealth and nothing more.

Emily pushed the branches away from her face as she walked through the forest. The folly was designed to look like an ancient building. Like a small castle that had been left in disrepair in the woods. It had been built at the same time as Bridlewood House and was often used for teas and luncheons when the weather was just right.

Some might have thought it pretentious, but Emily had heard Carstairs say that it was the fashion in Europe and England on vast estates. She often marveled at how many of the servants treated Bridlewood with pride as if it were their own. Emily could not say that she shared this sentimentality any longer. Her allegiances had always lay with Miss Charlotte, but now she started to feel as if something had shifted. In Charlotte and perhaps in herself. She wondered if Anatole had felt it as well. She knew that he had long dreamed of traveling and leaving Terrebonne Parish behind, though she hoped that never happened.

She stepped into the stone structure. There were no doors or windows, only the openings where those things would have been. The holes for the windows were tall with a point, like pictures of ancient castles she had seen in books in the library. Gothic, she had read.

Emily was expecting to see Captain Davies, but only found darkness. She began to feel an unease about being out here in the middle of the night to talk to a stranger. And Creole women did not have the protections of a white woman of means, like Miss Charlotte.

"You are not who I was expecting to meet."

The voice startled her, though she recognized it immediately. At first, she saw only the cherry red tip of his cigarette glowing. Captain Jonathan Davies became clear as her eyes continued to adjust to the darkness.

"I am so sorry; Miss Charlotte is unable to meet you. She sends her regrets."

As he exhaled the cigarette smoke billowed into the moonlight. He tossed it down and stepped upon the butt.

"I'm sorry to hear that. Is she unwell."

"She has the vapors."

"Then I hope she rests and makes herself well."

His voice sounded perturbed and did not match the sentiment of his words.

"She will be fine."

"I wish I had known earlier," he smiled "as I stand here in this old pile of damp."

"Do you not find it quite beautiful?"

"I look around and I see a rich man throwing money away on a place that cost more than the house I was raised in. A place that will be used for parties and the occasional midnight tryst."

Emily looked shocked for a moment. She could not think of ever hearing anything so scandalous an opinion about Mr. McCambridge. He was revered in the parish, in the whole state really. The words seemed oddly blasphemous. And yet they were notions that had often come to her own mind.

"Sir, do you not wish to marry Miss Charlotte and for this to be your life."

Captain Davies threw his head back in a laugh.

"You do not think for a moment that Mr. McCambridge would ever allow that to happen, do you?"

She considered this a moment and shook her head. There was not a great possibility that Mr. McCambridge would allow his daughter to marry a common army captain when his fortunes and society demanded more. But she could not say that.

"I do not know."

"Miss Emily, I know that you are friends with Miss Charlotte. But first and foremost, you are a maid. So don't tell me that you are ignorant of the limitations of this strata of society."

She heard herself begin to form a rebuttal, and yet she knew the answer was a resounding no. Charlotte's life and marriage had been mapped out for her and love did not appear anywhere on the legend.

"But doesn't she deserve to choose?"

"Of course, she does." He spoke. "But she won't. If she chose me her father would disown her and do you think I could ever give her this life?"

"Then why are you playing with her affections?"

He shook his head.

"If anything, she is the one playing with *my* affections. She knows better than any of us how this is going to end. Besides, something has changed."

"What has changed?"

"You."

"Me?"

"Yes, you have changed everything. I must confess that while I was enjoying the company of Miss Charlotte I have quite unexpectedly fallen for your charms."

"Don't try that with me, Captain Davies. I'm not some foolish rich girl."

"I know you aren't, Emily. I see who you are."

"Then who am I?"

"You're a lot like me. A poor kid who has found themselves sucked into the whirlwind lives of the wealthy because there really is no other choice for people like us."

"How does a supposed *poor boy* end up with the most coveted party invite in all of Louisiana?"

He smiled and shrugged.

"Beulah Sugarbaker."

Emily's brow furrowed and she involuntarily pursed her lips in response to the name.

"I met her at a dance she was hosting a party to benefit the army hospital. Many of us soldiers were invited to attend. But what I learned was that most of them wanted to support soldiers without ever having to be near one. Some seemed almost disdainful of our presence, like servants that you could not live without, but would not wish to have tea with. Such is the way of American patriotism. But not Beulah. Apparently, she was eager to meet us, so she had our regiment leader introduce her to all of us.

"That was nice of her."

Emily said, though she did not believe there was anything nice about Beulah Sugarbaker.

"She invited the five of us over for an after-dinner drink and dessert. We talked for hours and I found her quite charming. She said she thought I would meet some nice people if I came with her to a party. And I was so naive that I came to Bridlewood House thinking that I would, in fact, meet a nice girl who would take a chance on me."

Emily exhaled loudly.

"Those people don't take a chance on anything when it comes to money or position."

"But I was right. I did meet someone."

"But you said yourself that you knew you would never be able to marry Charlotte."

"I'm not talking about Charlotte. I'm talking about you."

Emily was stunned into silence for a moment.

"What?" She said, stepping back.

"I'm saying that I have grown quite fond of you over this time. You're a beautiful girl and I am glad to know you."

"Captain Davies, that is most irregular."

He seemed so earnest. His usual bravado cast aside.

"I can't help if it is *irregular*. It is how I feel." He said passionately. "Besides, we are not from their class. What does *regular or irregular* have to do with us? Why would we pretend to adopt their sensibilities?"

"What about Charlotte?"

"She doesn't want me! She wants a life that I cannot give her. She only wants me to make her father nervous. She wants me because she can't have me, and maybe that's the reason I wanted her. We have enjoyed all that either of us can give the other and now I am serious about moving on with my life."

"With..."

"With you." He said firmly.

"I don't understand." Emily said. "If neither of us have anything, how would we live."

"I will stay in the army and we can marry. I can't offer you much, but I can offer you love."

Emily's head spun in confusion. He was so handsome and too close. His eyes were far too piercing.

"I can't leave this house and my family for a man I barely know."

"Are you saying that you do not feel the same attraction that I feel?"

Emily looked up into his magnetic eyes, his perfectly chiseled jawline and she could not lie. She wanted to because she knew that would make it all so much easier. But she had found that the man's charm was quite inescapable.

"I do not say that I do not find you both attractive and quite charming, sir. But I understand my place very well. If there is anything that a creole understands it is their place in society."

"What does society have to do with anything?"

"We will be impoverished as a couple as I am too black to be an army wife and too white to do other jobs. You do not understand the complexities of my race."

He pulled her to him and kissed her with all his strength. All his passion flowed into her, flushing her body of all restraint. He then let go and looked deeply into her eyes. Emily felt momentarily confused and drained. He was an emotional vampire. His kiss had drawn not her blood, but her resolve.

"I ask again, do you not feel the way I do?"

She peered into his eyes and saw herself reflected. All the beauty and longing that he saw in her was in his eyes.

"I will not lie." She said again. "I do."

"That's all I wanted to hear."

"But that doesn't mean that we can do this."

"Why?"

"Because we will starve."

Jonathan was quiet a moment as he seemed to consider her for a moment.

"I'm sorry I cannot give you more." He said. "Perhaps you are right, Perhaps I should not ask you to make these sacrifices."

"I have a friend; he is a footman here. He is so protective of Miss Charlotte. He was nearly discharged for his distrust of Mr. Beau. And he has also said he does not trust you."

"He is a good man to be protective of his friends. But are you sure it is not merely jealousy? Perhaps he had hoped to have her for himself?"

"Truly, I do not know. Anatole has been our friend for most of our lives."

Emily thought for a moment about her life and her future. How Charlotte seemed less and less like a friend and more like an employer. In a few years would she cease to remember their friendship at all? But love. Was love a chance worth taking?

"But perhaps there is a way." He said.

"What?"

"What if we had the means to escape to the north where we would be accepted as a couple?"

"How could we ever afford to do such a thing?" Emil asked. "Especially if you are to leave the army to do so?"

He smiled. The plan that he had been waiting to share spilled from his mouth with abandon and ebullience.

Chapter 29
Cumulonimbus

Anatole had no idea what his mother was cooking for Sunday lunch. He was starving and he did not care. It smelled warm and delicious. It smelled like home. The house was just past the gates of The Bridlewood Estate. Leaving the manicured driveway and turning down his own overgrown road was always a study in contrast of his upbringing and his friendship with the McCambridge family. In his childhood he had been embarrassed by the meager home, but now it was a comfort.

His mother embraced him as if they did not see each other every day. But their roles were such that they did not greet each other in such an affectionate manner. They were at work and while he was not directly under her, there was a standard to maintain.

He looked over at his father sitting in his chair.

"Hey, baba."

His father ignored him.

"What's for dinner, maman?

"I made your favorite. Jambalaya."

"I was hoping that was what I smelled. I hope you made a lot."

His mother laughed.

"You have always had the appetite of a horse; I swear I don't know how we ever afforded to feed you."

"The McCambridge's own him now, they can feed him." His father called from the other room.

Anatole ignored him. He could tell when his father was spoiling for a fight. Instead, he went into his bedroom, as he did each week, to put his weekly pay into the box he kept on the shelf next to his few books. His books were his prized possessions. He read them over and over. Mostly tales of adventure that had molded his ideas for his future. Running away and making it on his own. Those ideas had been inspired by his books and now his savings sat next to them in their own treasure box.

Anatole picked up the box and immediately knew something was wrong. The weight was wrong. He opened it and his heart sank as he found it empty. It was not a lot of money, but it was everything he had saved this year, minus what he had given his mother to help with the bills. He knew immediately where it had gone.

Anatole stormed into the living area of the modest home.

"What did you do with my money." He said, keeping his head calm.

"What do you mean *your* money?" His father asked.

"The money I have been saving since I started working at Bridlewood."

"That's money for rent, son, that's how life works."

"I already give mother money for bills."

"Well, it ain't enough!" His father shouted back.

"It's more than you give her."

Anatole's father stood up and drew back to strike him. But the look in Anatole's eyes seemed to stop him.

Anatole had never felt rage like this. His heart and head felt like they might burst. The anger and hatred that he had felt for this man for so long had reached a point where he knew that if he did not escape this place he would not ever leave because he would kill this man. And the man would win because he would finally be dragged down to his level.

"Sir, you are finished ruining my life." Anatole roared.

"You have not grown so tall that I cannot still take you out to the woodshed for a beating."

"You two, please stop!" Fabienne screamed.

"Old man, you may try it but you will wake up next to Lucifer where you rightly belong!"

"I have no fear of you." His father seethed. "We've always known that you were a common sodomite!"

"NO!" His mother screamed.

Anatole could not say what happened next. He fell onto his father dealing the most terrible blows. They both crashed to the ground destroying a chair. The sounds he heard seemed to be coming from another room. It was if he were not even in control of himself.

He pulled himself back because he was not a murderer. He knew that he had to find control. Because he knew that he could be. He knew that if he did not control himself, he would be no better than his father. He knew that *that* part of his father lurked within him.

Anatole staggered back as he came to his senses. Where he had only seen red in that moment the clarity returned. His father lay on the floor bloody and crying. His mother knelt over him.

"Get out of here!" She yelled. "He'll kill you when he gets up. My baby what have you done!"

Anatole left the cottage with no fear of his father nor anything else. He made his way back to Bridlewood House. He looked down and his shirt was covered in his father's blood. He himself seemed unscathed, but he had no idea of the damage he had caused his father. He was somehow repentant, yet not sorry at all. He was regretful for the act itself, but he was not sorry for putting his father firmly in his place. He had needed it for so long. He had dreamed of doing this, of taking his father down.

He walked straight to Beau Chenevert's rooms and knocked. He was not sure of anything in this world except this was the moment.

Beau answered the door in his shirtsleeves, holding a book.

"Anatole." He said. "You don't have to get me ready for bed, I am-"

Beau looked down and his eyes widened as he saw the blood on Anatole's hands and shirt.

"What happened? Are you alright?"

Anatole pushed his way into the room. There was a look of terror and excitement in Beau's eyes. He stepped back as Anatole entered his chamber with the look of determination and lust in his own. Anatole shut the door behind him.

Anatole stepped forward and pulled Beau toward him and forced their lips to meet. His fire and passion were greeted and returned with equal intensity. Anatole pushed him back onto his bed with a force that seemed to be as instinctual as the force that destroyed his father. His entire body was engorged and on fire at once.

"What has happened to you?" Beau asked, still trembling with

With that a rip was heard as Anatole tore Beau's fine shirt from his body.

"Destroy me," Beau whispered into his ear. "Take every single thing from me and leave me useless."

Anatole stopped and looked into his eyes. He saw love and lust in equal intensity. How could it be like this? How could everything he had every wanted lay right in front of him?

Anatole fell forward onto him and bit his ear as Beau's body writhed under his weight. He had the passion he had the desire, but he did not know of sex. Instinctually he knew that it would come to him, but he did not want this to be like that.

"Teach me." Anatole whispered into his ear.

Beau looked up at Anatole and began slowly unbuttoning his bloody shirt. The movement seemed to calm Anatole. His hands explored Anatole's chest and lingered on his nipples. Anatole had never known that they produced a sensation. He had never known of a feeling like this.

Anatole leaned back as Beau traced a line all the way down to his belly button where a trail of hair led to more exotic destinations. Anatole unintentionally gasped and shuddered. The sensations of his body waking up to eroticism. His manhood strained his trousers in anticipation.

"You're a beast." Beau said quietly. "But I will tame you."

"You won't tame me." Anatole responded, "But I will bend to your will. Then I will take what I want, what I need right now. I *need* to be inside you."

Beau pushed Anatole back and unbuttoned his own pants. Anatole did not trust himself not to rip them.

Anatole placed his hand on Beau's chest directly over his heart. He could feel the rhythmic *padam padam* that sped up as he leaned closer. He could feel that Beau's desire matched his own.

"I am yours."

"Yes. Yes, you are."

Anatole could not believe he was talking to someone above his station in this manner, but he was ready to throw it all away for one night with this man. Beau had bewitched him in a way since the beginning.

Anatole did not know about pleasures of the flea aside from what he had read in books that had been secreted away at home,

but certainly not anything between two men. He allowed his
instincts to drive him to the places where they would and depend
on Beau to teach him what he knew.

Anatole leaned down and their mouths west again passionately. Somewhere between lust and anger the passion exploded
between them. His tongue traced a line from mouth to ear, whispering every filthy thought he had ever dared not say aloud. He
could not tell if Beau blushed, but he hoped he did. Beau's
moaning response let him know that he was responding to the
nibbling of his ear lobes.

Beau's hands explored the vast real estate of Anatole's well-
toned body and back. Down to his perfectly shaped buttocks that
had often been admired in his footman's livery trousers. Beau's
hands skimmed over the well-rounded flesh and grabbed tight to
them.

Beau grabbed tight then rolled them both over until he was
on top of Anatole on the bed. He straddled him. Anatole looked
up at the man who would be his master in more than one way.
For this moment he did not care about titles or their futures. He
only cared that this man was astride him with their cocks in
contact as if everything were exactly as it should always have
been and would be.

Beau backed off then knelt with his face in Anatole's groin.
He stroked his inner thighs in a teasing manner that drove
Anatole to the edge of madness. His tongue lapped at Anatole's
thighs and most intimate places creating ecstasy that he had
never imagined possible. Nothing like he had ever read about in a
book.

Chapter 30
The Intended

The carriage arrived with little portent. Charlotte was the only one who knew that she was arriving. The remaining footman, Charlie Mayes, stepped forward and opened the door to the carriage. Out stepped a plain but handsome young woman wearing a dark plaid gown. An expensive, yet unassuming garment. She did not appear to be an ostentatious woman, though her understated elegance was obvious.

"Ma'am." Charlie said, as he helped her down from the carriage.

She handed him an engraved card.

"Miss Charlotte is expecting me." She said.

Charlie Mayes read the card and palmed it so that he could place it upon the silver salver as he had been trained.

"Yes, ma'am. You are expected, I shall announce you."

A woman's maid stepped out of the carriage behind her.

"If you will ride with the carriage driver around back, he will show you where the downstairs are and Mrs. Blanchet will show you your quarters."

The two women looked at each other and the maid nodded and stepped back into the carriage.

The driver took her bags, along with her maid, around the back of house. As Charlie led her into the foyer and then deposited her in the drawing room where Miss Charlotte liked to receive guests.

"Quite a home." She mused.

"Indeed, ma'am."

The foreboding figure of Carstairs the butler appeared in the doorway.

"May I get you anything, ma'am?"

"No, thank you."

Allison Banfield sat quietly and assessed the room. She took in the art and the furniture. Her astute mind calculated the value of its contents. The style was a bit much for her personal taste, but she realized that it reflected the sensibilities for the nouveau riche.

Charlotte appeared at the doorway and entered the room. She was most surprisingly gay.

"Miss Banfield, it is so nice to finally meet you. I am Charlotte McCambridge."

Allison stood and they exchanged kisses on the cheek.

"My cousins in Atlanta speak so highly of you, Miss Banfield, and then I learned that you were known to my cousins Beau and Bernadette as well. I simply had to invite you to come and stay for a bit."

"I must admit it was a surprising invitation, but I am so pleased to be here in your lovely home."

Charlotte gestured and they both sat.

"Beau and Bernadette are also staying on for the month."

"It will be good to finally meet Beau," she said, "and his sister Bernadette as well."

"She's lovely, you'll get on well."

"Will their mother be here as well?"

Charlotte smoothed out her blue satin skirts.

"Oh, heavens no. Not until Bernadette's tea, of course. I was hoping for a more casual introduction first before assaulting you with the entirety of New Orleans and Terrebonne society."

They both laughed.

"Irregular, but honestly I prefer it."

"Carstairs." Charlotte called, "I think we'll have some tea."

"Yes, ma'am." He said and soundlessly disappeared.

"Lovely home you have here." Allison said.

"I imagined that you would think it a bit much."

Allison stifled a smile. It was as if Charlotte had read her mind.

"My mother, much like your mother, was a woman of breeding. And this is not the kind of home that she or my father would have built. They would have been too cautious of what society would say of this kind of display. They are still dreadfully old fashioned about some things."

"I understand." Charlotte said. "I am a child of two worlds. One devoted to the *old ways* and one financed by new money. When it comes to being *nouveau riche*, my father says that the *riche* is the only part that counts."

Allison could not help but smile at the charming young woman.

"I am a fairly direct woman, Charlotte. I would like to be direct with you."

"Of course."

"You live a life wrapped in the gossamer embrace of privilege. You are born from a mother from one of our oldest families. From what I hear you are conquering New Orleans society, which is quite the challenge. I can't imagine why you invited me."

Charlotte appeared taken aback.

"I simply wanted to meet you. You are marrying into my family and I wanted to welcome you."

"Nothing has been announced as of yet, but your cousin Beau and I do have an understanding. Was this meeting his idea?"

Charlotte blushed.

"No. Actually he does not know that I invited you."

Allison brow raised in surprise.

"This seems most unusual."

"I thought it would be a nice surprise, but now I am worried."

Charlotte lowered her head.

"He's been most melancholy lately and I thought it would help to see your face."

"Melancholy?"

"Nothing serious, really, just a post-holiday malaise."

Allison's eyes widened.

"It's already progressed from a melancholy to a malaise?" She exclaimed.

"I'm sorry, I've made a mess of all this." Charlotte said. "I was just trying to do a good deed for the two of you. Now I see that I have made a mistake."

Allison's expression softened.

"Not at all." Allison insisted. "But you should have been honest with me in your correspondence. I would still have come."

"I am sorry."

"No need to be sorry," Allison said, "let us have tea so that I can greet my intended."

"And anyway, in the past few days he seems to have made a remarkable improvement in temperament."

"Wonderful to hear."

"And also, I will get to introduce you to his sister, my dear cousin Bernadette Chenevert."

"I look forward to meeting her as well."

"Then it will be my pleasure to make those introductions."

"Carstairs." Charlotte called gently.

Carstairs stepped into the room from his post just outside the door.

"Yes, Miss Charlotte."

"I asked you to bring us tea but hold that."

"Yes, ma'am."

"Let Mister Beau and Miss Bernadette know that their presence is requested for tea in the conservatory in an hour."

"At once, ma'am."

"And show Miss Banfield to her rooms so that she may freshen up for tea."

"If you'll follow me, Miss Banfield."

Charlotte and Allison both stood.

"Thank you for coming, Allison." Charlotte said. "I hope that we can be friends and maybe even family."

Allison smiled and nodded.

"Of course."

She followed the butler out into the corridor. The footman greeted her again and took her from there.

"My name is Charlie and if you will follow me, I can show you to your rooms."

She followed behind the tall young man. She noted that his walk was more of a swagger. The kind of gate that tall and handsome men often held, no matter their station.

She followed him up the grand marble staircase. It reminded her of castles in France. The massive chandelier dominated the air of the room. While she had not been raised to display wealth in a manner as obvious as this, she did find Charlotte to be a charming young lady. The tinkling of crystal as a breeze blew through the house was so pleasant that she found herself reconsidering her initial appraisal of the situation.

She had thought she might encounter a typically raised child of extreme wealth who did not understand restraint. Instead, she found a charming young woman who held her family's best interest at heart. She was unexpectedly impressed. Soon she would hear Giselle's assessment of the situation from the down-stairs up.

At the top of the stairs, they turned left and the footman opened a door. He gestured her to enter. She stepped inside and found a sumptuous and sunny guestroom. Her maid Giselle stood solemnly by the windows.

"If you need anything we are at your service."

He smiled in a way that made her skin crawl.

"I won't."

His smile broke and he stepped back and shut the door behind him as he left.

"Cretin." She said under her breath.

"How was your meeting with Miss Charlotte?"

"Unexpected, actually. She is not quite the vapid heiress I had expected to encounter."

"Shall I ring for some tea or any refreshments?"

"No, actually we decided to have tea in an hour with my intended fiancée and his sister so I want to freshen up."

"I already prepared the basin with some water."

She did not look at Allison.

"What is it?"

Giselle exhaled.

"Are you certain that her scandal will not tarnish your good name if you marry her brother?" Giselle asked.

"You let me worry about that."

"I worry about *you*. That is a person's job when they care about someone. I don't want anyone making your life more chal-lenging."

"You don't have to worry," Allison said, "not many people on the east coast seem to be aware of the scandal. But what is puzzling is that I don't think anyone here really knows what happened either."

"Then how do you know?"

"My man Burton. He found out for me."

"Burton?"

"Yes, apparently he had been in the army with someone who knew the man involved."

"And what happened, if I may ask."

"I have no secrets from you, of all people. The Chenevert family has been known in society for at least a century. But the money has run out, leaving the siblings to look for marriages of convenience."

"Not so unusual."

"Not at all. Beau Chenevert was introduced to me through my dear friend Anna as a man who might understand my desire for a *white marriage*."

"And did he understand your desire for an unconsummated marriage?"

"We were both very much on the same page there. But Burton insisted on doing a thorough background search of my intended's family."

"And what did he find?"

"Apparently, she was engaged to be married to a man of means. Very unattractive, but a good name and plenty of money. But then she was caught with another man. An Army captain. A rather handsome devil, from all reports, who knew how to have his way with women of a certain class."

"An Army captain? As long as you don't think that scandal could taint your own good name."

"Why would it?" Allison asked. "It is over and this Army captain has not been heard of in New Orleans since, as far as I have heard."

"Good."

Allison stepped forward and pulled Giselle close. She kissed her hard on the lips.

"Careful, ma'am." Giselle said. "That moron could return at any moment."

Allison smiled wanly.

"You have already assessed his character, have you?"

"I saw the way he looked at you. I imagine he looks at all the rich women around here like that. I know the type."

"Indeed, they are common. But I can't fault him for making the most of his job."

They both laughed. It was good to finally be alone after weeks of travel.

"Now I shall lie down for fifteen minutes, and then we shall attempt to freshen me for tea."

"I shall do my best, madam."

Chapter 31
Gilded

Beau Chenevert came in from reading outside to find Anatole waiting for him. Seeing him there he could not help but smile as he stood just inside the doorway.

Anatole stood quietly in the corner near his suit of clothes, brushing the jacket that Beau would be wearing down to tea. The look on his face was tense.

"I do hope you are not having misgivings about what happened between us." Beau said.

Anatole stopped what he was doing and looked up at him.

"I am not. I can tell you that I have never been more certain of anything than what happened between the two of us."

"I am glad to hear it."

"My long-held suspicions about myself and my desires were proved right. By *you.*"

Beau made his way into the room and set his book down on the table by the bed. He walked over to Anatole and put his hand on his. He looked into his eyes and they shared a smile. But Anatole's smile was reserved.

"What is the matter, my strong St. Michael?"

"I have come to prepare you for tea."

Beau smiled broadly.

"Of course you have, my beautiful prince. As you should."

"There is a special guest today."

"Is there. Ah, well Uncle George did say that the governor might return soon for a business chat."

Anatole shook his head.

"Not Beulah Sugarbaker."

"No, not her."

"Don't keep me in suspense, my man."

"It is your intended. Miss Allison Banfield."

All the color drained from Beau's face. He was at a complete loss for words. He was hoping to make arrangements to meet her soon, but for her to come here unannounced was most irregular.

"It was meant to be a surprise, apparently."

"Indeed, it bloody is."

Beau now understood Anatole's look.

"Don't worry. I know that you have not given me your answer yet, but I assure you that she understands that I am to have my freedom."

"I am not worried, truly." Anatole said. "It was just a bit of a surprise after what you and I have been up to."

Anatole raised an eyebrow. Beau could not surpass a laugh. Anatole followed.

"What a different man you are today. Last night you were a wild animal. You came in here with your eyes on fire. I have never wanted anyone more than when I saw you last night. Your blood was boiling for release. And now you are calm like a lamb."

"Which way do you prefer?"

"I like both. Now I am going to have a whiskey, would you like one?"

"No thank you."

Beau poured himself a neat whiskey then sat in the chair next to the bed. He sipped it, then downed the entire glass. He could stare at his beautiful Anatole all day. He could not wait for him to take him up on his offer. To come and be his companion in Charleston.

Anatole helped Beau out of his jacket and trousers, setting them neatly aside. They touched lightly and sensuously, both knowing that they could not start this right now.

"If we don't stop, I won't be able to get your trousers back on." Anatole said.

They both laughed again. Then a quiet settled over the room. Beau could still sense some unease.

"It's still you and me." Beau said. "If you want it to be. All you must do is look in my eyes and say the words and we will leave this place and I will marry Allison and you and I can have our own life there."

"I will let you know tomorrow."

"I will meet with her privately this week. It will be easier to say things in person that neither of us would have wanted to commit to paper and ink."

Anatole returned to laying out the shoes for tea.

"I imagine that it seems unfathomable to you that I should weigh this decision so seriously."

"Not at all. You have your entire life and family and friends here. And I am asking you to leave it all behind for me."

Anatole focused his attention on polishing the shoes.

"I probably no longer have a family here. Not after what happened with my father."

"Are you ever going to tell me what happened?"

"And reveal the shame of my family? How could I?"

"What shame? My father spent every last penny we had on bad investments and worse women. And we didn't know anything about it until he was dead."

Anatole nodded understanding.

"My father stole all the money I had been saving for my escape. My escape from Bridlewood. Escape from Terrebonne Parish. Escape from service."

"You must have been very angry."

Anatole looked at him and shook his head.

"No, it was worse than anger. It was rage. Rage that had been building my entire life. He drank himself out of a job and then turned that failure into anger at my mother and myself. My whole life I was determined not to turn into what he was. But last night it happened. I lost control and I beat him to within an inch of his life. He could be dead, for all I know."

Beau sat silent. Stunned.

"We are *so* much alike. I do not want to poison *anyone* else's life if I have any of him inside me. And the worst part is that he is the way he is because he loved another man and he died."

"How do you know that?"

"My mother told me. She didn't say everything she wanted to say, but I could see it in her eyes."

"You don't have what makes him the way he is."

"How do you know? How can you be so *sure*?"

"Because I know those kinds of men. I have known a few. And you are not one of them. If you are debating coming with me because you fear turning into your father, just know that I am not afraid to take that risk."

Anatole knelt to where Beau was sitting. He took his face in his hands and kissed him deeply and passionately.

"No matter what I decide to do, I want you to know that that was the kindest thing anyone has ever said to me."

"I meant it."

"Now let's get you dressed for tea and we will talk more later."

Beau made his way down to tea after Anatole had helped him get into his attire. He could not get him off his mind.

Carstairs the butler waited at the bottom of the stairs. He had the practiced look of boredom and competence of a lifetime of service.

"They are waiting for you in the conservatory, sir."

Beau felt rather like a lamb to slaughter entering the situation where he was the only one who did not know what was going happening. He was well attired, thanks to Anatole, but feeling surprisingly nervous.

"Oh, cousin!" He heard Charlotte call out.

He looked over and saw her and another young woman chatting near a small table. Bernadette appeared at that moment right behind him.

"Hello, dear brother." She said, all smiles.

The pair of siblings walked toward his cousin and the young woman awaiting him. She was a comely thing. But not the fine boned China dolls that he saw so much of in society. The kind who bound themselves tight and pushed their food around on a plate. She looked like she knew her worth.

He strode directly to where she and Charlotte stood and tried to muster his usual confidence.

"Cousin, so good to see you." Charlotte said.

"You as well." He leaned in and kissed each of her cheeks.

"I would like you to meet Miss Allison Banfield."

Beau understood that in other strata of society it might be unusual being introduced to the person you are already practically engaged to, but things were different in high society.

"Miss Banfield, it is a pleasure to meet you."

"Please call me Allison."

"And I am just Beau."

"Beau is very interested in photography," Charlotte said, "he promises to take my portrait."

"Oh, that is quite a thing." Allison said. "I have read a bit about your Mr. Daguerre."

"Have you indeed?" Beau asked, astonished.

"Yes, I am fascinated by the art of the railways."

Beau could not hide the surprise on his face.

"In what way?" Beau asked.

"On the coast there is a growing interest in railway photography. They say that improved shutter speeds will only make action pictures more fashionable."

Beau was at a loss for words. She truly knew and understood his interests.

"Yes, indeed." He said. "And in the future, there will be the ability to take many shots in a row that will create a *moving* picture."

"A moving picture?" Charlotte laughed. "Surely you are joking.

"No, he's quite right." Allison said. "Technology is moving very quickly."

"I will leave you two to discuss this *technology*, whatever that means." Charlotte said, and gracefully bowed out to join Bernadette.

Beau looked at Allison and shifted on his feet.

"Now you about my hobby, why don't you tell me more about yourself."

Allison turned her head in a bit of a shrug.

"I have a variety of interests."

"Tell me."

"Why don't you tell me." She said. "Do you think that a woman should have control over her own assets."

"In modern society I cannot imagine that we are not moving toward a more equitable distribution of power."

"Interesting." Allison nodded. "And what do you think a woman's place in the world will look like in fifty years."

Now it was his turn to shrug.

"I can't say, really. But I imagine that women will vote and women will control property."

"Really?" She asked. "In as little time as that?"

"Little has progressed since Eliza Lucas Pickney, but I think that a reformation is coming to this country."

Allison's brow furrowed.

"What do you mean?"

"I mean that we may be headed for war in the next few years," he said, "and I think that the reformation years that follow will find a lot of widows in charge of plantations and businesses."

Allison's mouth was slightly agape with shock.

"That is a rather interesting way to look at it."

"I cannot take an emotional view of something that has not yet happened."

"And you see women taking a greater part of this *antebellum* society?"

"Yes, indeed. I see it as a necessary adjustment to the losses of war."

"Interesting."

"It is just what I see as the logical continuation."

"I must admit that I had not thought of it that way. You are an interesting man."

"And you are a woman of many interests."

"Indeed I am." Allison agreed. "I must say that I am rather surprised by you."

"In what way?"

"A broad-minded man has been, in my experience, difficult to find."

"If you will forgive me," he said, "is it not our mutual broad mindedness that has brought us together?"

A broad smile broke across her face.

"I suppose it is, Beau, I suppose it is."

Beau smiled to himself and thought about his future. After all that that he had been through he wondered if he might finally begin to see the light. Could he finally imagine a place where he was free? It was too early yet to tell, but could Allison Banfield be a wife and companion and an understanding friend? He knew that he could never tame Anatole's spirit for adventure, but could he convince him to let him join him on some of those adventures? Perhaps, and it was not important to know the answers to those questions just yet because for the first time in a long while he had *hope*.

Chapter 32
Metamorphosis

Emily finished hanging Miss Charlotte's fine things on the small indoor line inside the laundry area. By the time they were done with tea they would be ready. And then she would be able to fold and return the garments to their lavender scented drawers.

Downstairs was abuzz with activity. The arrival of Mr. Beau's intended had taken the entire household by surprise.

Emily turned when she heard someone else coming into the laundry room.

"Hello there, Miss Emily." Mini said, exhausted.

She entered the room carrying an empty basket.

"You don't have to call me *Miss*." Emily laughed.

"But you're Miss Charlotte's best friend. You're kinda fancy, like her."

"That is sweet of you, Mini, but you know I work here just like you do. Just call me Emily."

"Alright."

"When are you due?"

"My baby? Oh, I reckon I got another month."

Emily did not ask, because she already knew that a woman in their position did not have the luxury of staying home during pregnancy. Mini would likely go into labor at work one day and Mrs. Blanchet, the housekeeper, would call for the doctor.

Mini, unlike Emily, had been a housemaid for some time and probably would remain one. It seemed obvious that her natural timidity would keep her from rising in the ranks. But now with a baby on the way Emily hoped that she was wrong for the sake of Mini and her baby.

Emily would have been lying if she did not admit that she also worried that one day she would want to be married and that she would have to leave her job because married women could not be a lady's maid.

Being pregnant, Mini seemed perpetually behind of late. But like any servant, she could not afford to take a day off. Emily did not even know if such a thing were possible. so, it was not a surprise when she asked Emily to help her with laundry. And Emily did not mind as Miss Charlotte was not in need of her now.

Mini looked at Emily with pleading eyes.

"What is it?" Emily asked.

"Could I ask you a big favor?"

"Of course you can."

"I still haven't finished the linens in the guest rooms, and they'll need changing right now while they're at tea. Would you mind putting these linens on Mr. McCambridge's bed?"

"Of course I don't mind." Emily said.

She took the basket of linens and headed up the backstairs. She came out in the main corridor. She walked over to his door. Her footsteps changing from the thud on the wooden stairs to the crisp click clack on the marble of the corridor.

She knocked on the door to his suite of rooms. The door was ajar and swung open with her knocks.

Emily walked into the room.

"Mr. McCambridge, I am delivering linens."

She heard nothing but continued to the small library area of the room. To the side was a balcony that overlooked the conservatory. She had never been in the room before so she had never seen this view before. The conservatory was full of orange trees and palms and things that would not have otherwise survived the winter.

She turned to go back in and found herself face to face with Mr. McCambridge. She gasped.

"I'm so sorry, Mr. McCambridge." She sputtered. "Mini got behind so I am delivering your linens for her."

Without a word he grabbed her and put his hand over her mouth. She squirmed uselessly in his arms. Her reaction was slow and awkward because he was not only her boss, but he was also a man she had looked up to all her life. This could not be happening.

His hand slipped enough for her to cry out.

"Stop it, Mr. McCambridge, please!"

She said in a loud whisper, even now unable to break the social roles that had been bred into her.

She wanted to somehow end this moment without alerting anyone in the house. To somehow reverse time to a point only moments ago.

He pushed her back onto his bed and she felt herself begin to disassociate herself. With his enormous weight advantage, she could not hope to fight back. She felt as if she were leaving her own body. She looked up to the ceiling and focused on the ornate plaster. She did not think that she had ever appreciated it before. She felt nothing, she heard nothing.

Emily closed her eyes tightly and felt the beginning of a change. She felt herself open, as if from a cocoon. She soared upward, impervious to what was happening on the bed below.

Emily was above the room floating around the flickering candles of the chandelier. She was a moth. She flew close to the flames and felt their heat. And up from there around the crystals, sparkling delicately in the candlelight, and up the chain to the medallion at the base of the chandelier. In and out of the plaster flowers that had been crafted there. She saw nothing else, she felt nothing else.

Emily opened her eyes and she was in the corridor of the servants quarters. She had apparently dressed herself and tried to make her way up to her rooms but had fallen along the way. She was dazed but could make out a pair of shoes and a skirt in front of her. She looked up and saw the terrified face of Mini. Her mouth was agape.

"I'm so sorry, Emily." Mini cried. "I'm so *very* sorry."

"You knew." Emily whispered to only herself.

Mini knelt and pushed Emily's hair out of her face. Tears welled in her eyes and ran down her cheeks.

"Oh, no no no." Mini repeated nonsensically.

"You knew." Emily repeated, this time louder.

"I swear I didn't think he would hurt you too." Tears streamed down her face. "You're like their family. He wouldn't never hurt you."

But he did hurt her. Whatever trance Emily had been in, whatever self-induced state of mesmerization was over. The feelings began to return all over her body and she shook with a revulsion that she did not yet comprehend. Why was there pain in her female parts. Her arms were certainly bruised from being held down. With horror she began to recall flashes of what had happened.

"I swear I didn't ever think that old bastard would hurt you like her hurt me." Mini cried.

"It's alright, Mini." Emily found herself comforting Mini,

when she was the one who had just been...she could not bring herself to even think the word.

"C'mon, let's get you outta this hall and into your room and get you cleaned up."

Mini helped Emily to her feet.

"Are you hurt bad?"

Emily did not think that she was too badly hurt, only because she had stopped struggling. She knew that she had been powerless against the weight of Mr. McCambridge. And even if she had fought him off, what would her life be like afterward? He wouldn't let her stay at Bridlewood. Even now she was not sure that her position was safe. And what choice did she have. What had happened to her was something that her mother had warned her about all her life. That a white man would take his privileges out on her and she would be powerless to stop him or to do anything about it after.

She had felt a change indeed. Something inside her had snapped at that moment when her mind soared up into the ceiling of that master bedroom and found safety in the plaster swirls and flowers and acanthus leaves. There was rage. White hot rage. But then there was peace. But the rage was still there. She just somehow knew what she needed to do.

"I'm alright." She said.

Emily stood and followed Mini to her room. She removed her torn garments.

Mini poured water into the bedside basin.

"I swear, I- "

"Don't say it again." Emily said sternly. "It isn't your fault."

"I'm awful sorry."

Mini looked as if she were going to cry again.

"I'm sorry too." Emily added. "Of course you couldn't have known."

Emily sat down on her bed as Mini gently cleaned her body with the water and a washcloth.

"I shoulda known." Mini said. "But we all look up to you like you're one of them. We never thought he'd hurt you because you was like family."

Emily shook her head.

"Yeah, I used to think I was like family.

Mini shook her head.

"The first time it happened to me I told my mama and she slapped me across the face. She said *you a fool, Mini.* Then the next time it happened I didn't tell her nothin, but then my belly started growin and she knew. She slapped me again."

"Why?"

"She's not the type what does a lot of explainin'."

"You didn't do anything wrong, Mini, and neither did I."

"I know. My mama warned me, but I also still think she blamed me because it never happened to her when she was a maid. But she's real ugly so nobody bothered her."

"Mini!" Emily was so shocked she almost laughed. Mini had taken her out of her trauma for a moment.

"I'm real glad I made you laugh, Miss Emily."

Emily reached out and squeezed Minis hand.

"Thank you, Mini. Don't take none of this as your fault."

Mini lowered her head and nodded. She kept gently washing.

Emily closed her eyes and allowed Mini to clean her up. Soon she would have to meet Miss Charlotte in her rooms to change for dinner. She went back to that place deep within her mind and now she saw Captain Jonathan Davies. She remembered his plan. She had almost decided against it, and now everything had changed.

"Oh, I almost forgot." Mini said.

"What is it?" Emily asked.

"That handsome Mr. Davies sent this note to you."

Emily opened the note and stared at it for a moment. He was inviting her to meet at the folly again in a few days. She dropped the note to the floor. She could not think of anything else right now. Her mind seemed to shut down. Adrenaline had gotten her to this point, but now shock was setting in. She collapsed onto her bed and fell into a deep sleep.

Mini lifted her legs onto the bed and covered her with a blanket. She left the room carrying the wash basin. She would come back and make sure she was awake in time to take care of Miss Charlotte. One thing that Mini was sure of, it was that there was glory in work. Just like her momma had always told her.

Chapter 33
Lespri Mal

When everything had been taken care of for the moment, Anatole generally stood near front the door in the grand foyer to open the door for visitors or to receive instructions from Mr. Carstairs. He was the first person to ask if anyone needed anything. In the beginning his title had been Hall Boy, and that is literally where he worked and slept at night. In the corridor off the foyer.

Second Footman was quite a step up, and as he worked the position of valet, he could see the possibilities of a future in service that he had never planned.

He had just returned from the drawing room after having prepared the space for after dinner coffee and nightcaps, should Miss Charlotte decide to use it, which he doubted. But Miss Bernadette and Mr. Beau may. Despite all that happened he could not yet break the habit of calling him by the honorarium of Mister. Mainly because if he did, in fact, follow him across the country to be his servant in his household he would still need to address him as Mr. Beau. Or then even Mr. Chenevert.

Anatole had spent no small amount of time ruminating over

Mr. Beau's offer in his head. It turned and clicked in his head like the clockworks of a safe. What combination of outrageous possibilities would unlock this happy life for the two of them. What combination of events would lead to utter catastrophe?

His upbringing had been a simple one. He had read of romantic entanglements in great novels of the McCambridge library, but he had certainly never known of any personally. And the ones he had read about did not go smoothly. The fact that he was comparing his own life to novels that he had read made him queasy. Beau had in a short time brought an element of excitement to his life that he had wanted and read about but did not think he would ever find here at Bridlewood. Indeed, he was not sure he would find it anywhere. But he also knew that he was fantasizing about a life that could never truly be.

He imagined quick fumblings before putting Mr. Beau into his suit for dinner and stolen glances across rooms. Maybe even intimate discussions while getting dressed in the morning. But he could not imagine them being able to go to sleep or waking up together in the same bed. Romance? How could such a thing ever happen? Lying in bed kissing and contemplating their future together? It simply could not. Things might be slightly more progressive there, but they would never be like that. And who is to say that this bride to be would truly be as understanding of their situation as Beau seemed to think? Perhaps she might use this as bait and then demand more after the marriage? The possibilities where endless of how this could turn out badly. Far more so than how it might turn out to be a fairy tale.

"Hey, wake up!" The voice startled Anatole from his thoughts.

Charlie Mayes strode past Anatole, refusing to make contact, as usual. Their relationship was barely professional. Charlie had hated Anatole from the beginning. He had treated him with utter contempt and Anatole had never understood why. Perhaps it was just having to share the spotlight with another tall and relatively handsome man. Not that Anatole had control over either of those personal traits.

The urge to strike Charlie Mayes came easily to Anatole. A feeling he had never had with any other human being, except his father. And he knew that his punch would land true and solve the problem. But after what had happened with his father, he did not wish to tempt himself to lose control. He did not wish to become what he came from. He did not wish to ever repeat that history. He did not wish to solve a problem by creating a new one.

"Go lay a fire in the library for Mr. McCambridge. He's dining in there tonight." He said to Anatole, almost as an afterthought.

He realized that Charles, perhaps due to being a servant, needed someone to treat badly in return. He vowed never to do that himself. Even if he rose to the ranks of butler, he would never treat his staff as inferior. Everything he had learned from Carstairs was about encouragement and promoting his lessers to strive for better. Charlie Mayes only had one lesser and he spat on him.

But the task at hand beckoned. Dinner in the library was not unusual, as Mr. McCambridge often enjoyed dining alone since the death of Mrs. McCambridge. Anatole thought nothing of it. A table and two chairs had been placed there for exactly that purpose. Though now only one remained as one chair had been removed to the mausoleum for Charlotte's frequent visits with her mother.

Anatole walked into the library and the room had a chill from the days of rain and the lack of human presence for a while. He went about his usual routine of lighting candles and gas lamps. Mr. McCambridge did not like to enter a cold room, nor would anyone who had the wherewithal to prevent that.

Anatole gathered some wood from the stack in the corner. A

stack that he himself kept replenished as one of his duties. He laid a small fire in the fireplace, as he had been instructed. He looked at the table and realized with surprise that it had not yet been laid. He would have to go back to the kitchen to see that it was properly prepared before Mr. McCambridge's entrance at precisely seven o'clock.

At that moment he felt an icy cold sensation in his back and a great pressure. He drew in a breath but found his capacity limited and ragged. He turned and saw the face. He somehow knew that it was too late before he even knew what happened. The man stared quizzically back at him as Anatole felt a mix of shock and horror spread across his face. No pain had hit Anatole yet, merely the cold sensation of what he knew must have been the long blade of a very sharp knife. And as he looked at the man's face, a face that held either pleasure or remorse, he knew that it was an army issued knife. Captain Jonathan Davies stood before him looking only as if he had completed a grim but necessary task.

"Why?" Was all that Anatole could get out of his mouth.

His lung had surely been punctured by the blade.

He felt himself falling forward. He grabbed the dining chair to steady himself, but it tipped and toppled to the ground. Anatole toppled with it, driving the blade further into his back. Now the shock began to fade and a searing pain began to grow. An explosion from severed tissue and nerve. The room spun above him like a kaleidoscope then collapsed into blackness.

After a time, and Anatole could not know how long, his eyes fluttered open. He was still in the library on the floor, though he was not entirely aware of how he had gotten there. He took stock of what was around him. The rug Anatole looked up and saw shoes peeking out from under the hem of a colorful gown. He saw shades of red and purple. A few sequins sparkled in his blurred vision. He raised himself up and he saw a face he recognized.

"It's alright, mon cher." A woman's voice standing above him said.

"What happened?" He asked.

"You got into a little fracas, but you're alright."

"What *fracas*?"

"You ran into a *move*."

"A what?"

"A *lespri mal*." She reiterated. "An evil spirit, but in human form."

His head was cloudy but he had a feeling of deja vu.

"Wait, I know you?"

"Yes, I am Queen Marie. We have seen each other in the backstairs and back hallways of Bridlewood House. Where the likes of you and me belong."

"Yes, but why-"

"Oh, chile I'm so sorry."

"Sorry for what?" Anatole asked.

"Get yourself up off that floor, baby." She said.

"What are you doing here?" He asked.

"Oh, I'm always here." She said with now humor, "I seem to always end up back here."

He was puzzled to see Miss Marie, whom everyone called Queen Marie here in the library with him. Was she somehow part of this? Was she working with Captain Davies?

"Please, stop this."

"It wasn't me, baby. I would stop it if I could, but it's too late."

He sat up and looked around. The room was the same, but something was different. He stood up and found himself a bit wobbly at first. Like a newborn foal. He stood up to his full height and looked around the library. He saw the overturned chair and the table. As he looked more closely, he saw a pool of red. *Blood!*

Anatole ran into the conservatory. The room was filled with small orange trees and palms. It was black outside, the time when all you could see in the glass was your own reflection. The conservatory reflected the furnishings of the room back to him. But something was wrong. He realized that he himself was not part of that reflection.

He backed away in confusion. He turned back toward the library and saw an astounding sight. He saw *himself*. Not himself, but his body. Being dragged from the room by Captain Jonathan Davies. A false column in the library was open to allow for his murderers egress.

Anatole could not stop himself from stepping closer to the grisly scene. Closer to a maddening tableau of his own body being dragged through a pool of his own blood toward its unholy end. His mind could not comprehend what he was seeing.

Now his instinct to fight back kicked in. Now, at a time when he could do nothing. He would gladly use the force and the anger that he had been withholding against Captain Jonathan Davies, but it was far too late. The force he had wasted on his idiot father.

"Don't bother."

The voice of this woman, this Queen Marie came from behind him.

"It's too late." She said.

"Why did you not stop him?"

"I don't have the power to stop him." She said. "I only have the power to greet you and to tell you about where you are."

"I know where I am!" Anatole shouted.

"Believe me, honey, you really do not. You are here in the Bridlewood House. You are on the property owned by George McCambridge. But you're not on the same plane of existence anymore."

Anatole was on the verge of a panic like he had never known.

"What do you mean?" He screamed.

"You have been separated from your earthly body by this man. He killed you, mon cher. You are dead."

Anatole shook his head violently.

"That cannot be! I am still here and I am obviously still alive!"

"You have been caught up in the curse of this land, baby."

Anatole's eyes were wide with horror.

"What are you talking about?"

This land was cursed generations ago that none who died here would ever rest."

"By whom?"

"By Mahinto of the Chimakuan Indians. They were driven from their land by the white man and their blood curse on this land still stands."

Anatole shook his head, mute with astonishment.

"Then why are you here?" He asked, "You aren't dead."

"No, I am a medium. I am drawn here each time someone dies so that I may help them understand what has happened to them."

"But I don't understand."

"It will take some time."

"And why did he kill me?"

"I don't know the reasons of man," she shook her head and her curls bounced around carelessly. "But the actions of man echoes across time and they tend to kill for jealously or for money. In this case I fear it may be both."

Anatole watched as Captain Jonathan Davies returned and quickly began righting the chair and cleaning the blood from the parquet floor. He was trying to erase the existence of the crime. It began to occur to him that no one would know what happened to him. They would think he had merely chosen to run off in the night.

"Wait, you can tell my family what happened to me. You can let my mother know that I am alright."

"No, baby, I can't. When I am on the other side I am bound

by a set of rules. When I awake from this trance that I am in I will not remember most of this. Only that I helped someone cross over."

Anatole's mouth was open with shock and loss.

"This is a horror."

"I know, baby. This ain't fair. But life sure ain't fair, and you see that even death ain't fair."

Chapter 34
The Debt

Anatole leaving in the dead of night was shocking to her. She would grieve for the loss of him. He was as a brother to her. How could he not tell her that he was leaving? They had had a discussion just a few nights previous and he had not given her a warning that he might leave. Perhaps there was a clue in his words, but she had missed them. She wished that she could speak to her mother right now. Rather, she really wished she could speak to Mrs. McCambridge.

Emily had always thought of Mrs. McCambridge as a kind of mother figure, as her own mother was in New Orleans. She had always been kind to her and encouraged her friendship with Charlotte. Emily and Charlotte would lounge in her sitting room for hours and play games and ask questions about being a grown-up woman. Mrs. McCambridge would allow she and Anatole to be taught by the same governess as Charlotte. Making sure that they all had an education, which at the time was only within the sphere of the wealthy and almost unheard of among servants.

Emily had so many memories of Mrs. McCambridge dressing for parties. She loved those times so much. Watching her maids swirl around her in a hive of well-orchestrated activity. She tended to have a glass of champagne during those times and dispense the most amazing advice. Once she had told them both not to ever allow a boy to touch their treasure chest. They had compared notes later and neither of them knew what their treasure chest was. Charlotte was certain it was her dowry and Emily was certain that it was a buried cask of gold that her parents had never told her about.

For every important party, Emily had the memory of Mrs. McCambridge garbed in the latest fashions from Paris. It was a delight to her to get to see what they were wearing in other countries, and then to see someone here in Terrebonne Parish wear them. No one else could do what Mrs. McCambridge could do. She wore gowns that were on the edge of fashion and possibly scandalous...and always crowned with the emeralds that were famous throughout the parish, and perhaps the country.

The emeralds were famous as a set. A necklace, bracelet, ring, earrings, and tiara. A set that was called a parure. A collection of jewelry that is always intended to be worn together. This parure was emblematic of The McCambridge Family. It was said that you could tell the importance of a party based on whether Mrs. McCambridge wore the parure to your party, and Emily knew that there was truth to this. Over two decades of wear in Terrebonne Parish and New Orleans, the parure was well known.

She had watched many times as Mrs. McCambridge's maid had put them on her. Watched as she clasped the necklace around her neck. Watched as she set the tiara in place in her hair. Secured the bracelets around her gloved wrists. The ring and earrings placed.

To say that Emily understood the sentimental value of the emeralds far more than the intrinsic value was an understatement. She knew what they had meant to Mrs. McCambridge and she knew what they meant to Charlotte. Which meant that the decision to follow this plan was even more precious.

Emily had already decided before Captain Jonathan Davies even arrived at their rendezvous in at the folly in the woods. Charlotte's recent indifference to their friendship and new, strangely imperious attitude toward her had made it clear that her future here was purely as a servant. And if someone else was offering her more, then why should she not take it. The most handsome man she had ever met was offering her the world, and why did she not deserve it as much as Charlotte?

But more importantly, she felt she was *owed* the jewels. She deserved the money that the jewels would bring to her and to Johnathan. She had a baby coming and the father would pay in one way or another. He owed her at least as much as these jewels.

Why was it always for the woman to pay? Emily wondered.

She had not succumbed to the serpent of temptation. She had merely been doing her work when it happened. Doing Mini's work, to be precise. But Mini also did not deserve to be attacked. She had merely been in the wrong place at the wrong time and the curse of being a woman had landed upon her in a horrifying instant.

Charlotte would inherit a fortune that would dwarf the value of these gems. But these emeralds would secure a future for Emily and her child. Her child would never know its own misfortunate beginnings, for it would only know its own loving mother and father and never the rapist who began its life. The gems she planned to steal would support them in their lives ahead.

Emily vaguely remembered the dream that she had had before. The dream of the jewels and Queen Marie. She had seen Queen Marie since the dream but she did not acknowledge her and gave no clue that that the dream was anything more than a dream. Though it had seemed so real.

Emily had no way of telling the time, but Jonathan was late.

She had much work to do in the morning so if he did not arrive soon, she would have to leave before she was missed.

"I'm here." He called as he entered the folly.

"You're late." She could not see his face in the darkness.

He stepped forward and embraced her tightly.

"I'm sorry, I was detained by some loose ends."

"No worry." She spoke. "I have to tell you something."

"What is it, my sweet?"

"I have decided to go along with your plan. I cannot think of another way that will help us have a life outside of this wretched place."

She could not see his smile, but she could feel it in his embrace.

"You have made me very happy."

She felt as though she could even hear the smile in his response.

"But I want you to know something. Something that I just discovered and you must understand."

His brow furrowed in concern.

"What is it, my dear?"

"He forced himself on me."

"Who?"

"Mr. McCambridge. He forced himself on me and I think that I may be with child."

Jonathan's eyes widened in surprise.

"I need you to know that if you still want to go through with this that we may be raising another man's baby. And that I am only doing this because I am owed this money. I will have a baby because of that man and he owes me."

"I understand, my dear. He owes you and I am going to take care of you and our baby far away from here."

Emily felt tears sting her eyes.

"Our baby?"

"Yes," he said, "we will travel to the north and raise it as our own."

"Where did you have in mind?"

"I should like to go to Boston." He said. "I believe there are opportunities for men like me there. I would like to open a tavern. I would like to get something started there before the Irish take over."

"The Irish?"

"Yes, the goddamned immigrants are taking over this country."

Emily did not know what he was talking about but understood that she knew nothing of the world outside Terrebonne Parish.

Jonathan leaned down and kissed her passionately on the lips. He held her head in his hands and he pulled back and stared into her eyes glistening in the darkness.

Emily ran her hand down his back. She pulled her hand away quickly as it encountered a crusty patch on his coat.

"What—"

She began to ask, but even in the errant rays of moonlight that filtered into the folly she could see that the black smear was blood.

"Don't trouble yourself." He said, "I got into a fight at the Le Corbeau."

"That is a lot of blood, I—"

"I said, don't worry. That's why I was late, but everything is alright."

"I can't help but worry, Jonathan. You want me to trust you with this plan but I must know that you aren't going to go and get yourself killed in a bar fight and leave me and this baby alone."

"It was just a misunderstanding, don't worry. It won't happen again."

"Tell me again about the plan."

"After the party I will come to Charlotte in her rooms. You will make it so that I can find my way up there. You will then take that moment to gather the jewels that you have removed from Charlotte. While I am with her you will be sewing the jewels up into the hem of your dress."

"That won't work. Carstairs, the butler, always picks up the jewels after a party and locks them up in the safe before bed."

"Then I will see to it that Carstairs is unwell and unable to retrieve them."

"Do not harm him." Emily was stern. "He is a decent man."

"I will not, but I do have a potion that will upset his stomach in such a way that he will be indisposed for the evening."

"Then we can leave?"

"You need to stay one more day to make sure that no one knows they've been stolen. Disappearing right away will cast immediate suspicion onto you."

Emily thought about his words.

"I suppose you are right."

"When is Miss Charlotte's next party where she will wear the jewels?"

"Perhaps two weeks?"

"Then you will be for a week after you give me the jewels, I should think."

"And you will wait for me nearby?"

"Yes, I shall be nearby at the home of a friend."

Emily thought about what she was planning to do. There was no more loyalty between she and Charlotte. Mr. McCambridge had ruined what she thought had been a familial relationship. She had so looked up to him at one time.

She wished she could sit with her mother or her father one more time and talk to them. To tell them what had happened and ask their advice. But she feared that her mother would blame her.

She knew that she had done nothing wrong, and yet she

knew that the onus was on her. The woman. The servant. Original Sin. She was Eve and the apple was all her responsibility. The serpent was merely the instrument of her downfall. The more she thought of it the angrier she became.

She had done nothing wrong but she had paid for it anyway. And now as the rage began to well up again inside her she knew that she was ready to own that sin. The McCambridge family had ceased to be her friends or her family on that afternoon and nothing would ever be the same again.

Around the corner another pair of eyes watched from the darkness.

Chapter 35

The Note

So much hope. So much promise. Dashed away like boat on the rocks. Sebastian Beau Chenevert could not sleep. He was wide awake as the mantle clock struck one and then two. He had tossed and turned and finally threw back the covers and sat up in bed. He raked the lock of blond hair out of his face and straight back. He stared past the panes of glass into the darkness of the Terrebonne Parish night. He had barely slept. Several days had passed since the news of Anatole's disappearance had been so shocking that he had feigned illness since. Something was not right.

Then *the note* had been found.

How could I let myself fall so fast? He chided himself. *How could I allow myself hope?*

When Charlie Mayes arrived at his rooms that morning to dress him, he had been surprised.

Where is Anatole, he had asked.

He packed up and left in the night, Charlie had replied.

A note had later been found to corroborate this.

The day had passed by in a daze. Meals had been brought up

to his room and Charlie Mayes had been dismissed after realizing that he had no intentions of dressing. He did not wish to dress. But at the same time, he worried that his absence might betray his feelings. That he had asked too many questions of Charlie Mayes. Eventually he lay down and tried unsuccessfully to sleep.

He stood up and walked to the window and looked out at the inky waters of the brackish swamp glinting back slightly in the moonlight. Was Anatole out there somewhere in the night experiencing his first taste of freedom?

The night before had been cloudy and a terrible night to leave, Anatole could not help but think. *There would have been complete darkness. How badly he must have wanted to leave.*

Beau had spent the better part of his upbringing hating the social system that he had been born into. In a world of wealth and privilege his family barely clung to either. He did not have enough of either to live a life of luxury, but too much to be completely carefree of his family's machinations. Perhaps if his father had not accumulated massive debt before dying, he might think better of his position.

His mother had planned a marriage for Bernadette that would have set their fortunes back on track. But when Bernadette had been caught up in a scandal the engagement had been withdrawn and her reputation ruined. A scandal that his mother would never disclose and he never asked about.

His mother now treated him as the family's only savior. She had arranged a marriage that would be beneficial to the family and to him. He could pursue a life of luxury in a way that he saw fit if he followed through. And it seemed impossible not to.

His mother had never forgiven her McCambridge cousin for dying and not leaving anything to her, despite knowing of their situation. The entitlement of this imagined aristocracy was staggering, sometimes.

When he met Anatole, aside from the attraction, he saw in

him the kind of person he would like to know. To talk to. When he saw him reading and enjoying nature there was something so pure and virtuous that he had to know him. And the more he talked to him the more something else grew within him. He knew that Anatole did not know at first, but he sensed a tacit understanding. That there was a feeling that was shared, if not understood or spoken.

When he had made the offer to Anatole about moving to North Carolina and becoming his valet he had thought that he would be thrilled for the opportunity. But then he should have realized what he was offering Anatole was merely another gilded cage. That Anatole would aspire for something more if he were ever able to escape service. Of course, he would, this lover of nature and adventure tales. Of course, he would want and deserve more. But he never imagined he would disappear without a word.

The entire household was in shock. Anatole had packed his belongings and disappeared in the dark of night. But no one was more surprised than Beau. Their last moments together had told a different story. Beau had misunderstood. He thought that Anatole was willing to give the scheme a try. But that did not bear out.

Perhaps he should have followed Anatole's lead and just disappeared with him. But unlike Anatole he did not possess a trade or a craft with which he would be able to earn a living. That had been bred out of his kind over the centuries. And knowing a skill other than for leisure was quite looked down upon. Leaving him trapped in his own kind of cage. The kind of cage that Anatole must have been so desperate to avoid.

Anatole was somewhere out there enjoying his first day of freedom in his lifetime. Beau's sense of loss was almost matched by his sense of envy. To be out there under the stars by now with him. They could have protected each other. But Anatole did not even ask him. Probably because he knew that he would not make it when he was taken away from his luxuries.

Beau wanted a drink or a book, or both. He could ring Charlie Mayes to bring these things to him, but he simply did not wish to see him. Something about him did not sit right. He had all the judgment and attitude of one far above his station and he found it impertinent. He decided to head down to the library to find something to soothe his mind.

He lit a candle and the window instantly became a black mirror reflecting his disheveled appearance. Beau slipped on his robe and stepped into his slippers. He made his way down the corridor and down the marble staircase. He stepped quietly to not wake the hall boy and crept back to the library.

He was greeted with the familiar scent of books, both new and old. The smell of George McCambridge's cigars seemed ever to pervade the air of the library, though not unpleasantly so. It was a warm and familiar smell.

Beau perused the table stacked with books in the library. They had not been shelved yet, so recent arrivals or recently read. In the middle of the stack was the volume of Swinburne's poems that Anatole had been reading when he first saw him in the woods by the water. His mind raced with the thrill of that moment as he relived it.

He had come out of the woods, the light change from dappled to full sun. The sound of babbling water had drawn him off his path and into this glade. He never could have imagined what he would find there. Anatole, his valet, laying in the sun. His naked and glistening body lay with a book over his face while his feet dangled into the water.

As he approached and Anatole raised up, he saw his loose waves hanging down and his full lips. Anatole seemed to blush with some embarrassment, perhaps uncomfortable with being caught by someone supposedly above his station but did not seem uncomfortable with his body. Nor should he have been. Beau had known men and he had *known* men. But he had never known one as beautiful as Anatole. He knew at that moment that he would need to be guarded. He had seen the dressed and repressed version of Anatole, but this wild creature in the glade was someone he had not anticipated.

Beau returned to the present. Once again, he was alone in the library in the middle of the night surrounded by volumes of books and the glass conservatory just beyond. He sat down in the chair and began to read. As he did so he could not get the lines that John Ruskin wrote to Swinburne.

For the matter of it—I consent to much—I regret much—I blame or reject nothing. I should as soon think of finding fault with you as with a thundercloud or a nightshade blossom. All I can say of you or them—is that God made you, and that you are very wonderful and beautiful.

The letter seemed to allude to something much more than friendship, and to Beau it always would. Two people who shared a love of nature but a love that was deemed unnatural. It would never make sense to Beau.

In Beau's own letters to Miss Banfield, his intended, seemed to bear out his assumptions that they would have a marriage only in name. There were none of the romantic overtones of Ruskin and Swinburne. That they may perhaps have children, as would be necessary. But that she had her own interests that she would continue to pursue. She was involved in some new movement called Women's Suffrage, which seemed especially shocking in the southern society.

He had briefly lived in a fantasy where he and Anatole would be free to be themselves, at least in private, in that home. But clearly Anatole had decided not to escape one prison merely to be ensnared by another. And as much as it pained Beau, he could not blame him.

Can you not sense me?

Beau heard the words as if they had been said aloud. And yet no one else was there. Had he nodded off to sleep?

What Beau did not know was that he was not alone. Anatole watched him from the other plane. As if he were on the other side of a watery piece of glass. He could see Beau and hear him. He could reach out to him, but he could not touch. His attempt would merely pass through Beau's arm like he did not exist. But Anatole was the one who no longer seemed to exist. Relegated to a mirror planet of loneliness.

At that moment a chill ran through Beau that he could not explain. It was as though someone had reached right through him and touched his soul.

Beau laughed. He was on edge and needed to get some sleep. He had a luncheon with Allison tomorrow and needed to be at his best. He had put her off with a tale about being ill. It was not exactly a lie, as he certainly was not well.

He could not shake the feeling of the presence in the room. He could not say what it was, but he had the chills. All he knew now was that it was late and he needed sleep and would hopefully feel better in the morning.

Chapter 36
Two Loves

Mini finished cleaning the library and the conservatory. Each day she tidied the space, but on Wednesdays it was her task to do a full clean. She would polish the wood and mop the parquet floors. Once a month she would use wood soap on the floors and woodwork and really make everything shine, as her mother had taught her.

Today was a day for cleaning and indeed when she turned around the entire room shone. She turned and knocked a candlestick off the table. She chided herself for her clumsiness. She knelt and picked up the candle and righted it on the table. While she was down on her knees, she noticed a missed patch of dust on one of the legs and proceeded to polish it with the rag she kept tucked into her apron.

Mini found the library to be the most interesting room in the house. The books and artifacts were so beautiful. She sat surrounded by the answer to so many of life's mysteries, and yet she could not know their meaning. All because of not being able to read.

Mini had come to realize that her mother feared many things.

She feared what learning to read would do to her. Mini had always thought her mother feared her learning and then leaving for better opportunities. But lately she had realized that her mother had most likely feared that she would read and understand how few escapes there were for a life like hers. That it would make servitude harder, and maybe it would have.

She wished that she had taken Anatole up on his offer to teach her to read. She was so stubborn and fearful of that knowledge and now he was gone and he would never teach her. No one else would, and she did not want anyone else to.

She would never again sit with him and get lost in the blue green of his eyes. Blue green like the pool in the glade where she knew he liked to go to be alone. She would never again sit next to him at supper and hear one of his funny stories.

Long ago she fell in love with how he made her feel. He treated her as an equal. He listened to her. So often she felt that her voice was lost, but not with him. She cherished that and would forever. He was the kind of man she would like to marry, but she somehow knew that he was not that kind of man. She knew for sure the day she had seen him at the pool in the glade with *him*.

She remembered that day when she first met him and how he was the one who came and spoke to her like an equal. His face was so beautiful and yet he was so friendly. The way he took the time to make her feel a part of the group, even when she was so obviously not.

He gave her something that no one else at Bridlewood House did. He gave her respect. He gave her a sense of importance. She could almost feel him now, in the room with her.

Mini shivered as a chill ran through her body.

As she sat on her knees reminiscing, she realized that soon Mr. McCambridge might return and she did not want to tempt him with her presence. Not that she did not do anything to entice him, she merely existed. Despite what her mother had led her to believe.

She pushed herself up and as she did, she saw something sparkling in the rug. Something that was not usual. She reached out and picked it up and recognized it immediately.

Mini walked swiftly from the room clutching it tightly in her hand. She started quickly up the stairs, mindful not to be caught running. She turned down the corridor and knocked on the door. After a moment the door opened and Charlie Mayes stood there.

"Yes?"

"I need to see Mr. Beau for a moment."

"What about?"

"I have to give him a message."

Charlie's eyebrow raised imperiously.

"Maids do not pass messages. You may tell me."

"Who is it?" She could hear Mr. Beau call out.

"No one." Charlie said.

Mini decided that she was not going to be spoken of in that way.

"It's me, Mr. Beau. Mini."

Charlie's eyes widened with shock at her daring to usurp his dominance.

"You can go now, Charlie." Beau said.

Charlie's face flushed with anger and seemed to telegraph that consequences were imminent. He left and proceeded down the hall back to his position.

"Charlie was just getting me ready for luncheon. Did you say you have a message for me?"

Mini was at a loss for words for a moment. She was not used to talking to her betters. She summoned her courage.

"Not really a message."

Beau's brow furrowed.

"Then what is it?"

Mini extended her dark hand to him and opened her fist. Inside was nestled a shiny object.

"What is it?" He asked.

"Look."

For a moment it seemed that he did not want to know.

* * *

Beau looked closely and then reached out and took it from her hand. He turned it over in his palm and recognized it immediately. It was one of Anatole's cufflinks. The ones that were swords. Saint Michael, Michael Anatole Blanchet's namesake.

St. Sebastian, Sebastian Beau Chenevert, had been his own. Each named for saints, as was often the custom. Each one with their own catalog of conflicts and martyrdom. But they had one thing in common, that their faith would carry them through anything. Anatole certainly seemed assured of that, at least more so than he was. He deserved to be named for St. Michael, the archangel. He had an inner strength that matched his outer strength.

"Is this...is this one of Anatole's cufflinks?"

Beau asked, knowing the answer.

"His momma gave him those cufflinks." Mini said. "He was so proud of 'em, I don't think he would ever lose one."

Beau had many thoughts at once that frightened him, but one rose immediately to the top.

"But why did you bring this to me?"

"I know that you and Anatole were friendly." She said.

At that moment Beau realized that she loved him. And that maybe she came to him because she *knew*. She knew that he loved him too. Had they not been discreet? Could something have happened to Anatole because of his own lack of discretion?

As he turned the cufflink over and felt a strange sharp feeling in his heart. This connection to Anatole. Then he noticed the dried substance. It almost appeared to be blood.

Anatole was fastidious with his appearance. It seemed impossible that he might lose a cufflink without knowing. Anatole losing a cufflink and then that cufflink being found soiled in any way seemed even more unlikely. Dark thoughts began to flood Beau's mind. Could it be that something happened to Anatole? If so, what, and why? Could it have been Anatole's father seeking revenge after the brutal but well-deserved beating that Anatole had given him?

Something began to fall into place. A mystery unfolded. What if Anatole had not left under the cover of night? What if something had *happened* to him instead? He could not bear to imagine, yet he could not stop himself from imagining.

Perhaps it was all in his head. What if it were just his own ego wishing for some byzantine excuse for why the man that he loved had vanished. What tremendous narcissism he displayed at times. Yet he could not get the niggling thought to leave his mind. Perhaps he should just leave the cufflink with the other footman. Perhaps it was all a fantasy that he had concocted in his own mind to assuage the sting of abandonment. And, worst of all, perhaps he might never know which.

Beau turned back toward his room so that she could not see his face. The cufflink still in his hand. He did not know what to do with it. But he felt like holding on to it for the moment. He would find the right moment to hand it to Anatole's mother. She was the housekeeper, after all. Now it was all he had of Anatole. A bitter reminder of what might have been.

"I have to tell you something else."

"Can it wait until after lunch?"

"No, I think I better tell someone."

"Alright."

"The other night I was out at the folly. Sometimes I go out

there to smoke and meet up with my boyfriend who works at the farrier."

Beau seemed to be losing patience.

"And?"

"And I saw Miss Emily there. She was with a man. I heard them talking about a plan to steal something."

"Steal something?"

"Ye-yes."

Emily stammered. Suddenly she was not sure she should be telling on Miss Emily. But she was afraid it had something to do with Anatole's disappearance.

"To steal what?"

"He was talking to her about a plan to steal Miss Charlotte's jewels. The emeralds."

"Who was the man she was talking to?"

"I don't know. It was so dark, and I was tryin' to stay hid. I wasn't tryin' to spy on 'em."

"That's alright, Mini. I know you were not trying to spy."

"I felt bad listening to Miss Emily's private conversation and tellin you, but I am so worried she is gonna get herself in trouble."

They both realized at that moment that they were each thinking the same thing. That she had perhaps already gotten herself into trouble.

"Mini, I must go meet Miss Allison for luncheon now. Will you meet me tonight so we can talk about this further?"

"Yes sir, I sure will."

"Meet me in the library."

"Yes sir."

Chapter 37
Notes on a Scandal

Allison Banfield sat in her suite of rooms looking out at the forest that surrounded this side of Bridlewood House. She rather enjoyed the isolated nature of the estate, though she could not imagine living in this cultural desolation for long.

The door opened and Giselle entered looking harried and holding a letter.

"What is it?" Allison asked. "Did you find a pin?"

"Yes." She said, holding up a pin with the other hand. "And also, I have some correspondence from a friend in New Orleans."

"By the look on your face I can tell it is something interesting."

"Indeed. It is about your possible future sister-in-law, Miss Bernadette."

"Oh, you know I do not care for idle gossip."

"Of course you do not. No lady does. I will simply keep it to myself, of course."

"Is this about the supposed scandal that ruined her in New Orleans society?"

"Oh, I would not want to spoil the delicate nature of your ladyship's mind with this *idle gossip*."

She teased.

"Giselle, I shall get very cross with you if you do stop calling me *your ladyship* as if we are in one of your Jane Austen novels."

"According to the letter—"

"Who is the letter from?"

"I shan't disclose my sources. *Now*, if I may continue?"

Allison rolled her eyes.

"Please do."

"Apparently Miss Bernadette was engaged to marry, but she was caught having an affair with an Army captain, as you know."

"Yes, we already know that."

"What you don't know is that he is none other than Captain Jonathan Davies."

"The one who—"

"Yes, the very one."

"Do we tell someone?"

"It is most delicate." Giselle said.

"But we must." She Allison said flatly.

"How do you intend to *delicately* broach this subject?"

Allison thought for a moment as Giselle placed the last pin into her hair.

"I am to have luncheon with Beau shortly. We are to be getting to know each other better. I would not normally wish to take that opportunity to discuss such a matter, but I feel like I have no choice."

"I think it would be wise to find out if he is aware."

Allison judged the situation for a moment, then nodded.

"You are right, of course. But I do not think he is aware."

"Perhaps not." Giselle agreed. "But it certainly is telling of the character in that family."

Allison had those thoughts in her head as she headed down

the marble staircase. Her steps echoed throughout the cavernous entry hall. The chandelier sparkled in the afternoon sun. She had been raised in immense wealth and luxury, yet she was still overwhelmed by the grandeur of Bridlewood House.

She walked back across to the drawing room where she found the room warm and welcoming. A fire had been lit. She was alone in the room with only the table fully set for tea service.

"Please make yourself comfortable, ma'am."

She was startled by the voice of Charlie the footman.

He seemed to appear out of nowhere, which was appropriate. Yet she found herself finding irritation with everything he did. He pulled out the chair for her to sit at the table.

She heard footsteps at that moment and looked up and saw that Beau Chenevert had arrived and stood in the doorway.

"Please excuse my tardiness." He said.

"Oh please, do not worry about that. We are all enjoying the leisure of country life."

Beau walked over to her and clasped her hand. He leaned over and kissed it delicately.

"You are a true gentleman, as I had been told you would be."

"Thank you, Miss Allison. My appearance as a gentleman is due entirely to governess who demanded it so."

"True of all gentlemen, I fear."

Beau seated himself in the chair across from her. The small table was empty save for the settings of a small luncheon. A side door opened and a young maid wheeled in a cart of refreshments that tinkled with the elegant clank of silver and China.

The cart was loaded with a tea service and a tower of sandwiches cakes that would barely be touched. The maid parked the cart at the table and left it for them to serve themselves, as was custom.

"I enjoyed our conversation yesterday. I must say I am impressed to hear you speak on issues that affect women."

"Women will have their day."

"And if you were to find yourself involved with a woman who was not content to just wait for the times to catch up? A woman who was *involved* in the cause?"

Beau seemed to understand the implication and did not back down from it.

"Then I would be glad to find myself in the company of a kindred thinker."

Allison smiled.

"I am glad to hear you say that."

"It is easy to declare the truth."

"There is more." She said.

"Of course."

"My family has two businesses, as you are aware. Rail and banking. And I am wont to be involved in each."

"If that is possible then I support it."

"I appreciate that." She said. "But I will need some support that I will explain to you at length later."

"Of course." He said. "But do I detect that there is something more you wish to say?"

"Y-yes. I suppose so."

Allison's facial features were an anxious contradiction. Her smile belied the furrow of her brow. She seemed unsure of how to continue and stumbled over what to say.

"Beau, please understand that I find you most charming and surprisingly appropriate. I would very much like for us to make this arrangement work."

Beau smiled.

"I am most pleased to hear this."

"But I have to ask you something most delicate in nature."

For a moment Beau looked as if he had seen a ghost. As if the next question might be too much.

"I personally do not care about idle gossip but my mother

does. If she gets wind of anything that I cannot explain away then this union will not happen."

Beau looked forlorn, his eyes were glossy, as if he were about to cry. She had heard a rumor of him and Anatole.

"I understand."

"Are you aware of what happened with your sister Bernadette's engagement?"

A look of relief crossed his face.

"I cannot say I know anything about it. Neither she nor my mother ever spoke about it. All I know is that one day she was engaged and then another day she was not and my sister's standing in the social world changed overnight."

"Did you not ask your either of them?"

"I did not." He admitted. "My sister and my mother had long had their confidences in the world of matchmaking. I had never been privy to it and I did not wish to be."

"I need to tell you something. It is not gossip, but merely something you need to know."

He sat up, alert.

"What is it?"

"My maid is a penniless member of a respected family and has many connections in New Orleans. This morning, she received this."

Allison pulled the note from her pocket and set it on the small table. She pushed it across to Beau. Beau picked up the note and unfolded it. It was not in an envelope so he could not see who it was from. He opened it and looked at the words.

As she may become a member of your mistresses family, it may interest you to know that Miss Bernadette Chenevert was caught cavorting with an army captain named Jonathan Davies.

"Captain Jonathan Davies?" Beau said, astonished. "But we just met him for the first time at Christmas. At Réveillon."

"No, I am afraid not."

His facial features contorted in a way that suggested he might argue the point, but then fell as he relented. His eyes and mouth were open, yet he could not speak.

Allison leaned forward and placed her hand on his.

"I am sorry to share this." She said. "But it was important that you know."

"I had no idea, I swear."

She pulled her hand back and looked down at her lap.

"I can see that."

"Are you sure you can be involved with someone from such a family?"

"I can handle my mother."

He sat and gently shook his head.

"There is something else bothering you." She said.

"I am afraid so." He admitted. "But I would rather not talk about it at the moment."

"Of course not." She attempted to change the subject. "I understand that one of the footmen disappeared in the night."

He looked as though someone had stabbed him with one of the pastry forks.

She changed the subject again.

"I believe I shall try one of these cucumber sandwiches." She said, feigning interest as though cucumber was a flavor sensation she had not yet experienced.

Beau merely looked off into the middle distance.

"I want to apologize."

"For what?" She asked.

"For you coming all the way out here to the wilds of the Louisiana jungle. The bayous full of alligators and vultures. The swamp gasses and moonless nights. Only to discover that your intended came from a financially insolvent family with a series of sordid scandals and lackluster morals, even for ruling class standards."

Allison sat for a moment. The cucumber sandwich limp on her plate. She had not prepared for this level of honesty and now she felt like she owed him some of her own.

"Beau. My father was engaged to my mother when they he was fifteen and she was twelve. He deflowered her at thirteen. And then they were married at sixteen and twenty. My mother had no choice and my father had no accountability. We have plenty of money on both sides, but strong moral fiber on neither."

Beau turned and nodded with a wan smile.

"I understand you better than you think." She added.

"I appreciate that."

"And whatever happened with the footman," she whispered, "please know that I understand that as well."

A single fat tear rolled down Beau's cheek and landed on his trousers.

"I am not usually like this." Beau said. "I promise you that I normally have my life together."

"Then you are doing better than most."

They both laughed.

"I wanted him to come with me."

She did not ask; she knew who he was talking about.

"But I have reason to believe that something happened to him."

"You do not believe that he left in the middle of the night?"

"I do not." He said. "Right before I met with you, I discovered that one of his cufflinks had been found in the library."

Allison's eyes widened. She was in new territory. At first, she thought she had been merely dealing with his sister's scandal. But now it seemed that there was something much darker.

"And I cannot help but think that it somehow involves this Captain Jonathan Davies. He has been making secret advances toward Cousin Charlotte."

"But she has an intended, no?"

"She does. But she and my sister have created some arrangement where my Bernadette will marry her intended and Charlotte will be able to marry the army captain that she secretly loves. And now, thanks to you, we understand what that relationship is really about."

"I am so sorry." Allison said. "Now what?"

"Now I must speak to Uncle George. He will be furious. He will be back late tonight; I will tell him first thing in the morning."

"That is the only thing you can do."

"Again, I apologize that you had to be here during this disgusting turn of events."

"Beau, if I may be frank, I feel like you and I are going to have a very long friendship."

With that Allison Banfield stood and smoothed her skirts. She smiled and placed her hand reassuringly on his shoulder. She patted it lightly then turned and walked away from the room.

Chapter 38
Samael

The next morning Beau Chenevert sent word to his Uncle George that he would need to meet him as soon as possible. He did not know why, but he did not trust the footman Charlie Mayes to deliver the message. Instead, he gave the note to Carstairs, the butler, who seemed rather peeved at the minor duty.

Uncle George was not his uncle, of course. He had been married to his mother's cousin. He had been raised to call him uncle, as was common. He had never had a warm familial relationship with him. He was not that sort, nor was his own father.

George McCambridge had an incredible business mind, as was well known throughout Louisiana, despite having no formal education. He had seemingly parlayed a number of opportunities as a young man into ever growing success. But no one ever questioned how a poor lad from Scotland had found opportunities to make him one of the wealthiest men in the new world. Money and success were all the pedigree needed in his world. Nor how he had even made his way to the new world in the first place.

Beau stood outside the door to Uncle George's suite of rooms and waited for Carstairs to deliver the message. He felt a tingle of nerves break out across his skin as he went over what he would say in his mind. He feared not being believed, but also feared that he *would* be believed. For neither offered a good consequence.

Soon Carstairs emerged from the room and nodded for Beau to go in. Instead of returning downstairs Carstairs merely stood next to the door gesturing his entry.

He stepped into the suite of rooms and wondered at the grandiosity. The draperies had been opened, though little sunlight seemed to filter into the room on the overcast morning. Fine paintings dominated the walls. Beautiful furnishings had been brought over from George's homeland in Scotland.

He found his Uncle George sitting at a table in his night attire and robe enjoying his coffee and toast. Newspaper in hand. The table was laid with silver coffee service, a toast rack, and small plate.

"Good morning, lad."

Beau recognized the luxuriously grotesque painting over the bed. The Death of Lucretia.

"I see you appreciate fine art and that you appreciate the Hamilton."

"Indeed, sir. His neoclassical style is a favorite of mine."

"A great Scotsman. Were he alive today I would sit for him."

Beau grew impatient to impart his information yet dared not interrupt Uncle George.

"You would make a worthy subject, uncle."

"Alas, the great painters of my homeland are all gone now. I have amassed a fine collection of antiques from Scotland. Gathered here they remind me of when I was a lad in service in a grand home. Before I made my way to America and made my fortune in the Caribbean with sugar cane."

He looked back down at his newspaper and continued what he had been doing.

"Uncle George. I am sorry to have disturbed you so early, but I assure you that it is most important."

George remained focused on the newspaper.

"If the abolitionists don't start a war in this country, it will be a miracle. Why can they not leave well enough alone?"

Beau did not disagree with the abolitionists so he felt best to stay quiet on the subject.

"Sir, something came to my attention yesterday that I must share with you. I warn you that it may be unpleasant."

George McCambridge put his newspaper to one side and gave Beau his full attention.

Beau continued.

"I have heard some disturbing news about a plot to steal from you."

George put his hand up.

"Carstairs!"

Carstairs opened the door, obviously having been told to stand by.

"Fetch Mr. Blacksmythe. He should be downstairs at breakfast."

"Continue." Uncle George said.

"Yesterday Mini came to me with something she had over-heard out at the folly one night. She heard Emily and a strange man discussing stealing The McCambridge Emeralds from Miss Charlotte."

"What?" He demanded.

"Apparently there is a plan to steal them after a party and hide them away for a couple of days before absconding."

"Who was the man?"

"I can only guess—"

At that moment a quick knock was followed by the door opening. A tall and grim looking man entered. He wore black clothes that could easily be mistaken for clergy. He held his hat in his hands. He was perhaps forty, tall and strongly built. He came closer, but not too close, and stood silently in a way that Beau found disquieting.

"Mr. Blacksmythe will need to hear this. He is my *Samael*, if you understand the reference. He handles things for me that I do not wish to handle myself. Please continue."

In the Apocrypha, which predates the Bible, Lucifer was known as Samael. The arch nemesis of St. Michael. To Beau it was so odd to hear his Uncle George reference a book that was forbidden. One that he himself had read.

"Hello, Mr. Blacksmythe." Beau said nervously. "I am Mr. Chenevert."

"He knows who you are."

The sentence made Beau queasy. He understood what kind of man Mr. Blacksmythe was and it was not comfortable being *known* by him.

"As I was saying, Mini came to me with information about a plan to steal your emeralds."

"Is that all you know?" Uncle George asked.

There was only the sound of breathing from Mr. Blacksmythe behind him. The sound grew louder as if he had moved closer, yet he dared not turn and look at him again.

"No, there is more, I'm afraid. After she told me this, I met Miss Allison for luncheon and she told me of some new information that had been imparted to her maid."

He realized that he did not know how to continue without implicating his own sister. Anything he said could be her doom. And yet he had to tell Uncle George what he knew or Captain Davies could get away with everything.

"And what was that?" George asked.

"That a Captain Jonathan Davies had been overheard to be planning to seduce my dear cousin Charlotte. I suspect that *he* was the one in the folly that night that who was planning this crime against your family."

George McCambridge exchanged glances with Mr. Blacksmythe.

"There is more." George said flatly.

"Yes, sir."

Beau swallowed hard. He felt hot and perspiration erupted all over his body.

"It has come to my attention that my sister Bernadette may have been involved with Captain Davies in New Orleans."

"Are you saying what I think you are saying?"

"I do not know, sir." He said honestly. "I only know that a note received by Miss Allison's maid told her that Bernadette and this Captain Davies were intent on arranging marriages for themselves. Charlotte and Bernadette had a scheme where Bernadette would marry Robert Mayhew, thus securing the familial connection. And then Charlotte would be able to marry this Captain Davies."

Uncle George's eyes narrowed and his face reddened.

"I would never allow that to happen."

"I suspect that Captain Davies realized that and thus the plan to seduce Emily and steal the jewels came about."

"Carstairs!"

Carstairs opened the door and stepped inside.

"Yes sir."

"My daughter wore the emeralds to a party two nights ago. Did you then secure them in the safe as usual?"

Carstairs looked confused for a moment then suddenly paled.

"After the party I was unwell and Emily said that she would secure them herself."

"You were *unwell*? A fortune in emeralds was in your security and you felt *unwell*?"

"Sir, I started vomiting and I could not stop."

"Widow's Thrill." Mr. Blacksmythe said.

George looked up to him inquisitively.

"Someone gave him Widows Thrill.

"What?"

Mr. Blacksmythe turned to Carstairs.

"Who brought you tea that night?" He asked.

"Emily, as usual. She brings me my after-dinner tea."

"Widows Thrill." Mr. Blacksmythe turned back to Uncle George and continued. "It is a plant also known as kalanchoe. Sometimes made into a tea that induces vomiting. It grows wild all over the bayou parishes."

"Carstairs." George said, his voice low and deadly. "Go downstairs and check at once. And if those jewels are not there you are going to pay in ways that even I have not yet imagined."

Carstairs turned and moved quickly from the room. His footsteps down the backstairs echoed his speed. Mr. Blacksmythe followed.

"If those jewels are not in their place, do you understand what is going to happen next?"

"I do, sir," said Beau.

"No one steals from me. No one."

"I want to help you find this Captain Jonathan Davies and bring him to justice."

"Good lad."

"But please sir, Emily is a just a young girl and does not understand what she has done."

George nodded and seemed to weigh the matter.

"She is not sophisticated and, like Charlotte, fell into the web of lies of this master manipulator."

George sat solemnly quiet.

"Emily has been a part of this household and this family for most of her life." George said. "I do not take lightly this incident, though I surely do understand the power of a man like this Captain Davies over the weaker sex."

Beau felt a relief. He did not know her well, but he knew that she was close to Anatole and that he loved her.

"One other thing, uncle."

"What is that?"

"I do not think that your footman Anatole Blanchet left of his own free will."

"Do you think he was involved in this plot?"

"No, I do not. He had expressed to me some distrust in this Captain Davies."

"Why would a servant have occasion to discuss such a thing with you?"

"As my footman we often talked while getting ready or after evenings."

"Yes, as I often do with my own."

"He did not go into great detail, but he did say that he had overheard this Captain Davies speaking and that he did not trust him."

The door opened after a quick knock. Beau turned and saw Mr. Blacksmythe step into the room. His face was dark with portent. He knew instantly that the jewels were not in their place.

"Goddammit!" Uncle George shouted.

Beau winced. He had never seen his Uncle George angry and it was frightening.

George McCambridge sat completely still for a moment staring into the middle distance. Perhaps he was contemplating, but his poker face brooked no expression. Beau found it almost more unsettling than when he had looked furious. But it was clear that machinations were in progress.

George picked up his newspaper again began to read again. He picked up his cup and took a sip.

"If that is all you needed," George said without looking up, "then I need to get some work done."

Beau rose from his chair unsure of what to say. He realized that he had just set a chain of actions and consequences in motion. But how could he let Captain Davies get away with the chaos he had caused within his family? He could not. And whatever he may have done that involved Anatole. He could not even think about that.

As if reading his mind, George spoke.

"You were right to tell me." He said.

Beau nodded and turned to go. He inadvertently made eye contact with Mr. Blacksmythe and the man's dead eye stare sent a chill through him. His face expressionless yet intent, like a primordial creature who lived entirely by instinct. Like one of Darwin's lost discoveries that he had read so much about.

Samael, indeed. God's sword of justice and dealer of punishment. Uncle George clearly saw himself as God and Beau was smart enough to know that God's enemy was never Lucifer. Perhaps Bridlewood was the story of Apocrypha after all and all who entered this Eden did so at the will of master chess players who ran the game.

Chapter 39
Into The Gloaming

Emily placed each of the pieces of emerald jewelry on the petticoat one at a time. Quickly, but with care, she sewed each piece in place. She did not have a lot of time, but did not want the jewels to clank together and make noise as she made her way through the house and out to the location of their rendezvous.

As she sewed, she thought about all she was leaving behind. Her friendship with Charlotte had lasted most of her life. But too much had changed. And after what had happened with Mr. McCambridge, she no longer felt safe in this house. She could already tell that she was with child. And the thought of raising his child with no help and getting attacked again. She could not bear it.

Her heart raced with excitement. She had so much less moral confusion about what she was doing that she had expected. The decision was far easier than it should have been. Her mind repeated the phrase *There is a debt and it would be repaid.*

She had made peace with the idea of never seeing her family

and friends again. Not because she was in love with Jonathan Davies, but because she had to escape and he was the only one offering a way out. An escape for herself and for her baby. She would not continue working in this house, as Mini did, giving birth to the bastard offspring of that man who would then ignore her and the child.

Emily began to imagine never seeing her mother again and it hurt her heart. But maybe she could see her again someday in a few years. After everything had calmed down here. Perhaps they would understand.

She could not help but think of Mrs. McCambridge. Big Maman, they had called her. A great honor coming from a creole. She had looked up to her and now she was the only one whose opinion she would have worried about. But she was dead. And perhaps she was looking down from heaven and saw what her husband did. Perhaps she thought she deserved the jewels as well. But it just did not really matter to Emily anymore.

Emily had the strangest feeling that she had never had before in her life. She was able to do exactly what she wanted to do and she had chosen what that would be. She had agreed to the terms. She had agreed to the risk. The feeling associated with this alien to her. She realized that the feeling was freedom.

The ability to make decisions based entirely on her own wants and needs was new to her. She had not experienced it before in her life. Emily had realized that even Charlotte had not had all the freedom that she desired. She was tied to what her parents would want her to do.

Freedom was something that people take for granted, she realized. She had previously thought that she had freedom. And yet, now, as she made these plans, she realized that she had never known real freedom.

Charlotte wished to be dressed for dinner early and to undress herself, which gave Emily the evening off. This was the perfect opportunity to leave Bridlewood. To disappear and not be noticed until the morning. If she left a note that she was ill she may even have them not notice her disappearance until the following afternoon.

Emily stepped into the petticoat and tied it securely around her waist. She moved from side to side and heard nothing. She moved more vigorously and heard a slight tink of the pieces of jewelry hitting each other. She then pulled up her heavier woolen skirt and buttoned it in place. She then twirled and heard nothing. Finally, she felt secure.

She stepped outside her room and walked down the corridor. She could not pack a bag. She could not afford to be seen carrying anything from the house. The night before she had packed a small bag of things she needed. Her few items of clothing to make do until they were able to get to New Orleans and sell at least one of the stones to get by. Then they would make their way to Charleston to sell a few more. Jonathan had made the entire plan clear and she felt like it would work.

Time seemed to stand still as she walked as normally as she could down the hallway. In her heart she felt like she was making an escape, but time seemed to have a string around her waist that held her in place.

Emily padded quietly down the backstairs.

"Emily!"

Emily's heart nearly burst. She turned to see Fabienne Blanchet standing in the doorway to the downstairs.

"Emily." She said. "I need to speak to you."

Emily was frozen in place at the foot of the backstairs. She could not run. Not now. She eyed the backdoor, it was only a few feet away, but running would be an instant admission of guilt. She would merely speak to Mrs. Blanchet and then say she had a duty to attend to and then she would disappear outside.

"Yes, of course." Emily said. Her cool voice belied her terror.

Fabienne turned and walked slowly toward her office across from the kitchens. She walked into her office and sat at down at her desk, Emily followed closely behind.

"Shut the door." Fabienne instructed.

Emily shut the door behind herself. She seated herself at the chair across from Fabienne.

"I need to talk to you about something...*delicate*."

Emily felt her pulse begin to quicken again and she hoped that she hid it well on her face.

"Yes, ma'am. I just have to get back to Miss Charlotte soon."

"Emily, I have known you for most of your life and I feel like you would be honest if I asked you a question."

Emily's mouth was dry. She chastised herself for not drinking something first. For even coming into this room. It was a trap and she immediately fell for it. How did she ever think she would survive on the run?

"Yes, ma'am, of course I would!"

Emily answered more enthusiastically than she had intended.

"I have to show you something."

"Alright."

Fabienne held out her closed hand. She shook slightly. Emily's hands focused on her hand as if Fabienne held her entire future in it. And perhaps it did. Had dropped a piece of the jewelry somewhere? Had she implicated herself in some other way that she could not fathom? She wracked her brain.

"Do you recognize this?

Fabienne's trembling hand opened. Emily bent down to have a look at what was contained there. For a moment she was confused, but then she realized what it was.

"That is one of Anatole's cufflinks?"

Fabienne did not answer, she merely nodded. Her red rimmed eyes spilled tears.

Emily did not understand what was going on, but she did know that the cufflinks were Anatole's prize possessions. Fabienne had given them to him at Christmas and they meant the world to him.

"Where did you find that?" Emily asked.

"Mini found this in the library."

"But surely he would have taken these with him when he left."

"I have to ask you." Fabienne said. "You are one of his closest friends. His father is at home with his jaw wired shut. Anatole nearly beat him to death."

"Is that why he disappeared?"

"I don't know!" Fabienne nearly shouted. "I am so sorry; I am just at my wit's end."

"It's alright, Mrs. Blanchet." Emily said. "I can see that you are upset."

"What was going on with him?"

"I wish I could tell you something?"

"I do not believe that Anatole would leave without telling me."

"I do not believe he would either."

"Then I want to know what happened to him." Fabienne was forceful again. "Mini tells me that there has been a man around this house that she is worried about."

"What man?"

"This Captain Jonathan Davies."

Emily felt the wind knocked out of her. She had been so wrapped up in the plan that she had not even considered it. She remembered the conversation in the folly where she had told him that Anatole was suspicious of him. But he would not have killed him for that. Jonathan was not a murderer.

"He is a suitor for Miss Charlotte," Emily said, "do you think he would have reason to hurt Anatole?"

Emily's mouth was so parched. She needed just a drink of water, but she felt it suspicious to ask.

"I don't know, Emily. But I will find out."

The look on Fabienne's face convinced Emily that she would find out. And now it was more important than ever that they make their escape this evening and to never look back at Bridlewood.

When Anatole disappeared, she had been surprised, but not shocked. He had talked for years about leaving Point Cèdre behind. He wanted to find his own adventures and his own life. But she never imagined that he would do so without saying goodbye to his family and friends.

She remembered their last conversation. While they had sat eating mincemeat pie late one night.

"He told me that he felt like things were changing with Miss Charlotte." Emily said bluntly.

"What?" Fabienne asked. "What do you mean?"

"He seemed to think that she had been changing and that their friendship was different somehow."

"What do you think?"

"I told him that I did not know what he meant and that he was probably imagining it."

Emily heard herself lie but she could not risk implicating herself in whatever had happened to Anatole.

The more she thought about it the more she *knew* what happened to Anatole. They had been friends for most of her life and now he was gone. Could she have misjudged Jonathan? Could her anger at the McCambridge family have blinded her judgment to the point that she got her best friend killed? She knew the answer. She did not know how, but she knew the answer with a sickening dread. Horror and grief crept into her body. Her thirst now unquenchable.

She was now inextricably linked to Captain Jonathan Davies

and nothing could change that. She would get up from this chair and go meet him in the woods. Near the bayou's edge. But what would stop him from making *her* disappear if she displeased him?

"I think he probably dropped the cufflink on the way out." Emily said.

Fabienne furrowed her brow.

"What?"

"I think he probably stopped by the library to pick up a book for travel and it simply fell off his shirt."

Fabienne simply looked at Emily with her mouth slightly open as though she were looking at an imbecile.

"I am sorry." Emily said. "I just know that Anatole always dreamt of running off and I think probably he did after what happened with Mr. Blanchet."

"Did he mention anything about it?"

"He did not, but I did not really get to speak to him much lately."

"You really think he could have just dropped it by accident?"

Emily did not think so but could not implicate herself at this point. She did not wish to end up at the end of a rope.

"Yes, I do. Now that I know about what happened between him and Mr. Blanchet. I imagine he thought it best to leave town."

Emily stood and looked at Fabienne. Fabienne sat back in her chair and exhaled.

"If you'll excuse me, I need to get some things done for Miss Charlotte before bed."

"Yes, of course." Fabienne said absentmindedly.

Emily turned and walked from the room. She walked down the corridor and straight out the backdoor, closing the screen door gently behind her. She walked toward the wood.

She looked up at the sun that began to descend into the tree line and the orange glow that surrounded it. She turned back for one last look at Bridlewood. A trick of light and the disappearing sun made it appear that someone was looking down on her from the cupola atop the house. Then the sun dipped and the gloaming of Bridlewood turned gray with mist and to anyone who observed she disappeared into it forever.

Chapter 40
Twilight Falls

The misty afternoon would soon become a foggy evening. The sun had been hidden behind the clouds for the better part of the day and the air had remained cool and damp in a twilight from which it seemed it would not emerge.

It was that time of year in the south when winter toyed with returning one last time before spring. A chill rose up but had not decided if it would stay. The canopy of wetland trees kept the remainder of the sun from penetrating the woods.

The land that was now Bridlewood Estate had once been the home of native American tribes. These fields had been soaked in their blood before they were forcibly driven from their home to reservations to the north leaving nothing in their wake but curses.

Legends of the curses of those people were rampant in Terrebonne Parish. Stories of *Skinwalkers* who had avoided capture and lived in bolt holes deep in the woods. Stories of bloodthirsty *wendigos* who roamed the night hellbent on vengeance and blamed for every disappearance in the parish.

The fact was that the real curse of Bridlewood was neither

Skinwalkers nor *wendigos*. The real curse was not known to any living person. Queen Marie herself did not fully understand the nature of the rage of the blood curse of Bridlewood. The blood of the slaughtered ancestors of the natives of the land they called Bulbancha, the place of many tongues.

Captain Jonathan Davies strode purposefully through woods of the McCambridge estate. He was on a mission to rendezvous with Emily Delphin. She had dutifully stolen the storied McCambridge emeralds for him. He had tied his horse at in the woods near the road, but not close enough to be seen.

Emily was a beautiful young creole girl. She was smart, he could tell. But smart girls who are dissatisfied can be dangerous. He knew immediately that she would be his willing infidel against the McCambridge family. It was not a personal vendetta, merely opportunity knocking. He always answered the door.

Jonathan Davies had realized what he had when he had met Beulah Sugarbaker. As soon as he understood the nature of Beulah's hatred for the McCambridge family he knew that she would help him with his plan. She was not privy to the entirety of the plan; she thought his plan was merely to deflower the princess. But as soon as he realized the true staggering wealth his eyes widened and focused on a far greater prize than her cunny.

She was a beautiful young woman, and taking her flower was more than enticement enough. He was almost embarrassed at how easy it had been. She fell for his charms, as they always did. Because he did not push himself. He merely let his personal charms do the work. He knew his own face to be comely, and his body taut. He allowed his cool demeanor to attract the women of privilege and it always worked.

Movement in the distance piqued his interest. A man appeared in the opening in the wood and seemed to be heading in his direction. As he drew closer, he recognized the blond man as Beau Chenevert, catamite brother of Bernadette, though they had not yet met he had seen him at the Réveillon party at Christmas.

"Good day, sir." Beau Chenevert said.

"Is it?"

"I wonder what your intentions might be on my uncle's property on this fine day?"

"I do apologize, sir. For I was out for a walk and did lose my way."

"No worries at all, it is easy to get tangled in these woods. No one around for a mile."

"Yes, I was out looking for a good place to hunt pheasant."

"Ah, you must have been coming from the property next door. I know they allow game shooting. But it is typically a bit late in the season for pheasants and you have not a gun to shoot one. Did you intend to strangle one?"

Jonathan laughed wryly.

"To be honest, today I am merely out for a walk to see if any game is about. My father will join me for a hunt tomorrow."

"I wish you best on your hunt." Beau gestured far behind Jonathan. "In the future, the bottom of those trees is painted red a few hundred yards back. That is the beginning of Uncle George's property."

"Thank you for your hospitality, sir." Jonathan nodded. "I will be on my way."

Jonathan turned and headed back toward the property line was. He would perhaps have a clean getaway.

Then Beau called to him.

"Hold on."

Jonathan stopped and turned around slowly. Unsure of what would happen next.

"Have we not met?" Beau asked.

"I am not sure that we have."

A look of realization crossed Beau's face.

"Yes, Captain Davies, I believe. We met at my cousin's Réveillon party."

Jonathan's eyes narrowed in surprise for a moment. The possibility of a bloodless getaway now disappearing. His appearance on this very property at a time when the disappearance of the jewels would soon become known to the household would not go

"Ah, yes of course." Jonathan was caught off guard. He knew that he had not met the young man. They had seen each other at most.

"I thought you said you did not know the estate?"

Jonathan's eyes darted back and forth.

"Indeed, I just did not realize that the property was this large and that I was already walking upon it."

"Of course." Beau smiled.

The gears of Jonathan's mind produced a plan.

"I do hope you will forgive my ignorance."

"Of course." Beau repeated.

"I do remember seeing you at Réveillon." Jonathan said. "I hope you do not mind my saying that I thought you stood out that night. You cut quite a figure in your impeccable suit."

"Thank you. A change from my hunting attire I don today."

Captain Jonathan Davies began to walk slowly back toward Beau Chenevert. His eyes locked in on his in an aggressive manner meant for fighting or fucking.

"Indeed, you are also hunting without a gun. Perhaps you are hunting for another type of bird? A cock perhaps?"

Jonathan leered at Beau and grabbed his crotch.

Beau eyed the man's package. He smiled seductively and raised an eyebrow but said nothing.

"Why don't you walk with me into the woods where we will not be seen and show me yours and I'll show you mine?"

Jonathan turned and began to walk into the visual safety of the woods.

Beau's smile turned into a grin. His eyes seemed to glaze over with lust. He turned and followed Jonathan into the lush vegetative cover of the dark Terrebonne woods.

Jonathan walked for several minutes with Beau following wordlessly. Then Jonathan stopped and turned. His eyes were aflame with desire. His look was mirrored in Beau's own eyes.

Jonathan stood as Beau approached him. Beau stopped and stood unnaturally close to Jonathan. His face only inches from his. Beau reached out his hand and caressed Jonathan's chiseled face. The beauty of his bone structure could not be denied.

Jonathan stealthily reached into his coat and unsheathed his knife. It was a perfect spot. No one would see or hear a thing and the alligators would soon hide all evidence. The plan he had for Emily would work just as well for this man.

Beau's caress traced a line from Jonathan's jaw and down his chest to the laces of his breeches. They stared into each other's eyes for a moment.

The flash of the blade came quickly out of nowhere. The blade was at Beau's throat with preternatural speed, his eyes wide with terror. Jonathan's eyes, however, began to shine with mirth.

"I didn't want to do this, but you were in the wrong place at the wrong time. In deference to my friendship with your dear sister I will kill you quickly and painlessly, just as I did your lover."

The rope seemed to drop from the sky. It was instantly around Jonathan's neck, tightened, and pulling him backward. The Army issued knife dropped from his hand.

A new smile spread across Beau's face. Relief and revenge. Hearing Jonathan admit to Anatole's murder gave righteousness to his anger and

"You will pay for what you have done."

Jonathan appeared to be ready to speak but before he had the chance Mr. Blacksmythe slapped the flank of his horse, thus pulling Captain Jonathan Davies straight up into the air with a snap of the neck like thunder. There was no struggle, just jerking appendages.

Beau appeared to be in shock that the plan had worked. An expression of shock turned to a twisted amusement.

Mr. Blacksmythe looked nonplussed, as though it were an average day at work.

"Don't be angry with yourself, lad." Mr. Blacksmythe said. "It is the most natural thing in the world to enjoy seeing an enemy smited."

Beau stood confused.

"You can go on, now." He said to Beau. "I will take care of this."

Beau seemed to understand the need for him to exit the wood as quickly as possible. He hastily retreated to the open field and the out of sight.

* * *

Meanwhile Emily made her way through the wood toward the meeting spot designated by Jonathan. She pushed her way through the dense vegetation. The feeling of freedom was beginning to thrill her. Her heart raced.

"Stop right there." A low voice called to her.

The voice had the power to stop her in her tracks. Her blood went cold.

From behind a tree stepped Mr. Blacksmythe. She had never met him nor spoken to him, yet she knew exactly who he was. She had seen his countenance darken the corners of Bridlewood for years. There was no reason to know him. To know him was to understand that something had gone terribly wrong.

His face was plain and somber, but his skull was visible underneath. She could make out the indentation of each bone. He was a living ghoul and now he stood between her and freedom. But Jonathan would make quick work of him and then they would be on their way.

"I don't wish to interfere with your afternoon stroll, but there is something I wish to retrieve from you."

"I don't know what you mean."

"You know what I mean." He replied, his eyes deadly cold. "You do not want me to search your person."

Where is Jonathan? He would be here shortly and save her from this.

As if he could read her mind, Mr. Blacksmythe pointed upward. Her eyes followed his finger up to the sky. She saw the thing hanging here from the tree but her mind could not immediately identify it. A scream caught in her throat as she realized that it was her conduit to freedom, Captain Jonathan Davies.

She instinctively reached under her skirts and unlaced her petticoats. They fell to the ground silently. She stepped forward, clearing the way for Mr. Blacksmythe to pick them up.

Mr. Blacksmythe felt the material and tore open the hastily made seams. He held the necklace in his hands. Satisfied that the rest of the jewels were there he pocketed the necklace and took the petticoat somewhere behind her.

Emily's mind raced as she wondered what he was doing, but she dared not turn to see. The wait was interminable. But then with horror she felt the rope drop over her head.

"Say hi to Jesus for me." He said.

Then she heard a noise as he slapped his horse's flank.

She felt herself pulled high in the air and before she knew it, she was next to Jonathan's lifeless corpse. There was a snap that exploded in her ears as her neck snapped and then blackness.

A moment later she opened her eyes and looked around.

Confused. She had to adjust her head, as it was crooked. She looked up and saw not just Jonathan, but also herself. Without her petticoats she could see her underdrawers. For a moment she was embarrassed. But then, with a sickening realization, she understood that she was dead.

"I don't understand."

She turned and Jonathan stood next to her. She shook her head.

"Are we...?"

"Yes, of course."

It was then and only then that the true curse of Bridlewood was revealed to Emily. That she would walk these woods with Captain Jonathan Davies with their broken necks for eternity. She did not have the energy to be angry.

Epilogue
Gotterdammerung

It has been many years since that horrifying day. For a long time, I, Sebastian Beau Chenevert, tried to block it from my mind. But now those memories have dulled to a point where I can recall with them without injury. A gift that only age can afford.

For a moment I am back in the wood that day. I remember as I began walking away from Mr. Blacksmythe and the grisly scene. My feet could not propel me fast enough. I found myself breaking into a run. My heart was racing as I ran up the steps to the door of Bridlewood House. I stood at the door unsure if I should go in. My disheveled state would alarm any person I encountered.

Before I had the chance to decide the door swung open and the footman Charlie Mayes stood there with an expression of concern on his face.

"Are you alright, Mr. Beau?"

I was not alright, but I was damned if I would let this fool know. I had seen a man brutally murdered. And while he richly deserved it my humanity rushed back to me and I soon felt that I had made an egregious mistake in witnessing it. I should have left the wood without seeing while I still had the chance. Before I heard the sickening crunch of the man's neck. The vertebrae snapping like a dry twig.

I was determined to compose myself.

"I am quite fine, thank you."

"Of course, sir."

"Have you seen Miss Charlotte?"

"Yes, sir." He replied. "I gave her her wrap so that she might go out for a walk."

"Please let her know that I wish to see her when she returns." I said.

"Yes, sir."

He replied, as always, as a servant who had been asked to do a job he considered beneath him.

I climbed the stairs back up to my rooms. I did not wish for anyone else to see me in the state I was currently in. I felt as though something had changed drastically within my person. For all my love of nature and humanity I could not have denied the horrifying joy that I had felt when I heard that bastard's neck snap.

I shut the door behind myself and just stared forward at the scene before me. Just days ago, I had lain there in that bed with Anatole. His muscular body overpowering my own lithe figure. For one moment in my hubris, I thought I had it all. I had figured out how to have the life that society told me that I could not have.

I needed to relax and pull back from this episode of nerves. I closed my eyes began to think about that last evening with Anatole. We lay together and talked about our futures. I had tried to convince him to come to Charleston with me, but I do not know if I succeeded. I understood his doubts, but I also hoped that he would trust me. Perhaps he would have, but now we would never know.

The beating of my heart began to return to normal. My eyes

Epilogue

still closed tightly as I remembered and relished the feel of his hands on my body. He made me feel both fearless and protected at the same time. His strength could have been intimidating in a lesser person, yet he used it to make me feel safe.

When he first pushed his way into my rooms, I could not deny that I felt both terrified and enthralled at the same time. His eyes had been aflame with a lifetime of unfulfilled desire. I cannot say the value of being the person who he had finally chosen to explore his passions with. I was ready and I was more than willing but I was not prepared for the savagery he brought to my bed. He was insatiable and demanding, but also willing to learn.

In all the explosion of passions and torn clothing I was left feeling satisfied and spent. I was exhausted, he was like a machine that first night. I would never forget.

Leaned against the door with my eyes closed I felt him. Not just in my mind but on my skin. I felt his caress. I was terrified to open my eyes that I might see him or that I might not. What if he was not *really* there? I might stay blissfully unaware for a moment longer, had I not earned that?

Can you not feel me?

I heard the words; I had not imagined it. But I dared not open my eyes.

Open your eyes.

I shook his head, but my curiosity would not allow me to wait. I opened his eyes to the now darkened room. The sun had dipped below the horizon and the last drops of sunlight glittered off the swamp. I looked around the room and the shadow moved. I could make out the face of Anatole Blanchet, and then it was gone.

I let out a gasp.

I was immediately startled by a knock at the door that I was still leaned against.

Epilogue

I composed myself and quickly turned and opened the door to find Charlie Mayes standing there.

"Mr. McCambridge would like to see you in his rooms."

Of course, he would want to hear that everything had gone according to plan.

"Yes, of course."

Charlie nodded then backed away before walking back to his position at the front door.

I closed his door behind myself and headed down the corridor back toward Uncle George's rooms. In doing so I nearly ran headlong into Cousin Charlotte. Her eyes were rimmed red with tears. She must have just discovered about Captain Jonathan Davies. I felt for her. I understood completely, yet the punishment had indeed fit the crime and I was now glad that my cousin would not marry a fortune hunter and a murderer.

"Charlotte, can I- "but she was inconsolable and she was gone before I could say anything more.

At the end of the corridor, I knocked at my uncle's door.

"Come in."

I entered and found Uncle George sitting at the same table where he had breakfasted earlier. Now dressed and having a gin and tonic that he favored before dinner.

George gestured to a table to his right laden with spirits in decanters and various glassware.

"Help yourself to a drink, lad."

I could not stomach the thought at the moment, but I poured myself a scotch and hoped it might steel my nerves.

I sat in the chair across from George.

"I assume from the dour expression on your face that the deed is done."

"I am sorry, Uncle George, I do not yet have an appropriate facial expression for this. But yes, the job is done."

"The matter of justice is not one for the weak of stomach,

Beau. I have always known that you are of a more sensitive nature. But you must toughen yourself to the needs of this age. To the needs of the life that you have and the one you wish to have."

"I understand, Uncle George."

But I did not understand. I did not wish to ever understand. Did I wish to become a ghoul like Mr. Blacksmythe for whom murder was merely an errand? Never.

"You are right to be horrified by death." George said, sipping his drink. "But I have to ask you a question."

"Yes sir?"

"Did you not, at some point, have that delicious feeling of revenge?"

As hard as I wished to deny it I could not. For what he did to my Anatole I would snap the bastard's neck a hundred more times.

"I am sorry to say that I did."

"But I can tell that now your conscience has returned."

"Indeed, it has."

"Good." Uncle George nodded. "You are not meant for this."

"Now that he is dead, how will you punish Emily? Will you take the jewels back from her and cast her from this house or will you be lenient?"

George McCambridge laughed.

"She stole a fortune from me, my dear lad. From this family."

"Surely she was manipulated by this fortune hunter?"

"Certainly, she was, but how could I allow a theft of this magnitude to go unpunished?"

It was then that it began to dawn on me that Emily would indeed be punished as well. Perhaps I knew even then that she had already been punished.

"My daughter has already found the bodies of the thieving lovebirds in the wood on the edge of the bayou. She came into the library screaming accusations and horrors that I did not wish for her to see. But now she has and understands the price of disloyalty."

"Emily is dead too?" I don't know why I asked, I already knew the answer.

"I imagine so." George said. "That was certainly what my dear daughter said that she saw. That was the plan. I could tell that you could not stomach the entire plan.

"I understand." I said, though I did not. I also did not wish to become an enemy of the man who easily wrote death warrants for people in his home.

A scream tore through the quiet of Bridlewood House. Uncle George looked up at me.

"Sounds like the household has heard about Emily."

Uncle George shook his head as if decrying an unfortunate incident that he had nothing to do with, as he himself had not arranged it.

"Do not worry," Uncle George said to me, "no one will know of your involvement."

A knock at the door was quickly followed by his butler.

"Sir, come quickly!"

"What the devil is it?" He asked, cross.

"Just come quickly!"

Uncle George stood and followed Carstairs out of the room and down the stairs. I did not know if I had the courage or stamina to follow him into this fresh hell, but I felt that it was necessary. I took my shot of scotch in one go and stood.

By the time I made it down the stairs I saw staff running toward the conservatory. I followed them and the cacophony of shoes on marble. I entered the library and peered into the conservatory as the crowd stood. There was wailing from the housekeeper, Mrs. Blanchet and others of her staff.

"No!" I heard a shrill scream from the man himself, Uncle George.

Epilogue

My skin broke out into shivers. What was he screaming about.

"Not my baby!"

I ran toward the crowd of staff and I saw her in her pink dress with the roses. It was such a pretty dress. A simple but gay dress. George sat on the floor with her head in his lap. His darling Charlotte did not move. A trickle of blood seemed to form at her mouth and spill out.

"No!" Uncle George screamed again in vain.

I was so confused and could not understand what I was seeing. I looked up and saw my Allison Banfield. My intended across from me. Her face was a rictus of horror that matched everyone else's. My face was of confusion, but then it unfortunately dawned on me as I saw it beside her. A bottle rolled forward as Uncle George pulled her lifeless body toward him and shook wildly in his torment. A bottle of photography fixative. Arsenic.

She had gone to my darkroom and taken the arsenic. It was as if the bottom of my soul had dropped out for the third time this week. It was as if she had died at my own hand. As horrified as I was at what was happening, I was now equally terrified that my life would soon end at the hands of Mr. Blacksmythe.

I turned and left the conservatory. The wailing and screaming continued but my mind began to frantically make sense of the scene that had played out before me.

They were all there. I saw them. I could not help but see them even in the full darkness of the Louisiana evening. The door was open to the outside and Emily and Jonathan Davies stood on the porch with their curiously bent necks. But their dead eyes looked at me and I felt their confusion turn to anger. But they could not enter the house nor touch me.

I turned and walked up the grand marble staircase for the last time, for I knew that I would leave this place and never return. I would leave Bridlewood House a lesser man. I knew that Allison Banfield would no longer have me and that I would need to find a way to make my own way in the world.

As I topped the stairs Charlotte and Anatole greeted me wordlessly. They both seemed to yearn to tell me something that I could not hear. It was as if they were waiting on the other side of a slightly wavy glass. What Anatole needed to say he said with his eyes and then, just as they had appeared, they were gone.

I had never known loneliness like it. I returned to my rooms and began to pack. I wanted free of this home immediately, though I had no idea what reality I might face.

The knock at the door was expected. I knew that my time was up. I would find Mr. Blacksmythe on the other side and he would invite me into the wood so that I may pay for the crime of having brought arsenic into the house.

I opened the door, but to my surprise, instead of Mr. Blacksmythe I found Allison Banfield.

I could only shake my head. In doing so I discovered that tears were flowing freely down my face.

"I am so sorry, Miss Banfield. I am so sorry that you had to see this dark day. I understand that you could not possibly marry me now."

"Get your things." She said. "Giselle is packing and we wish to leave this house immediately."

"You wish to take me?"

"You are, more obviously than ever, a friend to me. And you do not belong here. If you still wish it, I want to have a wedding immediately and for you and me to start our lives back in Charleston. I cannot allow you to stay in this mausoleum a moment longer."

A relief crossed my face, for indeed I had found a friend in Allison Banfield. It would be bittersweet to start my life as so many had just ended, but the opportunity would not be ignored.

Epilogue

"I am almost packed."

I took her hands and kissed them with the love of a great friend.

I quickly settled in Charleston. Our marriage was a large and beautiful affair. Indeed, it was the event of the season. Mother and Bernadette attended and they were welcomed by Charlotte society. Eventually they sold the New Orleans townhouse and relocated to Charlotte in a small home near our massive residence so that they may enjoy the largesse of the Banfield family.

While I never again encountered the presence of Anatole Blanchet, I knew that his spirit and his energy was still out there. While I did not see him, I *felt* him. And I thought of him constantly. And though his body was never found I knew that one day I would see him again.

While I found many lovers along the way, I knew that I would never meet another Anatole Blanchet. My St. Michael who would continue on as my guardian angel.

Uncle George soon went mad from the loss of his wife and then daughter. The war came and he lost his sugar fortune. They say that he lost Bridlewood in a hand of poker and that it became a house of ill repute.

People later gossiped about a curse. The true nature of the curse of Bridlewood House was never entirely known to me. But I saw with my own eyes those that it took down.

And as I sit at this desk at Palm House and appraise my good fortunes, I cannot help but think how perfect it nearly was. To have been greeted each morning by his beautiful face and to have kissed those full lips in the cover of each evenings' darkness. The Camelot that I was nearly afforded.

I was reminded of a quote by HL Dietrich:

We are all victims. Our destinies are decided by a cosmic roll of the dice, the winds of the stars, the vagrant breezes of fortune that blow from the windmills of the gods.

Epilogue

And while I did not wish to imagine myself as a victim, there was no doubt that my destiny had been changed by whatever forces inhabited and controlled Bridlewood House. While I felt the spirit of Anatole Blanchet there I would never return. I would look to know another like him until the end of my days and would not succeed.

THE END

About the Author

Jerry Lambert is an American author from the Deep South who likes to write about the scary, funny, and/or sexy things. He now resides in Las Vegas with his husband and dachshunds.

To find out more about Jerry, visit his website:
   JerryLambertBooks.com

www.ingramcontent.com/pod-product-compliance
Lightning Source LLC
Chambersburg PA
CBHW051332250626
47155CB00007B/2563